PRAISE FOR WINTER RENSHAW

"My heart is in a tinderbox, and Winter Renshaw has thrown the match! The Queen of Angst blends fire and ice in this five-star, opposites attract forbidden romance!"

—Sosie Frost, *Wall Street Journal* bestselling author

"Winter Renshaw is the queen of being unpredictable in the best way possible! Angst, chemistry, and all the feels will have you glued to your Kindle."

—Ava Harrison, *USA Today* bestselling author

"Winter Renshaw makes my little dark-romance-loving heart pitter-patter with her fast-paced, sultry, intense thrill rides. Her books are addicting, drawing you in with nail-biting suspense and intimacy so hot I usually devour them in one sitting."

—Angela from Shameless Book Club

"Winter Renshaw is my go-to author when I'm looking for a book with a sexy alpha male and strong heroine."

—Claire Contreras, *New York Times* bestselling author

"Renshaw gives us an angsty, forbidden romance full of twists and turns that not only keeps us turning pages but gives us the happily ever after we crave."

—Kaylee Ryan, *New York Times* and *USA Today* bestselling author

"Utterly captivating! Renshaw delivers another emotionally satisfying, page-burning romance that kept me up until dawn."

—Adriana Locke, *USA Today* bestselling author

"What happens when fate steps in and provides you with everything you didn't know you needed? Anneliese and Lachlan find out in *Love and Kerosene*. Anneliese's strong resolve and compassionate heart, along with Lachlan's determination and kind soul, made for the type of characters I love to read about. They had both been through so much at the hand of the same person. Yet, despite having opposite goals, their empathy toward one another provided me with that heart-pumping ache, wondering what would happen next. Winter Renshaw captivated me from the first chapter to the last. I thoroughly enjoyed *Love and Kerosene* and definitely recommend it."

—Carina Rose, romance author

love
AND
KEROSENE

OTHER TITLES BY WINTER RENSHAW

THE NEVER SERIES

Never Kiss a Stranger

Never Is a Promise

Never Say Never

Bitter Rivals

THE ARROGANT SERIES

Arrogant Bastard

Arrogant Master

Arrogant Playboy

THE RIXTON FALLS SERIES

Royal

Bachelor

Filthy

Priceless (an Amato Brothers crossover)

THE AMATO BROTHERS SERIES

Heartless

Reckless

Priceless

THE PS SERIES

P.S. I Hate You

P.S. I Miss You

P.S. I Dare You

THE MONTGOMERY BROTHERS DUET

Dark Paradise

Dark Promises

STAND-ALONES

Single Dad Next Door

Cold Hearted

The Perfect Illusion

Country Nights

Absinthe

The Rebound

Love and Other Lies

Exmas

Pricked

For Lila, Forever

The Marriage Pact

Hate the Game

The Cruelest Stranger

The Best Man

Trillion

Enemy Dearest

The Match

Whiskey Moon

The Dirty Truth

love
AND
KEROSENE

winter renshaw

Text copyright © 2022 by Nom de Plume LLC
All rights reserved.

No part of this book may be reproduced, or stored in a retrieval system, or transmitted in any form or by any means, electronic, mechanical, photocopying, recording, or otherwise, without express written permission of the publisher.

Published by Montlake, Seattle

www.apub.com

Amazon, the Amazon logo, and Montlake are trademarks of Amazon.com, Inc., or its affiliates.

ISBN-13: 9781542038423
ISBN-10: 1542038421

Cover design by Elizabeth Turner Stokes

Printed in the United States of America

For Lindsay Dickey and Rachel Rongstad,
the queens of new beginnings and happy endings

I curled up
with my trauma
and gave it
a name.
It had your eyes,
his hands,
my voice,
your face.
Comfortable
and warm;
an eerily
familiar place.

—Etta Gray
@ettagraywrites

ONE

ANNELIESE

solivagant (*adj.*) wandering alone

They say everyone has a doppelgänger. Statistically speaking, there could be seven people sharing the same face at any given moment. But the odds of meeting someone's double are in the neighborhood of one in a trillion.

Highly unlikely.

Impossible, even.

"Anneliese?" Florence, the owner of Arcadia Used Books, waves her hand in my face. "Did you hear me?"

I peel my attention from the brooding man on the sidewalk outside the shop—one who shares the same messy auburn mane, hooded gaze, and chiseled jawline as my late fiancé.

"You look like you've just seen a ghost," she says with a hesitant chuckle as she places her palm over my hand. "Sweetheart, you're trembling and pale as a sheet. Is everything all right?"

Cool sweat blankets my forehead as I focus on the small stack of used books on the counter. The words on their spines fade in and out, growing blurry before turning clear again.

"Um, I'm sorry. What was the total again?" I steal another glimpse outside. He's still there—standing the way Donovan used to: one hand in his pocket, the other tapping out a text message with his thumb. Same build. Similar height.

It's uncanny.

"Fifteen dollars and twenty-eight cents," Florence says, her stare weighing on me. "You sure you're okay?"

No. I'm not sure.

"I just . . ." I shake my head, a feeble attempt to pull myself out of this daze, and then I slide my debit card her way. "I thought I saw someone I knew."

Her crinkled gray gaze drifts to the man on the sidewalk. She squints, but her efforts are in vain. Florence wouldn't know him from Adam. We'd only lived in Arcadia Grove for two months before his untimely passing. Granted, this was Donovan's childhood hometown, but Florence isn't a local—she's as fresh off the boat around here as I am.

"That guy right there?" She swipes my card and hands it back. "In the brown jacket?"

"Yeah." I draw in a steady breath. My heart has yet to calm down, but it's not for lack of trying. "But it's not him."

It couldn't be.

Even if it were, Donovan would never dress in a leather bomber jacket, ripped jeans, and dusty boots. And he certainly wouldn't leave the house without running a comb through his hair. This guy looks like he's been riding on the back of a motorcycle for days.

"Well, he *is* a looker . . ." She slides me a pen and the receipt to sign before placing my haul in a thin canvas bag with *have a great day* in faded red print. "If I were your age, he'd make me break out into a sweat too."

Florence winks. Maybe she thinks I was checking him out. Or maybe she's trying to make me smile.

"I'll call you when the next shipment comes in," she says, referring to the vintage and international baby-name books and rare dictionaries she sources for me. As a part-time naming consultant, I'm always looking for new and unusual terms and monikers to add to my arsenal. Florence never fails to deliver.

I wait by the exit, feet frozen on the wooden floor, and watch as the man who isn't Donovan scans his surroundings, shoves his phone into his back pocket, and exchanges it for a set of keys. A second later, he climbs into an olive green vintage Ford pickup, proving me wrong about the motorcycle. Cranking the window down, he fires up the engine and backs out of the slanted parking spot.

I emerge from Flo's shop as soon as he disappears over the hill, and I continue my Saturday-morning shopping with that stranger's image burned into my mind's eye.

Wandering the flower-lined merchant district of Arcadia Grove, I mostly shop the windows. It's all I can afford these days, though it's not like I'm in dire need of a new outfit for a hot date. I'm half-tempted to mosey into a home-accessories boutique to grab something pretty for the house, but then I remind myself I'm putting the cart before the horse per usual. There's no sense in buying kitchen accessories when my current one consists of a folding table, microwave, dorm fridge, electric teakettle, and single-burner hot plate.

I spot an empty park bench and take a seat, flicking through one of my books. While my eyes scan the words on the pages, nothing registers. It might as well be a jumble of nonsensical letters. I close it and return it to my canvas bag, opting to close my eyes and take a second to simply exist in this moment.

The late-morning sun is warm on my skin, trickling through the treetops and wrapping me in a much-needed hug—something I haven't had in three months, three days, five hours, and thirty-two minutes.

Not that I'm counting.

Before I met Donovan, I was content to wander alone. I wasn't trying to land a significant other, tangle myself up in some fairy-tale whirlwind romance, or wind up in some quaint town in the middle of Vermont. I also wasn't trying to uproot my entire life and pour every last cent of my savings into renovating a dilapidated Queen Anne.

But love—real or imagined—changes a person.

Some days, I hardly know who I am anymore.

Most days, I struggle to remember a time before he came into my life.

When I glance down at my left hand, there's a void where my engagement ring once glimmered.

After Donovan passed, it took me thirty days to take it off. I kept thinking *one more day*, and then that turned into *one more week*, which inevitably turned into *one whole month*.

I couldn't rip the thing off my finger fast enough when I found out he'd lied about the money I'd given him for the renovations. I'll never forget showing up at the Arcadia Grove Savings and Loan to find out if there was enough in our joint account to cover his funeral costs . . . only to be told there *was* no joint account.

The bastard stole my heart, and then he stole my life savings.

And now he's six feet under—a world away from having to atone for the mess he left.

My stomach rumbles when I notice a little pop-up coffee shop ahead. Collecting my things, I head that way, order a small latte and petite blueberry scone, and call it brunch. The sooner I get home, the sooner I can finish sanding the floor in the dining room.

Eyeing the sidewalk on my way back to my Prius, I look for the auburn-haired stranger in the brown leather coat, but all I spot is the usual cocktail of tourists and locals. Young couples holding hands. Families pushing strollers. Grinning teens taking selfies. Retired couples dining al fresco.

All around me, life moves on.

Yet here I am, wandering alone.

I make it back to my car and load my books onto the passenger seat. A white sedan pulls into the spot beside me, and a lovely-looking couple exits a minute later. They meet at the sidewalk. She picks something from his dark-chocolate hair, and he kisses her blissful strawberry-red smile. Before they vanish into the crowd, he wraps his arm around her shoulder as if to show the world she is his and he is hers. That was us once. I can only pray that what they have is real and not some get-rich-quick scheme.

I start my car, shift into reverse, and glance into the rearview. It's in that exact moment that the olive green Ford passes by.

I pull out of my parking space and end up behind him at the light on the corner. A sticker in his back window says In Transit, and the spot that should hold a rear license plate is vacant. With my knuckles white against the steering wheel, I catch a glimpse of his eyes in his side mirror as he peers my way . . . and my stomach drops.

I'd know that copper-hued gaze anywhere.

I tap my fingers against the wheel, focusing on the beat of the tinny pop music playing low from my speakers, and try not to make eye contact.

The light flicks to green, and the truck turns right.

Without giving it a second thought, I do too.

"Oh my God, oh my God," I mutter under my breath. "What the hell am I doing?"

This is crazy.

I am crazy.

I stay a few car lengths back, as if that could possibly make any of this less obvious given we're the only two vehicles on this side street.

Five blocks later, he takes a left, pulling into the parking lot of the Pine Grove Motel.

My chase—if that's what I want to call it—comes to an abrupt end. It's all for the best, though, because I didn't have an end goal. I don't even know why I was tagging him. My fiancé is long gone, and he's never coming back. And it doesn't matter who this look-alike stranger is or how much he resembles Donovan—because he'll never be *him*.

And thank God for that.

Snapping out of it, I continue home to my empty house on the other side of town: past the main drag with the charming shops, beyond the cozy park with the shiny blue slide, miles from Arcadia Grove K–12 and all the places that remind me of the life that was never meant to be.

Once home, I slip into a pair of coveralls, crank my favorite Madison Cunningham playlist to drown out the echo of my lone footsteps, and sandblast the hell out of the dining room floor.

By three o'clock, I'm chugging a glass of ice water in front of an open window to cool off, debating whether I want to continue to the point of collapsing in exhaustion—or call it a night with a five-dollar bottle of twist-cap wine and a few episodes of *Curb Your Enthusiasm* . . . a show Donovan would never watch with me because he didn't get Larry David's offbeat humor.

It's then that I see him again . . . the striking look-alike in the vintage truck.

He slows down in front of my house, his piercing stare homing in on my front door.

But before I can do anything insane—like chase after him on foot this time—he's gone.

TWO

LACHLAN

rantipole (*v.*) to be wild and reckless

"Well, well, well. Look what the dog dug up." Lynnette Hornsby steps out from behind her screen door, arms folded across her chest like she has a bone to pick with me. Not that I'd blame her. I'd tell her to get in line.

"Lynnette," I say. "Sorry to show up unannounced. Bryce isn't around, is he?"

Her stoic expression softens, and a smile that feels somewhat like home meanders across her face.

"You show your face at my door for the first time in years, and you ask for *Bryce*?" She feigns annoyance.

"Good to see you, Lynnette," I say. Bryce has worked in construction since we graduated high school. Last I knew, he's a foreman. I was hoping he could find me some quick work while I'm in town.

"That's better." She looks me up and down, like she's taking me in for the first time in forever. "And you just missed him, actually. He's working in New Hampshire for the next month. Why don't you come in, take your shoes off, tell me where you've been all these years and why you didn't so much as write a letter."

"You didn't get my Christmas cards?" I ask with a straight face.

She hesitates, and for a second, I almost have her.

"Nice try, kid." Lynnette's smile turns into a shit-eating grin. "You can't bullshit a bullshitter. Get in here."

She props the door open with her bare foot and motions for me to step inside. I kick my shoes off on the rug and take in a view that hasn't changed since the last time I was here. The same old brown floral couch is shoved up against the wall, a knit blanket along the back. The same saggy chair is positioned for prime TV viewing, next to an end table with an ashtray full of cigarette butts.

"You going to stand there gawking, or you going to give me a hug?" Lynnette opens her arms wide and waits for me to meet her halfway. I've never been a touchy-feely guy, but I'll make an exception for Bryce's mom.

She practically raised me.

Not in a traditional sense.

But she picked up the ball that my asshole father dropped more times than I can count.

She fed me, at times clothed me, and showed up to all my football games to cheer me on as if I were her own.

Lynnette's trademark Calvin Klein perfume, stale cigarette smoke, and Diet Pepsi breath wrap around me like a blanket, and she holds on a little longer than necessary. She's smaller than I remember. Or maybe I'm bigger. When I was growing up, she was always larger than life to me. It's fair to say my perspective has warped over the years. Time will do that to a man.

"There," she says when she's done. "I gave you extra—in case I don't see you again for another ten years."

Shuffling to her favorite chair, she sinks down, crosses her pencil-thin legs, mutes the TV, and lights one of her Virginia Slims.

"Bryce is going to freak when he finds out you're back in town. You know that, right?" she asks.

"That's not saying much." I take a seat on the couch, which sags deeper than I remember.

Lynnette chuckles, her voice raspy. I tried like hell to get her to quit smoking when we were kids, going so far as to break those damn cancer sticks in half every time she bought a new pack. In the end, she'd always make me pay her back. And if I didn't have the cash, she'd make me mow the lawn or wash dishes or pick up dog shit.

"Bryce has always been . . . excitable. Unlike you." She points her lit cigarette my way. "Getting any kind of reaction out of you required pulling teeth with dull pliers."

"Forgive me for not wearing my heart on my sleeve."

"Sorry about your brother." She takes a long drag, her eyes crinkling at the corners. "Such a shame. Just wanted to get that out of the way."

"We all get what we deserve in the end," I say without pause.

She doesn't flinch. "Time doesn't heal all wounds, does it?"

"Not all of them."

The flash of headlights in the driveway steals Lynnette's attention, and she pops up to check the window. The car backs out a second later, as if they got the wrong house.

She flicks her wrist. "Thought it was the pizza I ordered. Anyway, what are you back in town for? Thought maybe I'd see you at the funeral . . ."

She doesn't finish the sentence—she doesn't have to.

My one and only brother died in a horrific car accident, and while some preacher read his eulogy and a crew of funeral home workers lowered him into the frozen ground, I celebrated with beers and strangers at a pub in Glasgow.

It's not the kind of thing I expect anyone to understand.

"Just got back to the States," I say. "Thought I should tie up some loose ends with his estate before I figure out my next move."

"Ooh, a worldly gentleman now, are we?" She lifts a shoulder and gives me a teasing wink.

"Nah. Just wanted to get as far away from this place as possible."

Her demeanor shifts. She gets it. No need to rehash what took me from point A to point B.

"Well, are you at least having a good time?" Lynnette takes a long drag. "Seeing the world?"

"The best."

She exhales a plume of opaque white smoke before stubbing her cigarette against her crystal ashtray. "Then that's all that matters."

"Say, what's the deal with the house?" I scratch my temple. "Drove by earlier, and it looked like someone was living there? Saw lights on inside and someone standing by the window."

I had to slow down to make sure I wasn't seeing something.

My guess is it's a squatter.

Her forehead creases. "Yeah. That'd be Donovan's . . . fiancée. I guess that's what you'd call her? She's not his widow since they weren't married . . . anyway, I hear she's finishing the renovation they started."

I chuff. "She realizes she doesn't actually own the place, right?"

"Honestly, I've never talked to the girl. And actually, I didn't even know Donovan was engaged until after he died and someone at the coffee shop was talking about his fiancée. I was going to introduce myself and offer my condolences to her at the funeral, but the poor thing was inconsolable. Since then, I've only ever seen her around town in passing. She mostly keeps to herself. Just works on that house day and night. It's sad, really."

The sad part is that anyone would be that heartbroken over losing Donovan.

"So wait. *Why* is she pouring money into that dump?" I'm still confused. The thing leans to the left and needs a new roof, a full electrical rework to bring it to code, *and* a complete gut job inside. You look up *money pit* in the dictionary, you'll see a picture of that shithole. Maybe it was a beacon of beauty in its first life, when some local 1900s doctor built it for his growing family, but once my mother passed and my father was left to care for it, it took a one-way trip downhill.

"You'll have to go straight to the source on that one," she says. "Like I said, I've never talked to her. I think her name is Annie? Annielynn? Something like that."

"Hate to break it to Annielynn, but I'm about to raze the damn thing. Hope she hasn't put too much time and money into it . . ."

Lynnette cocks her head. "You can't do that, can you?"

"My father left Donovan the house after he died," I say. "Donovan died childless and unmarried and, as far as I know, without a will. As his closest living relative, that makes anything and everything he owned legally mine. Once I get the paperwork in order, I'm donating it to the fire department, watching them burn it to the ground; then I'm out of here."

"Oh, come on, kid. You really want to cause all that trouble over a house that isn't worth anything anyway?"

"It has nothing to do with what it's worth," I say.

"Oh, honey. I know you want to burn your past to the ground and you think it'll make you feel better, but it doesn't work that way. In the end, there might be a pile of ash where that house once sat, but you'll still feel the way you feel right now."

"Maybe. Maybe not."

"That poor girl is so heartbroken." Lynnette splays a bone-thin hand over her heart. "I wish you could've seen her at the service. The way she cried, you'd have thought they'd been together a lifetime."

"Obviously she didn't know him very well."

"Still." Lynnette doesn't disagree. "Just because your last name is Byrne doesn't mean your life needs to be all fire and brimstone all the time."

"Is there any other way?" I give her a wink, keeping a straight face.

"You need a place to stay while you're here?" She changes the subject. "I can make up the pullout couch in the basement. My sister's coming later this week, but it's yours for the next couple of nights if you want it."

"I got a room at the Pine Grove Motel."

She wrinkles her nose. "Oh, hell no."

"What?"

"That's the last place you should be staying. Nothing but hooligans hanging out on that side of town."

I choke on my laugh. "*Hooligans.* You're really showing your age, Lynnette."

"You know what I mean."

"Rest assured I can hold my own against hooligans, riffraff, *and* ruffians," I say.

"I'm not worried about that." Her eyes scan me from head to toe, and she stifles a chuckle. She always used to say I was built like a brick shithouse—in fact, she's the entire reason I went out for football in high school. "It's an inconvenience thing. If you want your catalytic converter stolen or your room broken into, then by all means, stay there."

A Monte Carlo with a busted muffler and a neon pizza sign on the roof pulls into the driveway.

"That's dinner," Lynnette says. "You're staying, yeah?"

"Who eats at four o'clock?" I tease.

"Oops, am I showing my age again?" She swats at me from across the room before getting up to meet the delivery guy. "Set the table, smart-ass. We've still got more catching up to do."

THREE

ANNELIESE

lagom (*n.*) not too much, not too little, just right

"Good morning! Hello, hello." I plaster a smile on my face Sunday morning and wave to the couple on my computer screen. Several weeks ago, they hired me to come up with three name options for their baby girl, who's due any day now. "Are we ready for the big reveal?"

These moments are just as nerve racking as they are exciting—for both me and the parents. The vast majority of the time, I'm met with smiles and laughter and clapping and general fanfare. On rare occasions, I miss the mark by a mile. In those cases, the parents are generally stiff lipped and give me a fake smile and a curt thank-you, and I never hear from them again.

I have a good feeling about these two, though.

Jake and Seraphina Dybeck are a picture-perfect, nice-as-pie couple from Montpelier, who describe their perfect baby name as the kind of classic moniker you'd see in a Pottery Barn Kids catalog but with a vintage twist. During our initial consultation, they gave me a list of names they couldn't or didn't want to use (ones they loathed, they disliked, or other friends or family had already used), as well as a list of names they liked but didn't love.

"We've been counting down the days," Jake says, slicking his hands together.

Seraphina grins wide, covering her face in excitement. "I'm so nervous I think I might pee my pants."

"Ha! Well, we definitely don't want that, so I won't keep you waiting any longer," I say, grabbing my notebook and flipping to their page. "Okay, so the first name I have for you is . . . Adeline Iris Dybeck. Adeline is a fresh take on names like Madeline, Madelyn, or Madeleine. You can pronounce it however you prefer, and you can call her Addie for short if you're into nicknames, which, Jake, I know you said you wanted something that could be formal and shortened. We also have the mismatched syllables—three in the first, two in the last—as well as the long *i* sound in all three names."

I was in high school when I first found out I had a penchant for choosing names. I was the youngest cousin in a big Catholic family, and our extended family was growing by leaps and bounds. After one too many accusations of "name theft" and watching a handful of family members fight over "the good names," I sat down and made a list. Then I made another. I dispersed them to all my pregnant cousins, who then referred me to their friends and colleagues and their extended families. After a while, I started charging. First it was twenty-five dollars per name, then fifty, then a hundred as it became more involved. By the time I was out of college, I'd turned my little side hustle into a full-fledged business—helping expecting parents all over the country come up with the perfect monikers.

Seraphina and Jake exchange watery-eyed looks, their hands clasping.

"Adeline Iris," she says, slowly, letting it linger on her tongue.

"Adeline Iris," he repeats.

"We love it." Seraphina turns back to the camera.

"Awesome, that's what I like to hear," I say. I throw a celebratory fist in the air. "Ready for name number two?"

"I don't know if you can top Adeline, but we're ready," Jake says, leaning closer to the camera.

"All right, next up we have . . . Ivy Cate Dybeck," I say. "Again, we're carrying that long *i* sound in the first and last name, and we've got Cate with a *c* as a classic but modern middle name. Also, Cate is a nod to Jake's grandmother, Catherine. I don't tend to match syllables with first and last names, but I'm making an exception here because visually, Ivy is a shorter name, and I think that, overall, it's a strong contender."

"Ooh, I really like that," Seraphina says to her husband. "I don't know which one I like better . . ."

"Before you get too attached to Ivy Cate, let me put number three out there," I say.

Jake nods, and Seraphina rests her cheek against his rounded shoulder as they wait.

"Violet Evelyn Dybeck," I say. "Violet, Evelyn, and Dybeck both have the short *e*. Violet catches the vintage charm you both wanted, while Evelyn is a nod to Eve, Seraphina's mother's middle name. Violet and Evelyn both share the *v* sound, which is a bonus combination."

"Those are . . . wow," Jake says.

"We love them all," Seraphina echoes.

These are the moments I live for—the home runs.

"I don't know how we're going to choose." Jake runs his hands through his thick dark hair, turning to his wife.

"We have three more weeks to decide." She rubs her round belly. "God willing."

"Pro tip? Keep an open mind," I say. "Wait until you meet her. You'll know instantly if she's an Adeline, an Ivy, or a Violet."

Seraphina draws in a deep breath and gives me a grateful smile. "Thank you so, so much, Anneliese. We're not creative at all."

Her husband chuckles.

"We're accountants, and we think in numbers and logistics, and trying to come up with the perfect name for our little girl was just . . . not in our wheelhouse," Jake continues for her. "We're so glad we found you."

"Aw, anytime, guys. I'm just happy that you're happy," I say, giving a quick wave over the webcam. "Take care, and don't forget to send me her birth announcement! I can't wait to find out which one you go with."

In my pre-Donovan prime, I used to charge $1,500 for three names, which included hours of research and a handful of meetings to narrow down final options. People would pay those kinds of prices in Chicago, where most of my business came from word of mouth, and I had a monthslong wait list.

As it turns out, Arcadia Ridge doesn't have the same cutthroat baby-naming demand. Most of my business these days comes from my Etsy shop, where I've had to slash my prices to book clients, and I'm lucky if I garner enough business in a month to keep the lights on in this house and a full tank of gas in my Prius.

I end the video conference and flip to the last page in my notebook—the one reserved for my personal favorite names . . . the ones I was saving for *us*. Perfect monikers that are forever bittersweetly tainted.

Donovan and Anneliese Byrne had such a ring to it with all those *n*'s. I planned on continuing the pattern, and Don promised I could have free rein when it came to naming our future children. He said names were my thing and he'd be remiss to veto a single one that I found to be perfect.

It was always the little things.

From the moment we met, I'd never come across anyone so charming, so observant, so willing to do whatever it took to put a smile on my face. He wasn't like the other guys I'd wasted my twenties on—the ones who would ghost me after a string of amazing dates or match with my friends on dating apps despite insisting we were exclusive. The ones who spent more time in the gym than anywhere else and thought that going over their newest bench press record made for fascinating dinner conversations.

From the start, Donovan was different.

He was one of a kind.

He wasn't too much; he wasn't too little; he was just enough.

He wasn't overly chatty—only speaking when he had something important to say. Silence never bothered him. He didn't have to constantly fill the space with meaningless sound, though he was a huge fan of leaving me little love notes in unexpected places or showing up with flowers for no reason at all. Surprise date nights were his specialty. He also respected the concept of personal space. He wasn't constantly touching me twenty-four seven, but he'd never miss an opportunity to steal a kiss or sweep my hair from my cheek or brush against me with a hug in passing while I was cooking dinner or uncorking a bottle of wine for us. He never dominated the TV—taking interest in my shows, even if they weren't necessarily his favorites. And he was dynamite in bed— like he intuitively knew how to work my body without any guidance.

Being with him was easy and effortless. I'd never clicked with anyone the way I clicked with him—which is why six months in, he was proposing, and I was packing up my apartment, and we were moving to his hometown to renovate his childhood home and start our life together.

It's been challenging these last few months—reconciling the Donovan I fell for with the con artist he truly was. Nothing adds up, nothing makes sense, yet at the same time it does.

He played me like the love-drunk fool that I was.

A hot thread of embarrassment traces through my veins, the way it does anytime I think about him for too long.

I close the lid of my laptop and trek to the kitchen to heat up a frozen lasagna for lunch, the kind that smells better than it tastes but only costs ninety-nine cents. While I wait for my ancient microwave to do its thing, I walk to my room and change out of the blouse I wore for the video call and into an old T-shirt with a hole at the hem and a stretched collar. The unparalleled comfort of worn-out clothing is the only luxury I have these days.

The microwave dings, and I go back, twisting my hair into a messy pile on top of my head along the way and mentally mapping out this week's renovation schedule. But something catches my eye on the way—an imposing shadow by the front door.

Gasping, I jump behind one of the pillars in the front hall, peeking out just enough to find a masculine figure standing on my porch.

He knocks three times.

My heart lurches into my throat, which is suddenly drier than the Sahara.

In all the time I've lived here, I've never had any unexpected visitors save for the occasional neighborhood kids selling cookies and magazine subscriptions or the handful of neighbors who dropped off a casserole or two after Donovan passed.

"Hello?" a man's voice calls through the door. "I know you're home. Your car's in the driveway . . . and I can hear you moving around in there."

I peek around the pillar once more, trying to get a better look, though the way the sunlight shines in on the east side of the house paints him as nothing but a tall, dark mystery man.

"Annie?" he calls. My blood turns to ice. It's not my name, but it's close enough. "Annielynn?"

Again, close enough.

He knocks a second time.

"I'm not leaving until you come out," he says. "And I've got nowhere else to be right now, so . . . I can play this game all day."

I freeze like a doe on a midnight highway.

"I'm Lachlan," he says.

My killer has a name—and I like it.

But that's not the point.

"Lachlan Byrne," he adds, pressing his face closer to the glass, though due to its opacity I can't make out his features clearly. "Donovan's brother."

Apparently my killer is also a liar. Donovan never had a brother. His mother passed when he was eleven, and his father died a few years before we met. If he'd had any siblings, he would've told me. That's the sort of thing you tell someone you've just pledged to spend the rest of your life with.

Then again, he failed to tell me he'd pocketed my life savings.

Tiptoeing to the dining room, I peek out the window that overlooks the driveway—where an olive green F-150 is parked behind my car. I clamp a hand over my mouth, drawing on a mental image of the guy from yesterday . . . the rugged version of Donovan with the copper eyes and messy auburn hair.

"Hello?" He knocks again, his tone demanding this time.

Scraping my skepticism off the floor, I clear my throat, remind myself I'm surrounded by hammers, crowbars, sanders, and saws, and answer the damn door.

"The name's Anneliese, not—" I say before I lose my voice entirely. Yesterday I saw him from several yards away, and his resemblance nearly knocked the air from my lungs. But now, standing mere feet from this man, it's like looking into the eyes of Donovan himself. I attempt to speak once more. Nothing but air makes it past my lips.

Lachlan peers past my shoulder, into my messy house, before settling his heavy gaze back onto me.

"Anneliese," he says in a cool, collected manner before leaning against the doorway with the conviction of a man who owns the place. "Let me guess . . . my brother told you I was dead?"

"No," I finally manage to say. "He never told me you existed . . ."

His full lips—*Donovan's* full lips—inch into a smirk.

"Of course," he says, as if the revelation amuses him.

I don't want to believe him. I don't want to believe that Donovan once paged through an entire scrapbook filled with shot after shot of his parents with just one child and intentionally neglected to mention there was ever a second.

But given everything that's come to light since his passing, it wouldn't be completely out of the question.

"I didn't see you at the funeral," I say. I didn't speak to many people that day, but I'd have noticed if someone looking nearly identical to Donovan were standing graveside.

"I was out of the country." He doesn't elaborate.

"I've never seen a single picture of you in any of the photo albums."

A painful expression colors his handsome face, but it's gone in an instant.

I cross my arms and square my shoulders. "I'm sorry, but why are you here? What do you want?"

"This house," he says.

Squinting, I attempt to process his words. "What about the house?"

"You asked what I wanted. I told you," he says without a hitch. *"This house."*

I'm going to be sick.

"Unless you can produce a valid will naming you as Donovan's beneficiary, I'm legally entitled to his estate," he says. "Lucky for you, I'm not after any money. I just want the house."

There is no money.

There is only the house.

The house *is* the money.

Before we moved here, Donovan suggested we combine our savings into a renovation fund. Excited and woefully in love, I cashed out my savings and wrote a cashier's check to our new bank, which Donovan claimed he deposited into a joint account he'd set up online. Over the months that followed, we wasted no time ordering cabinets, hiring electricians, and sourcing tools, materials, and subcontractors.

We were burning through it quickly, given the size and scope of this renovation, but now the bank won't let me touch the funds. They won't even give me a balance on the account.

I met with an attorney several months back—a free-consultation type of thing. She said legally, I had no claim to the house since we weren't married, but I could file a claim *against* the house to try to recoup some of the money I'd invested into it. All I needed to do was find a close relative to legally inherit Donovan's estate so they could serve as the administrator. I reached out to one of his distant cousins on social media a couple of times but never heard anything.

The trickiest part, I was told, would be to prove that I'm the one who funded the majority of the account while also proving that Donovan intentionally lied to me about placing my name on the account. On top of that, I'd have to prove that my funds were directly used to purchase materials for the house. She didn't sound overly optimistic, nor did she sound thrilled about taking on the case. On five separate instances, she reiterated how expensive this could get.

But I just may be looking at a silver lining—one I never knew existed.

"Can I buy it off of you?" I ask. I don't know any sane banker who would let someone mortgage this house in this condition—nor do I know any sane banker who would approve me given the fluctuating nature of my income—but I put it out there anyway. If I could buy this thing from him somehow, then I could continue the renos, flip it, and walk away with a little extra padding in my pockets.

Lachlan laughs. "Sorry, but no."

I bite my lower lip to keep it from trembling. This is the universe kicking me when I'm down, but I'll be damned if I fall apart in front of this asshole. If I'm forced to walk away now, I'll never recoup any of this. Everything I've poured into this house will have been for nothing.

"Do you have papers?" I ask. "Something official?"

"I'm working on it."

"By working on it, you mean you've hired a lawyer and started the probate process?"

He studies me, sizing me up perhaps. Donovan may have played me for a fool, but I'm sure as hell not letting his brother do the same.

"I just got to town yesterday, but it's on my list," he says.

"And you realize probate court can take up to a year . . ."

"Less if it's uncontested. You planning on contesting it?"

"I plan on filing a claim against it," I say. "I've funded the renovations on this house, and I've done most of the work. Why wouldn't I want to cash out my investment?"

He rakes his hand along his carved jaw. "How long did you two date before you went all in?"

He's not so much changing the subject as he is fishing for information . . . information that could help his case.

"I don't see how that's any of your concern." I meet his curious gaze straight on.

Lachlan inches back, slipping his hands casually into the front pockets of his jeans as if to make himself less intimidating. "Look, we can do this the easy way or the hard way, and I don't want to be in this godforsaken town a day longer than I have to. I'm sure we can come to some kind of reasonable solution—"

"Reasonable solution?" I move into his personal space, which causes him to step back farther onto the porch and nearly lose his balance. "You come pounding on my door unannounced on a Sunday morning telling me you're taking my house, and now you want to come to a *reasonable solution?*"

His own brother went to great lengths to erase him from his life . . . now I'm beginning to see why.

He's silent, though his eyes are glinting as he holds back his words.

"I'm only going to ask you to leave once," I say, nodding toward his parked truck.

Lifting his palms in surrender, he meets me with a wordless, unreadable expression.

With that, I return inside, shut the door behind me, and secure the dead bolt while I'm at it. Resting my back against the wall, I wait until I hear the heavy tromp of his boots down the front steps, the creak of his truck door, and the rumble of his engine.

Just like that, he's gone.

But something tells me I haven't seen the last of him.

FOUR

LACHLAN

brontide (*n.*) the low rumble of distant thunder

The hotel room is pitch black when my alarm goes off Tuesday morning. I toss the scratchy cover off and head to the window, convinced it can't possibly be 7:00 a.m. and still look like night. I'm greeted with a rumble of thunder and a flash of lightning. Pockets of standing water puddle the parking lot. The rain pours so hard I can barely make out my truck in its spot a few doors down.

Peeling out of my boxers, I hit the shower, cranking the ice-cold water to hot and giving it some time to get there.

My lower back is on fire—thanks to that saggy excuse for a mattress.

I'm supposed to meet with a local estate lawyer at eight thirty. It sounds like this whole thing could get expensive if Donovan's fiancée puts up a fight. I don't know her well enough to tell if she was bluffing Sunday when she said she was going to contest it, but I know my brother enough to know that his preferred type always tended to be naive. I doubt she has any idea what she's in for. If I know my brother, and I do, he probably sold her the sun, the moon, and the stars, plus some swampland in Florida.

The showerhead spits for ten minutes before barely getting luke-warm. I wash up with a thin white bar of motel soap and watered-down shampoo that barely lathers. When I'm finished, I wrap a thin towel around my hips and attempt to make a pot of coffee. The machine whirs and whizzes, but nothing comes out.

For crying out loud.

I finish drying off and change into clean clothes. By the time I leave, I'm uncharacteristically presentable, dashing through the downpour to reach my truck without getting soaked—and while I'm impressed with my timeliness and ability to assemble myself like a working-class stiff, I'm less than captivated by the shattered driver's side window waiting to greet me.

Glass crunches under my shoes as I get closer.

"Son of a bitch." I unlock the door and inspect the inside. I know better than to keep anything valuable in here, but it looks like the so-called hooligans ransacked my glove box and the storage behind my bench seat. As far as I can tell, nothing of value was taken.

With every passing second, rain soaks through my clothes, making the fabric cling to my skin like a suffocating hug.

Carefully, I pluck shards of glass from my damp seat before climbing inside to get out of the torrent.

Taking a deep breath, I massage my temples and get my shit together.

I can't walk into the attorney's office looking like a drowned rat who pissed his pants.

Heading to the local Walmart, I buy clear plastic, duct tape, a pair of khakis, a white button-down, an umbrella, and a towel for my seat. I rip the tags off, change in the bathroom, and head back out.

I'm two blocks from the law firm when my phone rings. The clock on the dash reads 8:45 a.m., though I didn't need to check the time to know I'm late.

"Mr. Byrne," a woman's voice says once I answer.

"I'm on my way—it's just . . . it's been a morning."

"Well, that's what I was calling about," she says. "You were scheduled for eight thirty, but Mr. Swank has been asked to fill in for another partner at the last minute at nine. He was wondering if you'd mind rescheduling so he has more time with you?"

I pull into a parking spot outside the building and pinch the bridge of my nose.

This is the cherry on top of today's shit sundae.

"Yeah," I exhale. "That's fine."

"We could do tomorrow afternoon at three o'clock, or we'll be looking into next week," she says. "Monday or Tuesday."

"Tomorrow at three is good." I end the call, pulling away and heading to the nearest coffee shop. I grab two black dark roasts—one for me and one for Lynnette—and then I head to her part of town so I can let her gloat about being right about that motel.

As much as I hate to admit it, Lynnette's never been wrong about much of anything.

She always had a saying about storms—that they were *lucky* and always had a way of washing away any stagnancy in a person's life. She'd even go so far as to lie in the driveway like a crazy person and let the rain soak her to the bone. Then she'd come in shivering, grinning, her mood completely uplifted. It never failed: within a day or two, she'd announce she'd gotten some promotion or her car had stopped making some weird noise or some lame ass she was dating had finally moved on. Once, she won three thousand bucks on a scratch-off ticket—some of which she used to take Bryce and me to Six Flags for an entire weekend, VIP passes and all. It was my first, last, and only time at an amusement park, and while I thought I was having the time of my life, my excitement paled in comparison to the joy on Lynnette's face as she watched us run from ride to ride and shove our faces with concession-stand junk food.

I thought of Lynnette often over the years.

I thought about her off-kilter advice too.

It rained all the time when I was staying in London years ago, but anytime I felt stationary, I'd just move along to somewhere new. And when the stagnancy followed me, I'd pick up and leave again.

As much as I've been a rolling stone gathering no moss over the years, there's a stagnant piece of me I haven't been able to shake. A piece that's still here in Arcadia Grove, a piece I'm ready to cut loose once and for all so I can finally be free.

Maybe I've gone about it all wrong.

Maybe I should've lain in the rain.

FIVE

ANNELIESE

pluviophile (*n.*) a lover of rain, someone who finds joy and peace of mind during rainy days

"Oh, honey, I've got this." Florence places her hand over the dinner bill Tuesday night. "My treat."

It's always her treat.

I look forward to the day when I can return the favor.

"You don't have to do that . . . ," I say, like I always do, knowing full well she'll insist until she's blue in the face. Florence is too good to me. We've only become friends in the past few months, but I get the sense that she's taken pity upon my situation and enjoys looking out for me. A couple of years ago, she lost her husband of fifty years, moved here on a whim because she thought it was a charming little town, and then bought a quaint cottage in the historical district and poured her life savings into Arcadia Used Books.

"Don't be ridiculous," she says, rolling her eyes. On a handful of occasions, she's made small comments about having never had children or the fact that her closest niece and nephew live in California and she rarely hears from them except on her birthday. "*I'm* the one who invited *you* out. You know I adore your company."

Flo is also well aware of my financial situation.

She slips two large bills into the black leather envelope and slides it to the end of the table. The restaurant has been packed tonight, and our waitress is spread thin. It's going to be a while before we get out of here, not that I'm in a hurry. I'm going home to a big, empty house.

In a way, finishing the house is my equivalent of Flo's bookshop. We both needed to pour our energies into something to distract us from our bleak realities.

"You know the other day at the shop?" I ask Florence. "When I thought I saw someone I knew?"

Her eyes crinkle at the sides, and she toys with her white Lucite necklace. "Ah yes. I do."

"He looked exactly like Donovan," I say.

Her mauve lips press firm. "That must've been upsetting for you."

It was a lot of things.

"He . . . that man actually showed up at my house on Sunday." I crumple my napkin in my lap.

"What? What do you mean, he showed up at your house?" Florence leans closer, angling her left ear my way.

"He says his name is Lachlan . . . and that he's Donovan's brother . . . but Donovan never mentioned he had a brother."

Florence frowns, straightening her posture. She doesn't like what she's hearing.

But to be fair, I don't like what I'm saying.

"Are you one hundred percent sure that's his brother?" she asks.

"No. Of course not. But he looks like him. Nearly identical. And he knows his name. Claims the house is legally his . . ." I exhale. "And he's not wrong. I mean, if he *is* Donovan's brother . . . there was no will and no heirs. At least none that I know of. He'd be the next of kin."

"Oh my, my, my." She fusses with the wedding band she still wears. "What did you tell him?"

"I asked him to leave," I say. "And he did. But he wants the house. I don't think he's just going to walk away—especially if it's legally his."

"Are you absolutely certain Donovan didn't leave a will?" she asks. "If he forgot to mention his brother, perhaps he forgot to mention that as well?"

She's giving him the benefit of the doubt—which I'd love to do, but Donovan was an impeccable person. Slightly type A. Organized and meticulous. If he'd had a will, he'd have surely mentioned it. But being thirty, perhaps he felt he was young and invincible and had more time to worry about those things. That and who knows what other secrets he was hiding—someone capable of ripping off an honest, trustworthy woman isn't going to put all their dirty dealings on paper.

"He wouldn't have *forgotten* something like that," I say. "He purposely didn't tell me."

"In all fairness, sweetheart, the two of you had a bit of a whirlwind courtship. It is likely there are certain things about him you'd yet to learn," she says. "I was with my Lou over fifty years, and there were still things I didn't know about him. Little things, of course. Nothing as major as what you're dealing with, but I think it's human nature to never fully show our hand to everyone we know. We're all entitled to keep a little bit of something for ourselves."

Swindling my life savings and pretending to be an only child aren't exactly "a little bit of something," but I digress.

I can't stop thinking about the photo albums and how Donovan must have painstakingly edited and removed every trace of his brother.

"Maybe he was trying to protect you?" Florence lifts a brow.

"Couldn't he have just said, *Hey, I have a brother, and he's not a nice guy, so we don't talk anymore, and if you ever see him, just stay away?*"

"Million-dollar question, my dear." Her lips mold into a sympathetic slight curl.

Our waitress grabs our check.

"No change, lovely," Florence tells her. "Thank you."

I grab my bag. She grabs her clutch. We slide out of the booth.

"Any plans tonight?" I ask.

"Why, yes, actually," she says. "I have a date with my television set. You know I never miss an episode of *The Manor in the Mountains*."

"That's right. It's Tuesday night." I walk her to the door. "We shouldn't keep your lumberjack and his society girl waiting."

"Guinevere and Johnny."

"Yes, Guinevere and Johnny," I echo as I walk her to her parked Buick. A burst of carefree laughter trails from down the street, where a group of women dressed in business casual sashay into a local bar.

I'd always assumed I'd find a friend group once Donovan and I were more settled in here. But the second we arrived, we poured all our time into that house, and any spare moments we had we poured into each other. I'm kicking myself now for not trying to get out of my bubble, but hindsight is twenty-twenty.

At least I have Florence. But it wouldn't hurt to put myself out more and try to meet a few new friendly faces. I'm not sure how much longer I'll be here. Before Lachlan waltzed into my life, I thought maybe a year at the most—assuming everything went smoothly with the reno and legal side of things. Now it's anyone's guess.

Flo sends me off with a hug and an air-kiss, and I eye the bar once more.

It's only eight o'clock. If I go home now, I'll waste away the rest of the evening doing a little bit of this and a little bit of that until I wear myself out enough to fall asleep. For someone as busy as I am, there are days and nights I feel like I do a whole lot of nothing. It's a strange paradox.

Thunder rumbles through the dark sky, and lightning crackles above the trees. Donovan always loved stormy weather. In fact, it inspired him so much he'd stand on the front porch and watch it roll through, ignoring the chilly raindrops that pelted his skin and the warning flashes of lightning illuminating the sky. But having grown up in the Midwest, I've only ever associated it with tornado season. I'd take cover in the basement while he was delighting in nature's visual performance outside, earbuds in his ears playing some melodramatic playlist, lost in his own world.

Looking back, it was almost as if he were challenging Mother Nature to a duel.

What I mistook for a charming quirk of his was nothing more than arrogance in disguise.

A sprinkle of rain pats softly and rustles through the leaves overhead before beading along cars and making its way to the sidewalk.

Trotting ahead, I duck inside the bar to get a drink and wait for the weather to pass.

I make it inside without getting terribly soaked, snag an empty spot, and order a four-dollar cocktail off the Tuesday-night-specials menu—a bottom-shelf whiskey-apple-cranberry concoction.

One sip later, I'm transported back to the night I first met Donovan in Minneapolis. It was a Tuesday afternoon in late June, and the skies were a sickly shade of blue green. Weather sirens wailed in nearly every suburb surrounding Minneapolis thanks to torrential winds. All flights at MSP were grounded, and the airline put me up in the Marriott across the street. With nothing to do and nowhere to go, I decided to kill my time in the lobby bar.

I was on my second drink of the evening—another whiskey-apple-cranberry invention—when a striking auburn-haired gentleman in a navy three-piece suit took the empty seat beside me. He placed his cell phone and hotel key on the bar, ordered an old-fashioned, and made a comment to the bartender that it looked like he wouldn't be getting into Chicago anytime soon.

"Flight 324? Into O'Hare?" I interjected out of boredom.

He angled himself toward me as I took a sip, and I almost choked when I caught myself lost in his imperious gaze. In that moment, I couldn't tell if the skies were green, blue, pink, or purple, because all the color was in his eyes.

We spent the hours that followed glued to our barstools, flirting and drinking and small-talking our way into one another's world. He was a social media manager for a Fortune 500 corporation—but his dream was to be a writer. He was in the midst of querying agents in New York with the hopes that one of his passion projects might one day take flight. He loved classical music and Rat Pack jazz, was currently restoring a vintage Aston Martin DB6 Volante. His guilty pleasures were Cameron Crowe films, Mexican chocolate, and sleeping in. And his five-year plan included restoring his childhood home and getting a dog.

I'd never met anyone like him in my life—and in the span of a single evening, I was certain he was the one I was going to marry. I was also growing drunker by the minute. But when you know, you know—sober or not.

Everything about him serenaded my soul in a way I'd never experienced before. His laugh? It gave me life. The scent of his expensive cologne? Intoxicating. Unspoken confidence undulated off him in waves. Even the cadence of his words and his extensive vocabulary sent an electric thrill down my spine. I counted over a dozen beautiful women sauntering past us over the course of the night, each of them stealing glimpses at the gorgeous man chatting me up. But he never took his eyes off me. Not once. Not for a second.

By last call, we were equal parts uninhibited and enamored.

He invited me to his room for one more drink . . .

I couldn't say no.

My head, my heart, my soul, and my body were all screaming in unison for me to go with him.

He paid both tabs in cash and wasted no time leading me to the elevator, his hand on the small of my back. The doors weren't halfway closed before he stole a kiss that catapulted my stomach to the floor . . . his hands in my hair, his tongue grazing mine . . . his commanding presence flooding my senses.

We barely made it to his room with all our clothes on, and I spent the entirety of the night tangled in his sheets. By the time the sun peeked through the blackout curtains, I'd lost track of how many orgasms I'd been gifted by Donovan's golden touch.

Exhausted, dehydrated, and running on sheer adrenaline, I clung to every millisecond of every minute with this man, going so far as to watch him sleep. Though truth be told, I was only trying to take a mental picture to remember him by. Half of me figured it was a one-night stand. The other half of me prayed to God it was the beginning of a beautiful love story. While he slept soundly, I scribbled my number on a pad of hotel notepaper on his desk, quietly dressed, then headed to my own room to grab a shower and get ready to fly home.

With every silent hour that passed, my hope grew thinner, and I grew more convinced that the connection we had was nothing more than wishful thinking on my end. While I've entertained my fair share of guys pretending to be interested for the sake of a hookup, this one was different.

He was different.

Then again, my grandmother once told me we're always seeing what we want to see, even if we don't realize it. Reality is subjective, not concrete. Two people can be sharing the exact same experience and attach completely different meanings.

I was boarding my three o'clock flight home that afternoon when a flight attendant approached me and asked if I'd like a spot in first class.

The woman beside me huffed, making a comment under her breath and giving me side-eye. But I accepted the offer, gathered my things, and followed the attendant to the front of the plane.

"We don't normally do this," she said as we walked, "but we've had a special request."

I bit my tongue and quieted my confusion as she led me through the divider curtain, past a row of wide leather chairs. The scent of champagne and high-priced perfume filled my lungs as I gazed down each aisle. I was three rows in when I spotted the auburn-haired Adonis from the night before.

Donovan greeted me with a smile that *sent* me.

And I couldn't even say where I went—only that my feet were surely off the ground.

"Anneliese," he said, motioning to the open seat beside him. His full lips arched into the sort of smile that made my insides somersault. "Hope you don't mind the upgrade."

We were inseparable from that moment on.

I sip my drink again, savoring it as if it could possibly transport me back to that night. Unfortunately, I'm still here in Arcadia Grove, living out one side of what should have been our happily ever after.

Thunder rattles the bar windows as rain pelts the glass. A young couple dashes through the front door, drenched and laughing. They cozy up in a corner booth, shrugging off their wet jackets. She wrings out her hair. He dries his hands on a stack of napkins. They order two beers, and he steals a kiss. I miss those ignorantly blissful moments—when nothing (and no one) else mattered. When everything else was background noise.

There are times I wonder what it'll be like with someone new some-day . . . if I'll be able to fully fall for another person the way I fell for him or if I'll be questioning everything, holding back, and waiting for the other shoe to drop.

Donovan didn't just steal my money; he stole my faith in love.

"You've barely touched your drink." The bartender checks on me. "Can I make you something else?"

I perk up. "No, no. The drink is fine. I'm just savoring it."

It may be strange, but I want to remember. I need a hit of the sweetness to remind me of the bitter because some days I forget. Every once in a while, there are little pockets of the day when I find myself wistful, nostalgic for the good times.

Reminiscing like this helps me remember the good times were all for show.

"You sure?" He arches a brow like he doesn't buy it.

No one savors cheap whiskey.

"Yeah." I offer a gentle and reassuring nod, opting not to explain. I think of Florence's advice earlier—that everyone needs to keep a little something for themselves.

"What the hell . . ." The bartender squints across the room, peering out the floor-to-ceiling windows. "That's not . . . is someone actually lying in the street right now?"

I follow his gaze.

Sure enough, a man is lying on his back in the middle of Main Street in the pouring rain.

All around us, patrons are drinking and chatting and lost in their own little worlds. The two of us are the only ones witnessing this maniac.

"Do you have an umbrella?" I ask.

"You're not seriously going out there, are you?" The bartender scoffs.

"He's going to get run over by a car." I slide off my barstool. Umbrella or not, I refuse to let someone die on my watch.

I don't wait for his response—clearly time is of the essence here.

Trotting to the front door, I jerk it open and burst onto the sidewalk, loping between cars until I get to the middle of the street. With my heart in my teeth, I'm bracing for the worst—fully expecting to find a delusional psychopath or an unconscious heart attack victim.

Only the man in the street is neither of those things.

"Lachlan?" I ask, the rain dousing me in angry sheets.

He opens his eyes, peering up at me. The glow of streetlights paints his handsome face, and I'm taken aback all over again by how much he resembles Donovan.

"You trying to get hit by a car or what?" Water droplets bounce from my lips with each word.

He slips his hands behind his head and shrugs his shoulders into the hard ground, as if to show me he's settling in and not going anywhere.

"Wouldn't be the worst thing to ever happen to me," he says.

"I don't know if you're trying to be charming, but this isn't cute. Seriously. Get up." I wave my hands, motioning for him to move.

The stubborn jerk remains.

"Come on. I'm not joking." I reach for him, offering a hand.

His gaze flicks to my outstretched palm, then squints back to the sky. The drops of water that land in his thick lashes don't faze him in the slightest.

Headlights beam bright in the distance—three blocks away if I had to guess. They stop at a red light, buying us a few extra seconds.

"Come on. There's a car," I say. "You have to get up."

After the year I've had, I'm not about to stand here and witness a man get run over in the street—even if he is a bona fide jackass.

"They'll go around," he says, unbothered.

The light flicks to green.

"What if they don't?" I ask.

He says nothing, only watches me.

"I *really* need you to get up," I say.

He laughs through his nose. "You *need* me to get up?"

"Yes. I need you to get up," I echo.

"I need a lot of things, but I don't go demanding them from perfect strangers who owe me nothing."

"Fair enough." My clothes are soaked, adhering to my skin like wet glue, and a shiver runs through me. "I would *like* to know if you're really Donovan's brother. And if you are, then I would also *like* to know why he never told me about you."

"I'm sure you *would* like to know those things." His mouth forms a tight smirk.

The car lays on their horn. I motion for them to go around, which they do—thank goodness.

Donovan doesn't so much as flinch as they pass.

"Two days ago you slammed a door in my face," he muses. "Now you're begging for favors. Funny how things change when you're the one who wants something. Are you always this opportunistic?"

My jaw falls. "Opportunistic? I'm trying to save your life."

"No one asked you to."

I'm making zero headway with him, and given the fact that I know nothing about this man, I'm not sure where to go from here to get through to him.

"I'm sorry we got off on the wrong foot." I cross my fingers that an apology will smooth things over—a last-ditch attempt. "You caught me off guard, and you just showed up at my house saying it belonged to you. I was defensive, and I'm sorry."

"Do you always do that?"

"Do what?"

"Qualify your apologies?" he asks.

I frown. "I was explaining. I wasn't qualifying."

"Same difference."

The headlights of another oncoming car turn onto the road. "Okay, for real. You have to get up. This isn't funny."

The car coasts closer, and I wave it around, only this time it crawls to a stop. The driver, an older gentleman with tortoiseshell glasses, rolls down his window.

"You need help, ma'am?" he asks. His wipers swish, throwing splatters of rain in our direction.

"Nope, we're good." Lachlan motions for him to leave, but the driver looks at me for reassurance.

Crouching down, I tell Lachlan, "If you don't get up, I'm going to ask this man to help me peel you off the damn concrete. Is that what you want?"

"Of course that's not what I want."

"Then get up," I say through a clenched jaw.

Before he has a chance to respond, the driver speeds off—as if he wants nothing to do with our quarrel. Can't say that I blame him. As of now, it appears to be a hopeless cause.

"All right, then," I say. "You leave me no choice."

I slump next to him, lying on the cold, wet cement like a fellow crazy person.

It's a desperate move, but it's all I've got.

"Feels good, doesn't it?" he asks.

Little shudders run through me, and all I can think about are things like hot chocolates and warm blankets and fireplaces.

"If I catch a cold, it's your fault," I say.

"That's a myth . . . that being cold is how you catch a cold. Colds are viral."

"That's great that you know that. Would be a shame for all of that knowledge to go to waste when you get flattened by a set of Michelins."

"That would be a shame, but only because I prefer Firestones," the smart-ass quips. "What do you think it would feel like? Getting run over?"

The rain softens, dying off by the second.

"Not sure," I say. "And not sure I want to find out."

"Do you think it'd be quick and painless, or do you think you'd be flopping around like roadkill, waiting to be put out of your misery?"

"Guess we'll find out soon enough." I slip my hands behind my head, same as him, though my heart is hammering so hard it's about to rupture my chest.

"You don't want to go out like this, do you?" he asks. "Next to me?"

"I don't want to go out at all."

"Then maybe you should get up?"

My teeth chatter. "I will when you do."

The soft drone of tires on wet pavement steals my attention. I pop my head up and see a car speeding by on the opposite side of the road . . . a little too close for comfort.

"So how much longer are we going to do this?" I ask.

The rain stops without warning, and nothing but the scent of damp earth lingers in the night air.

Lachlan sits up with a grunt, pushing himself to stand, and then offers me his hand.

"Oh," I say. "So we're done now? Just like that?"

I place mine in his, and he pulls me up with a steady grip, as if everything that just transpired were the most natural thing in the world.

He lets me go once I'm upright, and I steal a glimpse of the white shirt plastered to his muscled torso before finishing off with the drenched khakis molded to his lower half. It's a complete one-eighty from the ripped-jeans-and-T-shirt uniform he sported the last two times.

"You good?" he asks, heading for the sidewalk. I nod, watching his confident strut. The man walks exactly the way his brother used to. "You should probably get out of the street. Don't need you getting hit by a car after all of that."

He's certifiable.

That's got to be why Donovan wrote him off.

"Where are you going now?" I trot after him, but only because I'm curious.

He points to the bar. "Was going to grab a drink if that's all right with you?"

"I'm headed that way actually. My stuff is in there." I straighten my shoulders and glance at the door. I don't want him to think I'm following him.

"Ah, I see. So you saw me lying in the street and came to save me," he says. "How valiant."

"I was just doing what any decent person would do." Donovan was always bragging about his good deeds. He once came across an elderly woman in a grocery store parking lot who had taken a fall and spilled all her groceries. He wasted no time helping her up, rebagging her food, and driving her home. Once there, he placed her in a comfortable chair, gave her some ice for her knee, and put all her things away in the kitchen.

Good Samaritan was practically his middle name.

Of course, I never verified any of that.

I took his word as gospel.

For all I know, the sweet little old lady was nothing but a figment of his imagination—yet another story to feed me so I wouldn't question that he was anything but a saint.

Lachlan grabs the knob and props the door open with his foot. "After you."

The thick, stuffy atmosphere of the place greets me like a warm hug, chipping away some of the chill in my bones.

He goes his way.

I go mine.

The bartender gives me a wave when he spots me, placing my purse next to my drink. He must have tucked it under the bar when I dashed out of here earlier.

"Thank you," I say, taking a seat and trying my hardest not to worry about where Lachlan's going. From the corner of my eye, I watch him disappear into the men's room.

"So what was his deal?" he asks. "The guy in the street?"

I blow a burst of air between my lips and laugh before reaching for my watered-down cocktail. "Wish I could tell you."

"I was about to call the police when I saw him get up," he says. "You think he's okay?"

No. I think he's insane.

"For now," I say.

"Let me make you a fresh one of those." He points to my drink. "Top shelf this time. On the house. It's the least I can do since you saved a man from becoming roadkill tonight."

"Not necessary." I slide the barely touched drink forward. "I'm actually going to head home. I think I've had enough fun for one evening . . ."

I'm gathering my things when Lachlan appears out of nowhere and takes the stool next to me.

"Two shots. Vodka," he says, patting the counter. He turns to me. "Sit down, Anneliese. Let's have a drink. We're practically family, are we not?"

"I'll pass." I slide my purse under my arm.

Disappointment colors his chiseled features, and he places his hand on my wrist. "Seriously? We narrowly escaped death together, and now you want to bolt like we didn't just share a life-altering experience?"

"Correct."

The bartender places two shots on the counter and eyes Lachlan, who slides one of them closer to me. Something tells me he's used to getting anything his heart desires.

It must be a Byrne thing.

"You want to know why my brother never told you about me?" he asks.

"Yes," I say without pause, eyes growing wide in the dark as I gift him my full attention.

"Take this, and I'll tell you." He hands me the shot glass. "Bottoms up."

I toss it back, letting the cheap vodka burn my throat on the way down. It takes everything I have not to retch when I'm done. My eyes water, and my stomach curdles.

Lachlan laughs. He's yet to touch his shooter.

"You going to tell me or what?" I ask.

"The reason why my brother never told you about me . . ." He draws out his words, taking his time. My heartbeat pulses in my ears as I cling to every syllable. ". . . is because he was an asshole."

In less than a second, my desperate curiosity fades, and all I see is red.

I'd toss my old drink in his face, but I think he'd enjoy that too much. That and I've never been one for theatrics.

Without another word, I walk away knowing one thing and one thing only: all Byrnes are assholes.

If he wants the house, he's going to have to pry it from my cold, dead fingers, and I'll spend every last ounce of energy I have making sure of that.

SIX

LACHLAN

orphic (*adj.*) mysterious and entrancing; beyond ordinary understanding

"Shut up! Just shut up!" the man taking his morning smoke on the balcony outside my motel room Wednesday shouts into his phone. "No . . . you're not listening to me, Judith. I said I'd be there when I get there . . . if you don't quit fussin', I'm not coming at all . . . oh yeah? Is that what you're gonna do? With what? Huh? With what?"

I perch on the foot of my bed, a thin white towel secured around my waist and hair still damp from my morning shower. Grabbing the nearby remote, I crank the TV to top volume, but it does nothing to drown out the stomping going on above me. Last I gleaned, it was a family of six crammed into that room. When they're not stomping and parkouring off furniture, they're watching an endless loop of Nickelodeon cartoons on full blast.

A police siren wails in the distance, and I think of my truck with its busted window.

I've stayed in hostels ten times worse than this over the years, but at least their beds were softer than these sorry excuses for mattresses.

I don't know how much longer I can put up with the Pine Grove Motel, but the only other option in town is a three-star chain that costs quadruple what I'm paying per night.

I washed yesterday's clothes in the sink when I got home last night and left them in the bathroom to dry. Surprisingly, they didn't have a single speck of dirt after the whole lying-in-the-street incident. In an hour or two, they should be ready to be ironed, and I'll be strutting into the Swank, Grove, and Ledbetter law firm to get the ball rolling on my brother's estate.

I chuckle to myself at the thought of Donovan's girl lying down next to me in the street, thinking she was some kind of white knight sent to save me. She clearly has a savior complex . . . rescuing strangers, salvaging an old, ruined house, probably thinking she was saving my brother from a lifetime of loneliness.

There's an edge beneath all that softness, though, like biting into something sweet only to get an unexpected spicy aftertaste.

I'd be lying if I said I wasn't curious about her—specifically what she saw in my brother. She seems like a bit of a ballbuster, and he tended to go for the softhearted pushovers. Then again, I hadn't spoken to him in years, so what do I know?

As soon as I graduated high school, I sold my car and bought a one-way ticket to London. From there, I couch surfed and free roamed and train hopped and soaked in every sight, sound, and experience I could, never staying in one place long enough to grow attached to anything or anyone. I always knew once that unsettled restlessness started gnawing away at my bones from the inside that it was time to move on.

Over the years, I learned where to find odd jobs that would pay under the table. They were mostly manual labor in the construction realm—bricklaying, plaster patching, carpentry, tile installation, and plumbing repairs. At this point, I could probably build an entire house on my own if I needed to. But a house is nothing more than a vault for memories good and bad, and I've got no use for one of those.

"Judith, for the love of God, I told you, I'm on my way," the man outside my door screams into his phone again. I peer through the curtains and watch him light up another smoke. He's shirtless and shoeless, his hair's a mess, and his belt buckle is undone. He's not going anywhere anytime soon.

Sometimes I wonder if people live for drama because they've got nothing better to live for.

Maybe their lives are otherwise dull and it keeps things interesting.

The smoker outside stubs his cigarette against the handrail before heading back to his room, slamming the door so hard it rattles the mass-produced oil painting hanging over my bed.

After Anneliese left the bar last night, I stayed and nursed a beer, replaying our entire exchange in my head. I've met hundreds if not thousands of people over the years, and I don't know that a single one of them would've lain in the street next to me.

Reaching for my phone, I pull up an old social media account, log in, and prepare to run a search on her name before realizing I haven't got a clue what her last name is. I type in *Anneliese + Arcadia Grove Vermont* on the off chance something pops up . . . but I get nothing.

Pulling up a search engine, I enter the same phrase.

No dice.

I lean back against the headboard and let my phone fall on the pillow beside me. Slipping my hands behind my head, I close my eyes and picture her dirty-blonde waves and those icy-blue eyes the color of the Atlantic. Those full raspberry lips and that pointed chin were nothing more than the cherry on the sundae. And that peach-shaped ass.

My God.

I could eat my fist just thinking about the way it swung side to side as she walked away last night.

There's no denying she's a work of art.

I can't begin to imagine what she saw in my brother of all human beings on this earth.

Maybe if I stick around long enough, I'll find out.

I peel myself off the bed, iron yesterday's clothes, and finish getting ready. My appointment with Swank isn't until three o'clock, so I've got some time to kill. Locking up my room, I head to the parking lot and breathe a sigh of relief when my truck appears to have made it through the night unscathed.

Only my relief is short lived . . . because the damn thing won't start.

"It's probably your catalytic converter," a disembodied voice says after I pop the hood and climb out. I turn to find the smoker from earlier leaning against the dusty white Chrysler 300 next to me.

"I haven't even looked at the engine yet. How would you know that?" I ask.

"Saw some kids come through here last night, getting under cars and running off with parts." He lights a cigarette, pinching the butt between his thumb and forefinger before blowing a plume of wispy smoke out of the side of his thin lips. "They like to take 'em for scrap metal. They get about fifty bucks."

Hunched over my front end, I drag in a jagged breath and recall what Lynnette said when I first told her I was staying here.

Can't say I wasn't warned.

"You know where I can get another one delivered?" I ask. "Is that parts store on the square still around?"

The man shrugs. "How would I know? I don't live here. Not permanently anyway. I'm from Scottsbluff, just west of here. My old lady kicked me out. Asked for a break even though she blows up my phone all day and night and begs me to come back. Second I get there, she kicks me out again."

He takes a long drag, shaking his head.

"Then why keep going back to her?" I ask, though it's more of a personal remark that I didn't mean to say out loud.

"Because I love her." His words are curt and staccato, as if my question insulted him. "I'll keep going back until she finally tells me not to. That's what you do when you love someone."

It's also what you do when you're scraping the barrel with your barely existent self-esteem and you live in a town of five hundred residents and romantic prospects are slim pickings.

"She probably just wants me to mow the lawn," he says, taking another drag. "Last time she wanted me to clean the gutters. At least she fed me that time. Dishes weren't even washed before she picked a fight about some asinine shit and sent me out the door."

"You realize how pathetic you look to her, right?"

His face turns pinched, as if the thought had never crossed his mind.

"Have a little respect for yourself," I say. "Don't come to her when she snaps her fingers, and don't go with your tail tucked between your legs every time she swats you with a newspaper for being bad. I'm sorry, but she doesn't respect you."

Maybe he hasn't given her a reason to respect him, but still. There's a very clear lack of mutual respect happening here, and someone needs to be the one to point it out to him.

The man flicks his cigarette butt on the ground, grinds it under the toe of his sneaker, and stares blankly ahead, as if he's digesting my words. And I hope for his sake he is. I hope I've opened his eyes to an entirely new perspective that will allow him to rebalance the power in the relationship or get off that godforsaken hamster wheel of drama.

"Sorry about your truck, man," he says when he snaps out of it. "I can drop you off downtown if you'd like? Think there's a parts store not far from there. They might be able to point you toward the nearest junkyard if they can't help you. That thing's pretty . . . ancient."

"Shit. Yeah. Two secs." I check and ensure that my catalytic converter is indeed missing—and it is. Then I climb into the passenger side of his smoky Chrysler. He climbs in beside me and starts the engine. "Why'd they take mine and not yours?"

"I put a lock on mine," he says as we drive away. "Little habit I've been practicing most of my life. That's what happens when you grow up on the shit side of town, my friend."

He turns up his music—"Peg" by Steely Dan—and taps his fingers against the steering wheel.

Five minutes later, he pulls up to an auto-parts store just south of the main shopping district.

"Thanks for the lift," I say when I step out. "Hey, I didn't get your name."

"Vernon," he says. His gold wedding band glints in the sun as he grips his steering wheel. "Vernon Mayfield."

"Good luck with Judith, Vernon." I point at my eyes, then his. "And don't forget what I told you."

He gives me a nod and a wave before taking off.

A half hour later, I'm a hundred dollars lighter, but I have my universal-fit catalytic converter. The only problem now is I need a welder to attach it, which means finding an auto mechanic who can tow it in ASAP and not drain my bank account while they're at it. Bonus points if they can order me a replacement window, though more than likely it'll have to be pulled from a junkyard.

That's what I get for buying the cheapest truck I could find off Craigslist the second my feet touched US soil again.

I check my watch, grab a bite to eat from a food stand, and take a seat on a park bench to kill some time before I walk to my attorney's office. All around me, locals and tourists dawdle up and down the flower-and-tree-lined streets like they've got all the time in the world. A cluster of women passes by, their arms heavy with shopping bags and their eyes lit as they debate on which café to hit up for lunch.

Shoving the last bit of food into my mouth, I wipe my hands and toss the napkin into the nearest trash can. Up ahead is an endless buffet of gift shops, boutiques, and specialty stores—none of which cater to the thirty-year-old-male-grifter-wanderer demographic.

I settle my attention on a used-book shop and head that way.

I could think of worse ways to pass the time.

SEVEN

ANNELIESE

datsuzoku (*n.*) an escape from your everyday routine

I rap my knuckles against the glass countertop at Arcadia Used Books, humming along to a Celine Dion ballad being piped from overhead speakers. This is the first time I've been standing on the employee side of this thing, and it feels . . . unnatural. I've never worked retail in my life, but when Florence called me at six o'clock this morning sounding frantic and asking for a favor, I said yes before she could get to the point.

Sometime overnight, her ninety-year-old mother took a fall in her home in Arizona and hurt herself pretty badly. Florence was beyond upset, of course, and asked if I'd cover the shop while she flew out to assist her mom and get a handle on the situation.

Thirty minutes later, she met me at the shop and gave me the keys and a lightning-fast tutorial on how to open and close the place. On her way out, she almost forgot to show me how to operate the card reader. Poor thing was so flustered.

Now here I am.

It's been three hours since we officially opened, and we've only had a handful of browsers. I've yet to ring up a sale, but it seems easy enough. I just scan the sticker on the book, wait for the price to show on the iPad, then swipe the card on the reader. Receipts are emailed. Easy enough.

I locate a feather duster behind the counter and dust a few of Florence's knickknacks: a business card holder made of glazed ceramic, a small crystal vase filled with fresh lilies, and an amethyst paperweight holding down a stack of book requests.

The bells on the front door jangle, and I glance up from my cleaning to find a dark-haired woman about my age.

"Hi, welcome." I offer her a friendly smile. "Have a look around, and let me know if you have any questions."

Not that I'll be able to answer them—but I'll do my best.

"Thank you," she says, letting her gaze linger on me for a few extra beats. Securing her canvas tote over her shoulder, she heads for a non-fiction shelf along the wall.

Minding my own business, I continue dusting anything and everything.

I'm terrible at just being still.

It used to drive Donovan nuts. Not in a negative sort of way, but he couldn't understand how difficult it was for me to just *be*. Not moving, not speaking, not physically doing something . . . those things are torture to me. I think it's part of the reason why I've poured myself into refinishing the house. It's hard, exhausting, challenging work. And when I'm not sanding floors and scraping off old paint from wooden built-ins, I'm whipping up baby names like there's no tomorrow, my mind whirring like a mental Rolodex.

Some part of me is constantly moving. I know no other way to exist.

"Hi. Excuse me." The brunette pops her head around. "Do you know where the business section is?"

"Um . . ." I work my way from behind the counter and rack my brain. I only know where Flo keeps her small selection of baby-name books, but I'm sure I can find something. "Forgive me, it's my first day . . ."

"Oh, really?" She lifts a dark brow, watching me intently. Staring, almost. Maybe she's just one of those people who stare without realizing it? "Where did you work before?"

That's a pretty direct follow-up question, but some people are straight shooters.

"I have my own business," I say. "I'm a naming consultant. I mostly consult on the side, but I'm filling in for the owner of the shop while she's out."

"What kind of names?" she asks—another direct question. Then again, she could be making innocent small talk.

I remind myself it's okay to let my guard down. This isn't a big city. Florence once told me sticking noses into others' business is practically an Olympic sport in Arcadia Grove. Besides, I was just telling myself the other day that I needed to make more friends—or at the very least . . . acquaintances.

"Baby names," I say.

"Oh?" She follows me to the next row, her attention weighing on me as I scan rows upon rows of books for anything remotely business related. "Do you have children?"

I shake my head. "I do not."

I'd elaborate, but doing so would involve sharing the story of Donovan, and on the off chance I break down in tears, I'd hate to put this woman in the awkward position of having to comfort me.

"So you just . . . name other people's babies?" she asks with an amused chuckle. "That's . . . quite a unique line of work."

"Here we are." I lead us to the shelf in the corner and point to the middle row. "Is this what you were looking for?"

She chews the inside of her lip, her gaze passing from the books to me and back. "I think so."

The woman reaches for a novella about small-business ownership and flips through it too quickly to read any of the words.

"Were you wanting something more specific?" I ask.

"Maybe something on marketing?" She exhales, hugging the book against her chest. "I recently opened a floral shop—thought it'd be good to specialize in wedding arrangements since Arcadia Grove is sort of a mecca for weddings."

It's true. Donovan told me that when he first brought me here. People come from miles around, other states even, to get married under the two-hundred-year-old oak on Briar Hill or in the seventeenth-century church on Sweetwater Drive or the fully restored Victorian mansion on Fleur de Lis Boulevard.

"Running the shop has been . . . a little overwhelming," she says. "Turns out all my talent is in flower arranging and none of it is in marketing, accounting, or advertising."

"What's the name of your shop?"

"Stem," she says with a wince. "It's awful, isn't it?"

"Just . . . *stem*?" I ask. "Singular?"

She nods.

"I mean . . . you could probably do better," I say with a gentle blunting to my words.

"I was trying to go for one of those hip, one-word-type names with a cutesy modern font on the door," she says. "But I think I missed the mark."

"You can always change it."

She shrugs. "To what?"

Between running Flo's shop, working on projects around the house, and staying on top of my name bookings, I probably shouldn't be committing to anything else, but I know what it feels like to be on the verge of losing everything you've ever worked for.

I can't let this woman's livelihood go down over a poor choice of name—something that can easily be fixed with a little bit of time and effort.

"Would you mind if I played around a bit with some ideas?" I ask. "Maybe I can come up with something more marketable?"

Her dark eyes spark with light as her mouth inches into a hopeful smile. "Really? You'd do that for me?"

"Of course," I say. "Just give me a few days. I'm kind of buried at the moment."

"Whenever you have time would be amazing," she says, gushing. Her entire face is lit as she toys with a ruby pendant hanging from her delicate neck.

The bells on the front door jangle, followed by heavy footsteps.

"I'm going to let you browse the business books here, and I'll meet you up front when you're ready to check out," I tell her before heading up.

I'm halfway to the register when I spot the man standing by the greeting card rack. Those broad shoulders, the dark-copper hair, the hooded gaze that could cut glass. I don't have to take a step closer to know exactly who it is.

"Lachlan." I stop in my tracks.

He glances up, shifting his posture as if he's equally surprised to see me.

"What about this one?" The floral-shop woman appears from behind me with a marketing textbook with a slightly outdated font. The tag reads five dollars.

"I can't personally vouch for it since I've never read it, but it looks promising," I say.

"I found a few more." She shows them to me one by one before placing them on the counter by the checkout. I grab the first book from the top, and her eye drifts to my left hand, as if she's curious to see if I'm both childless *and* single. I brace myself for her to ask another personal question, but instead she offers a simple "I figured I'd get them all. What the heck."

I ring her up—easy as pie—and rattle off her total before placing her books in a plastic sack.

"Berlin," I say when I hand her card back. "That's a beautiful name."

"Thanks for pronouncing it like the German city and not like Merlin the wizard," she says with a chuckle. While her demeanor is soft, there's an intensity in her eyes as she drinks me in again. Her gaze settles on my naked ring finger once more before her attention flicks down for a moment.

I brush it off.

Some people are just socially awkward or unabashedly curious.

Or maybe she's heard of me before—everyone loves a heart-wrenching tragedy to gossip about.

"Here you go." I hand her bag of books across the counter. "Stop back in a few days, and I'll have those shop names for you."

"Will do. Thank you . . ." She doesn't ask my name but offers a smile and a wave on her way out.

"Well, that was . . . interesting," Lachlan says from the card stand as soon as she's gone.

"What are you talking about?" I lean over the counter and rest my chin on top of my hand.

"You and Berlin."

"What was weird about it?"

"Oh . . ." His lips press flat as he frowns. "You don't know?"

I roll my eyes. "What?"

"Berlin is Donovan's ex," he says. "They dated pretty much all through high school and off and on in college. There might have been an engagement somewhere in there . . . I don't really know what happened after that because, well, I had more important things to worry about than my brother's dating life. I can only assume it didn't end well."

"Why didn't she say hi to you, then?" I ask.

"I don't think she even noticed me. She was too fixated on you the whole time."

Thoughts swim through my head as I reexamine all her lingering glances in a different light. I thought something seemed off . . .

Lachlan plucks a pale-blue card from a holder and flips it open to read it before putting it back.

"You'd think with all the writing talent in the world today, greeting card writers would've upped their game a little," he says. "I could write better drivel than this."

"Then do it."

"My sentiments wouldn't be mainstream enough for the greeting card masses."

Donovan was a writer. He was always scribbling away in his notebook . . . ideas, prose, poetry. He mentioned once that he'd written an entire novel by hand when he was in his younger days. He promised he'd let me read it one day. Obviously that day never came, and I can't begin to know which box in the attic contains all his writings, nor do I have any desire to explore them.

"Maybe you should get a blank card then," I say. "Write your own message."

"Unfortunately, the only blank card I've found in this rack is a sympathy card. I'm in the market for one of the birthday variety. By the way, who sells greeting cards at a used-book store?"

"They're vintage." I head over to help him hunt for the perfect one. "Some people think greeting cards are overrated. Florence, the owner of this shop, loves them. She's saved every one she's ever received. I think her collection is somewhere in the thousands."

"What about you? Do you collect anything?" he asks.

"Names," I say.

I select a white birthday card with yellow lace edging and flip it open to find an empty white space begging for the perfect words.

"Here you go." I hand it over. "It's blank. Now you can write anything your heart desires."

He swipes it from me, and our fingers brush. My eyes lock on his, and for a second, I can't breathe. It's like looking into Donovan's eyes. A rush of blissful ignorance is followed by the sharp tang of anger, flooding my thoughts with everything I'll never get to say to the man who changed my life forever.

Turning away, I walk back to the counter, collecting myself with each step. By the time I get there, I've taken three deep breaths and the pressure welling in my chest has faded.

"Is there anything else I can help you with today?" I ask. It's strange being cordial with the man trying to take my home, but this is Flo's store, and he's a paying customer, and I'm a grown woman capable of acting like one.

"Yeah." He rakes his hand along his stubbled jaw and peers around the shop. "You have any Hunter S. Thompson?"

"I don't know who that is, but I can look?"

"You work in a bookstore, and you've never heard of one of the greatest American writers in the twentieth century?"

"What did he write?"

"*Generation of Swine* . . . *The Curse of Lono* . . . *The Rum Diary* . . . *Fear and Loathing in Las Vegas*—"

"Oh! The movie with Johnny Depp." I perk up. "I've seen that one."

"The movie based on the book, but yes. That one."

"Sorry, not a reader." I offer an apologetic shrug.

I head for the fiction section, and he follows, his boots heavy on the wood floor with each confident stride.

Scanning the *T* shelf, I pause when I get to the place where Thompson should be.

"I'm sorry. I don't see anything . . ." I bite my lip. "I'm sure Flo can order one, though. She orders lots of stuff for me."

"Thought you weren't a reader?"

"Baby-name books," I clarify. "For my business."

He scratches the space above his eyebrow.

"I'm a name consultant," I tell him. "For babies. Mostly. I've done some pet names . . . and I guess I just promised Berlin I'd help her name her flower shop . . ."

His gaze skims over me from head to toe. "That's a thing?"

"Everything is a thing," I say, head tilted. "But yeah. Anyway, can I help you with anything else, or are we ready to check out with your blank vintage greeting card?"

Lachlan's brows rise, and he scans his surroundings. "Kind of wanted to do a little browsing but seems like you're ready to get me out of your hair."

He checks his watch—which I can't help but notice is an antique piece and not a mass-produced Bluetooth-enabled device.

"I'm meeting with my attorney at three," he says. "Trying to kill a couple of hours."

"Your attorney?" I ask. It's happening. He's actually doing this. Not that I doubted him, but a part of me hoped maybe he'd get to know me a little better first and get to know my situation before moving full speed ahead with kicking me out.

"Yes." Our eyes meet. "I told you, the house is legally mine, and I'm going through the proper channels. Did I not make myself clear the first time?"

I swallow the hardness in my throat.

"We completely redid the electric," I say. "Which was thirty grand. And we did some foundation repair, which was ten grand. We ordered cabinets. That was another thirty grand. But they haven't installed them yet because they were waiting for us to refinish the floors in the kitchen and bathrooms. If I walk away now, they get to keep that money. We also ordered several thousand in light fixtures—which are in storage. The rest of the money—as far as I know—is sitting in an account in Donovan's name at Arcadia Grove Savings and Loan, and they won't let me access it since we weren't married and my name wasn't on the account."

"Wait, wait, wait. You gave him more than seventy grand of your personal savings and let him put it in an account in his name?"

I take a breather. "It's not that simple."

The heaviness of his stare pulls my attention back to him.

"Your brother lied to me," I add. "He took my money, put it in an account that only he could access . . . and then he died."

Lachlan's full lips press into a flat line as he exhales. I'm not sure if he feels sorry for me or if he thinks I'm the world's biggest fool at the moment. Either way, it doesn't matter. What's done is done, and he doesn't owe me a thing.

"I can get you your money back," he says. "Once I get through probate, I'll have access to everything of his."

"I don't even know if there's much left at this point. Most of it's wrapped up in the house."

His posture shifts.

"I take it the house means entirely different things to each of us," Lachlan says.

Placing my hand over my heart, I say, "I know it's where you grew up, but it was where Donovan and I were building our life together before. Now that he's gone, I've got no reason to stay in Arcadia Grove. At least let me fix it up and give it the renovation it deserves. Then we can sell it and split the profits? Actually, I don't even need the profits; I just want to get my initial investment out of it so I can move back to Chicago."

"What makes you think I want to sell it?"

My nose wrinkles. "Oh. Did you want to live there?"

"Not at all."

I'm confused. "Then what do you want with it?"

Last I checked, the place assessed at forty grand—mostly due to its deteriorating condition. The city was on the verge of condemning it until we stepped in and promised to restore it to its full glory.

"I want to burn it down," he says.

My stomach sinks, and I study his face, waiting for some indication that he's messing with me, but his stoic expression remains.

"You can't be serious," I say. That house might represent a mixed bag of emotions for me right now, but it doesn't deserve to burn to the ground. All that history, all that hard work, all that potential . . .

"Unfortunately, Blue Eyes, I am." He heads for the register, but I cut him off halfway there.

"But why? Why would you want to destroy a perfectly good home? I mean, it's not perfectly good yet, but it will be. Another family should get a chance to enjoy it and make their own memories there."

"I have my reasons." He steps around me and continues on. After placing his greeting card on the glass countertop, he then reaches for his wallet.

"I'm sorry, but I can't allow that."

Lachlan waves his Visa and points to the iPad as if to silently tell me to stay on task, but I'm too astounded to function right now.

"Wouldn't that be arson?" I ask.

"Not if I donate it to the fire department. They'll do a controlled burn and use it for training."

"I don't understand . . ."

"And you don't need to." He taps the card and glances at the iPad screen. "Looks like I owe you three ninety-five and tax. Should I ring myself up or . . .?"

I swipe his card with trembling hands and complete the transaction.

"What did that house ever do to you?" I ask.

While Donovan and I only lived together in that house for a couple of months, he told me enough stories about it to fill an encyclopedia. The first night we arrived, he led me around by the hand, giddy as a schoolboy, as he showed me his childhood bedroom, where his initials were scratched into the back of the closet door. He then pulled me outside, where he demonstrated how he used to climb the big pine tree in the backyard. When he was finished, he was covered in sap and smelled like Christmas, but every part of him was a contagious sort of shiny and euphoric. He also showed me the red peony bushes his mother had planted decades before along the east side of the house, the shed where his father used to work on his welding projects, and the peg in the garage where his favorite bicycle—an emerald-green Schwinn—used to hang.

He painted the picture of a charmed childhood.

I can't imagine how a house filled with so many joyful memories for one brother could be nothing more than trash to the other.

"Thanks for your help." He lifts the bag with the greeting card before heading toward the door.

I try to say his name, a feeble attempt to keep him from leaving so we can continue this conversation . . . but nothing comes out.

For the first time in my life, I'm speechless.

EIGHT

LACHLAN

logophile (*n.*) a lover of words

"You didn't have to get me anything, kid." Lynnette swats at my chest Thursday afternoon when I show up with a birthday card and a twelve-pack of Diet Pepsi. I'm sure she'd have much preferred a carton of cigarettes, but I don't condone that shit. "Get your ass in here and have some cake. My sister baked it from scratch—double-layer German chocolate. Our grandmother's recipe."

She sets the case of soda on the kitchen table and rips into the card.

"'Happy birthday,'" she reads from the front before flipping it open. "'Words are cheap and so am I. That's why I'm only giving you one this year . . . *tacenda*.'"

"*Tacenda*," I echo.

"Still obsessed with those obscure words, I see," she says, arching her mouth. "What's this one mean?"

"Things better left unsaid."

"So in other words, I'm the most amazing person in the world, you're sorry for not keeping in touch better over the years, you'll never do it again, and you love me," she says.

"Sure."

"Wiseass." She throws her lanky arms around me and gives me a bite-size bear hug. "I still have that calendar you gave me for Christmas all those years ago, the one with the word of the day. Never used it but never threw it out either."

"That counts for something."

"Maybe it'll be worth something someday?"

"Doubt it."

"No, I mean, when you're a famous writer. I can say Lachlan Byrne gave this to me when he was sixteen years old," she says.

"Ever the optimist." Some things never change.

"You still writing?" she asks.

"Not lately." Part of the reason I moved out of the country was to get away from my toxic upbringing, but the other part was to experience the kind of life I'd only ever read about in books and magazines. I thought it would inspire me and help me work on my craft. And it did. To a point. But somewhere along the line, I sidelined my passion in favor of beautiful women, late-night pub crawls, and thrill-seeking adventures of the European variety.

I can't remember the last time I picked up a pen for the sheer pleasure of writing.

"Sit down, Lach. I'll slice you some cake," she says. "But you can't have it until you sing me 'Happy Birthday.'"

"Guess I'm going hungry then."

She laughs as she slams cupboards and drawers, and a minute later, she places an over-the-top triangle of double-layer cake in front of me.

"You want a glass of milk to wash it down?" she asks. But before I can respond, she's already halfway to the fridge.

She was always like this when I was growing up—doting on me the same way she doted on her own flesh-and-blood son. I always found it bittersweet that her birthday was the same date as my mother's death.

The two never met each other, since Lynnette and Bryce moved here years after Mom died. But I like to think that they'd have been friends, and I always pictured them sitting side by side at my games in coordinating school colors.

"You hear from Bryce?" I ask between bites of cake rich enough to put me in an instant sugar coma.

"Yeah, he called me yesterday. Cell service is spotty where he is because they're pretty close to the mountains, but he's doing well. I told him you were in town. He made me promise not to let you leave before he gets back."

"Ha. I'm sure I'll be here awhile. I met with an attorney yesterday. Says we'll need to file to open an estate to transfer the house into my name. If everything goes smoothly, it could take four months, but if Anneliese files a claim against the estate, we're looking at a year, at least. Maybe longer. And I wouldn't be able to sell the house until the claim is resolved."

"Do you think she will?" Lynnette takes the seat beside me and props her head on her hand.

"Apparently she dumped her life savings into that shithole."

Lynnette shakes her head before throwing her hands in the air. "I don't want to judge, because I've made some crappy decisions in my day, but that's just . . . *oof*."

She doesn't mention Donovan—she doesn't need to.

Tacenda.

Some things are better left unsaid.

"I have a feeling she's going to fight me on this every step of the way," I say.

Yesterday Swank said to get the ball rolling he needed a copy of Donovan's death certificate—which I'm assuming Anneliese has. Once I get that, we can open an estate, and once I'm named administrator of said estate, I can transfer the house into my name, and the rest is history. Given the fact that both of our parents are deceased and Donovan had no wife, children, or will, Swank doesn't foresee an issue, as I'm

Donovan's closest living relative. The only hiccup would be if she files a claim against the estate to recoup renovation costs, but he said that could be tricky, proving that the money came directly from her, funneled into Donovan's account, then went directly to pay for materials and labor. The whole thing sounds convoluted and expensive—at least on her end.

"Speaking of Anneliese," I say. "I've run into her a couple of times this week."

Lynnette leans back, crossing her legs. "You don't say?"

"Saw her at a bar and then again at a bookshop." I decide not to mention the fact that I showed up at her doorstep last Sunday, because I have a feeling Lynnette would rip me a new one. It was a dick move, but there's no easy way to drop that kind of bombshell on someone. I've always been the kind to rip off the Band-Aid. Drawing things out only causes unnecessary suffering. "She's dead set on fixing up the house."

"I'm sure it reminds her of your brother. She's probably still grieving."

"She can grieve anywhere she wants—just not there," I say. "And I don't know how much grief has to do with it. Sounds like Donovan made off with her money."

"What are you talking about?"

"She didn't elaborate. Something about an account that was only in his name." It doesn't feel right to go into detail, to air her dirty laundry like small-town gossip.

"Good Lord." Lynnette clucks her tongue. "Well, it wouldn't be the worst thing to have a little heart."

I learned a long time ago that being soft gets you nowhere in this world.

"Anyway." I take a bite of cake.

"How's the Pine Grove Motel treating you so far?" Lynnette asks with a twinkle in her eye.

I fork another bite rather than answer her.

She laughs. "That's what I thought. Wish I had some space for you. My sister's staying until Lord only knows when because now that she's retired, she's got all the time in the world. I told you she's retired now, right? She takes the opportunity to remind me every chance she gets. Maybe one of these days I'll get to know what it's like to be *retired*. Then again, I don't know what I'd do with myself with all that free time. Anyway, Bryce gets back next month. I could put you in his room, but it'd be temporary."

"I wouldn't want to put you out."

Lynnette slants her gaze. "You just have shit timing, is all I'm trying to say."

I was thinking about finding a short-term rental, but the only places that will rent to someone with no job are the kind of places that make the Pine Grove Motel look like a Sandals all-inclusive resort.

"It'd be nice if I could stay at my own damn house," I say.

Lynnette pitches forward, shrugging. "Well . . . why don't you?"

I sniff a laugh and almost choke on my cake. "Highly doubt Anneliese would be on board with that. I may or may not have told her I plan to burn the place down."

She swats the air. "Just can't help yourself, can you?"

If there's anything I hate in this world, it's liars.

I'm honest to a fault.

"You told me the other day you did a lot of construction work overseas," she says. "Why don't you . . . I don't know . . . offer to help her fix the place up in exchange for a room there?"

"Work for free so I can stay in a house that's legally mine . . ."

"I'm not saying the situation isn't screwed seven ways from Sunday, but you need a place to stay, and I'm sure she could use some help cleaning the place up, and maybe—just maybe—by the time it's over, you'll finally pull your head out of your ass and realize you're better off selling it than burning it to the ground."

I've daydreamed about watching that place go up in flames more times than I care to admit.

I lean back in my chair, pull in a long breath, and give it some thought.

She may be onto something.

NINE

ANNELIESE

heimat (*n.*) a place that you call home

"What are you doing here?" I answer the door Friday night to the man who's beginning to become a regular fixture in my life.

"Sorry to drop by unannounced again. I'd have called, but I don't have your number." Lachlan's gaze skims past me and into the darkness of the house.

I've only been home thirty minutes—long enough to throw on some shabby, paper-thin pajamas, wrap my hair into a messy bun, and warm up some leftovers. I was about to uncork a bottle of red and cue a movie on Netflix when I heard the knock on the door.

I pull the baggy neckline of my shirt over my exposed shoulder, suddenly grossly aware of the fact that I'm not wearing a bra.

"Can I help you?" I ask, repeating the words I've said a couple of hundred times this week at the bookshop. I thought remodeling a house was a lot of work . . . it's nothing compared to retail. I don't know how Flo does it—standing on her feet for hours on end, forcing smiles to placate grumpy patrons, essentially being stuck in a twenty-foot-by-thirty-foot room all day that smells like paper and the passing of time.

"Yeah," he says. "A couple of things. I need Donovan's death certificate."

My lips press flat. I'm not a petty person, and I'm not going to keep it from him, but this is certainly not the way I wanted to kick off a relaxing Friday night.

"I'll have to dig it out of storage," I say, "but I'll get it to you."

His dark brows arch, as if he was expecting more friction.

"Anything else?" I ask.

He nods, his hands forming an upside-down V in front of his nose. "Yes. I have a proposition for you."

I lean against the doorway, arms folded. I know better than to make any kind of deal with the devil, but I'm curious.

"Go on," I say.

"We both want this house," he says. "And we both have entirely different intentions with it. We also both need a place to stay while we . . . sort out the next chapter of our respective lives and—"

"Hold up." I lift a palm to silence the man because my thoughts trot one step ahead of him. "If you're suggesting that you move in with me—"

"That's exactly what I'm suggesting," he says. "Hear me out."

There's nothing Lachlan can say to make me warm up to the idea of living with the one man my dead fiancé clearly didn't want in his life, nor do I have any desire to associate with yet another Byrne.

"I may know a thing or two about fixing stuff," he says. "If you let me stay here—and to be honest, I can't believe I'm asking for permission to stay in my own home—if you let me stay here, I'll help you finish the house."

"What's the catch?"

"Let's give ourselves a timeline," he says. "Six months. Tops. By the end of the six months, if you can convince me not to donate this place to the fire department, I'll sell it, you'll recoup your costs, and we'll split the profits and go our separate ways."

"And if I can't convince you?" I ask.

"This place burns to the ground." He slides his hands in his pockets, speaking as casually as if he were speculating about tomorrow's weather forecast.

"Seems like your mind's already made up."

He lifts a muscled shoulder. "Of course it is. But I'm giving you a chance to change it."

"Why?"

He blows a puff of air through his full lips. "Because this probate thing is going to take—minimum—four months, and I don't want to spend the next one hundred twenty plus days in this *Groundhog Day* town, sleeping on a lumpy mattress at the Pine Grove Motel, figuring out how I'm going to get through these never-ending weeks."

"So essentially, you're bored," I say. "You need somewhere to stay and things to do to occupy your time."

"Only boring people get bored."

I roll my eyes.

"I'm just saying, there's a way this could work out for both of us," he adds.

This house has five bedrooms—three of which are usable. Two functional bathrooms plus a powder room off the kitchen. I'll admit it gets lonely from time to time, and a little bit of company wouldn't be the worst thing in the world—but I don't know Lachlan from Adam.

I cinch my arms tighter across my chest. "Tell me the real reason Donovan cut you out of his life, and maybe I'll consider it."

"He didn't cut me out of his life," Lachlan says. "I cut him out of mine."

"Then why did he pretend you didn't exist?"

"The only person who knows why is no longer with us, so . . . unfortunately I can't answer that."

Squaring my gaze on his, I say, "I'll be straight with you. I'm not comfortable living with a stranger."

A beautiful stranger.

Perhaps a wicked one too.

"I'm sorry, but I can't just let you move in," I say, my stare dropping to his tatted forearms before lifting to the ink that snakes down the side of his neck and disappears under his shirt collar.

"It's not a matter of *can* or *can't*, Anneliese," he says. "It's a matter of *will* or *won't*. We both know this is the only chance you have at salvaging the work you've done here and getting any of your investment back."

The image of a local sheriff placing a court-ordered eviction notice on my door plays in my head. He's not wrong. Then again, I don't know what would be worse: being evicted from this house and losing everything I've worked for . . . or living with Donovan's estranged brother for the next six months and still losing everything I've worked for.

"What are the odds you'd see things my way?" I ask. "Honestly."

His whiskey-colored gaze skims the ragged framework of the front door. He runs his fingertip along a deep scratch.

"I don't know if I can give you a number," he says after a bit of contemplation. "But I can give you my word—I'll hear you out. That's the best I can do."

The leaves of the thick oak tree out front rustle in the breeze. Crickets chirp, and the streetlights come on. It's a night like any other, but there's also something different in the air: something I can't place my finger on.

The truth of the matter is that I can hem and haw and debate this all I want, but at the end of the day, his offer is the best chance I have at saving this house and walking away with enough money to start the next phase of my life—whatever that may be.

"Give me the weekend," he says, perhaps sensing my hesitation.

"Like a trial?"

"Exactly. I'll be here at eight a.m. tomorrow. We'll work on the house for the next couple of days. You can decide after that."

I drag in a humid summer breath and let it go.

It's not a terribly unreasonable idea, all things considered.

"Fine," I say after a brief pause. I don't want to seem too eager.

Lachlan's mouth arches into a perfect smile—and for a second, he doesn't seem so intimidating . . . or so infuriatingly determined.

"Get a good night's rest, Anneliese," he says before he goes, taking a second to rap his knuckle against a saggy plank of siding on the porch wall. "We've got a busy couple of days ahead of us."

I close the door behind him, resting my back against the foyer wall and replaying our surreal conversation on a loop in my head.

I only hope I don't live to regret this.

TEN

LACHLAN

natsukashii (*adj.*) suddenly, euphorically nostalgic

"Hi, so . . . yeah," Anneliese says Saturday morning when she answers the door. "I guess we're doing this."

She's wearing a faded Michigan State T-shirt. The bright green makes her eyes especially blue. I catch myself getting lost in them for a split second; then I snap the hell out of it.

She's a beautiful woman, no question.

And there's a fierce edge to her that I wasn't expecting given my brother's penchant for the naive types.

But I'm not here to steal that bastard's girl—as much as I would love to hold that over him. It's not the same when he's rotting in the ground. Plus I've got enough respect for myself that I have no desire to play second fiddle.

I place my leather duffel bag by the front door.

The last time I set foot inside this place, I was eighteen. A fresh high school graduate. I thought I knew everything about everything, and I was on a mission to prove it. I left with a backpack and two middle fingers to the world and never looked back.

My father didn't try to stop me. In fact, he stood by and watched me pack without so much as a word. Donovan was just getting home from a date with Berlin when he saw me throw my things in the trunk of my car. I'll never forget the wild look in his eyes when he realized I was leaving for good.

That was the thing about my brother—he only needed me around because it gave him the upper hand. Without me, he couldn't shine. Being the golden child wasn't as glorious for him when he couldn't rub my face in it.

"You okay?" Anneliese asks.

I have no idea how long I've been standing here, drowning in the heaviness of ancient thoughts.

"You look . . . really angry," she says carefully.

I drag in a loaded breath and let it go.

I'm going to have to let a lot of shit go if I'm going to stomach the next six months in this town.

"Nah. I'm good." I glance to the left, toward the living room where my mother used to read me stories by the glow of the fireplace.

For nine short years of my life, I had that warm, fuzzy, traditional childhood. After my mother passed, my life became somewhat of a Dickensian tragedy.

"I thought you could stay in the blue room," she says. "The one next to the primary bedroom. The other rooms . . . well, one's not furnished, and the other two are being used for storage. One of those is Donovan's old room, but I get the sense you wouldn't want to sleep in there."

When I was growing up, the blue room was—in many ways—my prison *and* my sanctuary.

I suppose life has a way of coming full circle when you least expect it.

"You're not wrong." I slip my bag over my shoulder and head for the stairs, instinctively skipping the ones that creak. Funny how chunks of my childhood are fuzzy memories or completely blacked out while little things like this have never left.

Anneliese follows me, her hand gliding up the rough railing of the banister.

"The bed's a little small," she says. "I'm assuming it's the same one from when you were a kid? There's a dresser, but I haven't opened it. We hadn't gotten around to that room yet. I assumed it was just a spare room . . ."

I open the door at the end of the hall, greeted with a musty scent. Dust particles float through the air along with the scent of clean cotton.

"I washed the bedding overnight," she says.

I'm placing my bag by the foot of the bed when a white envelope on the dresser catches my eye. I'm midreach when Anneliese clears her throat.

"Donovan's death certificate," she says, her voice low and soft.

For a moment, I feel sorry for her. I can't imagine any of this is easy. She seems like a decent, trusting person who fell for the kind of guy who ruins everything he touches.

I slide the certificate out of the envelope, scanning the words on the page.

Certificate of Death: State of Vermont
Name: Byrne, Donovan Nolan
Date of death: February 12, 2022

I don't know the specifics of how he passed, and I only found out when a distant cousin I hadn't heard from in years texted me with their condolences. My blood ran hot and cold at the same time, and I couldn't type my brother's name into Google fast enough. Two seconds later, I was poring over a two-paragraph article about a fatal car crash on I-93 believed to have been caused by deteriorating road conditions during a winter storm.

His obituary came out a couple of days later.

There was no mention of me.

I realize now that Anneliese was likely the one handling the funeral arrangements and subsequently providing information for the obit. If she didn't know I existed, it all makes sense. Not that I needed to be acknowledged. It's no skin off my back.

"I'll let you get settled," Anneliese says from the doorway. "I have a Zoom call in about ten minutes, so I'll be in the study. After that, I thought we could work on staining the dining room floors . . ."

I give her a nod, and she leaves, shutting the door behind her.

I take a seat on my bed, which suddenly feels ten times smaller than I remember it. I run my palm along the old bedspread my mother chose for me before she passed. She called it scintilla blue—because the threads had tiny specks of gold gossamer that could only be seen in certain light, and only for a brief moment. *Scintilla* was one of her favorite words. Along with *lucency*—a word that meant *radiant luminosity.* She loved anything that reflected light, and she was never without a gilded barrette in her hair or a polished sterling-silver locket dangling from her neck. Everywhere she went, she lit up the room—figuratively and literally.

As soon as she died, it was like all the lights went out.

It took nearly two years for my father to draw the curtains and let the sunshine back into the house, and even then, it was never the same.

Pushing up from the bed, I head to my old dresser, tugging hard on the top drawer because it always used to stick. It doesn't want to slide out at first, so I give it another pull. When it finally gives, I'm met with a handful of old T-shirts, a pile of knotted socks, a yearbook, and a stack of old Moleskine notebooks.

I grab the top one off the stack and page through it, perusing my angsty teenage poetry and trying my best not to cringe. When I'm finished with that brief walk down memory lane, I check the middle drawer, shoving aside a stack of sweats and gym clothes in search of my old handwritten manuscript. While it definitely wouldn't be up to snuff by today's standards, that thing took me two full years to write, and I've thought about it often over the years.

The title was atrocious—*The Neon Prince*.

And it was about a kid who saw his entire life in bright neon colors, while everyone else saw theirs in black and white. He didn't fit in. No one saw things the way he did. Eventually—after years of being gaslighted and told he was the crazy one—he learned how to wield his difference to his advantage. He learned how to describe color to people who had never seen it before. Soon people came from miles around to hear his stories and bask in his unique presence. One by one, the people believed him. And one by one, the believers began to see those dazzling neon colors the kid spoke so fondly of. In the end, they called him the Neon Prince because of his bravery and valiance.

I don't know what the hell I was thinking, but I loved it at the time.

I shove the clothes around a little more, but the old three-subject notebook containing my original masterpiece is nowhere to be found.

I check the bottom drawer next.

No dice.

Not sure who would've taken it or what they would've done with it, but there's nothing I can do about it now.

I head downstairs to get started on the dining room, passing the study along the way. When we were kids, my mom turned the room into a hybrid library (for her) and playroom (for us). Now there's nothing but a folding table-and-chair set.

When my parents first bought this house, my mother insisted that it was too much. We were a family of four, and she stayed at home full time. She wanted to spend more time making memories with her sons and not maintaining a gargantuan house. My father refused to see it her way, only focused on the size of the place and its history. He was consumed with having the biggest house on the block.

My mother eventually relented because she loved the bastard, but she set up the house to be efficient—ensuring each room had dual purposes. In the end, we didn't utilize half of this place. And in the very end, my father let it go to shit.

Talk about a waste.

"Hi, Jana! Hi, Greg!" Anneliese waves at the computer screen as I pass. "How are you? It's so good to see you again!"

There's a light in her eyes, the same one my mother used to have when she was in her element, doing something she loved or coming across something shiny and new to add to her collection. She came alive.

"Are you ready for the big reveal?" I hear her ask.

I head to the dining room to get started. She's already laid out all the materials—masks, gloves, cans of lacquer and stain, a roller brush, drop cloths, plastic sheets, masking tape, fans. I tape off the entrance to the room to keep the odors from coursing through the big empty house and open the four windows along the far wall to get some air circulating.

"All right, so I know you said you wanted something timeless and classic." Her voice travels from down the hall. "So the first name I have for you is Benjamin James. The *j* theme goes well with your last name, Johnson, and we have mismatched syllables, which is just . . . chef's kiss to me." She laughs. "I'm a total nerd about that, I'm sorry, but it gets me really excited."

I chuckle.

She's . . . cute.

"Number two, I wanted something that started with an *n* because there's a little-known trick you can do to take a name to an entirely new level," she continues, "so there's something just visually and audibly stunning about a name that starts and ends with the same sound. For instance, think of Taylor Swift. It just . . . flows."

Crouching, I crack open the first can of stain and slip on some gloves.

"So with that in mind," she says from the study, "my second name for you is Nathaniel Benjamin Johnson. In this case, I'm recycling Benjamin, but I think it fits."

I grab a roller and get to work, starting in the far corner of the room and working my way toward the taped-off exit.

By the time I'm halfway finished, the rustling of plastic sheeting steals my attention. I wipe my brow and turn to find Anneliese leaning in the doorway. I hadn't realized it before, but she's all done up— her sandy hair curled into waves that cascade down her shoulders, her lashes darkened, her lips a shiny shade of ruby red. She's even wearing a polka-dot blouse with a pencil skirt that hugs at her soft waist and accentuates her feminine hips.

An unwelcome surge of . . . excitement . . . runs through me, but I peel my gaze off her and return to the task at hand.

"Wow," she says, scanning the room. "You work fast. It would've taken me all morning to do what you've done in . . . what . . . thirty minutes?"

"I don't like to waste time." I've stained, painted, drywalled, and tiled more rooms than I can count, and at the end of every project, there's another one waiting. Another sight to see. A new adventure waiting for me.

A drunken, twice-divorced middle-aged woman at a bar in Dublin once told me that if I kept my eyes focused on what's in front of me, I wouldn't be tempted to look at what's behind me.

So far she hasn't been wrong.

It's only when I look back that I lose my footing.

"This looks really good," she says, stepping closer but keeping away from the wet planks. "I can't wait to see it all dry and lacquered."

"I couldn't help but notice it seems like you're sanding and staining each room at a time," I say. "Might be more efficient if you sanded everything at once and then stained everything at once . . ."

Her mouth twists into a knowing smile. "I know. Believe me, I know. I just . . . I like having my little projects. And I like having a room complete and done before moving on to the next one."

"That's *horribly* inefficient."

Anneliese shrugs. "It's the way I work."

"Yeah, we're not doing it that way anymore." I dip the roller into the stain and get back to work. Idle chat wastes time, and time is money—that is, *if* I decide to sell this place.

For now, I'm sticking to my original plan, but I'd be lying if I said I hadn't run the numbers a few times. Money has never been a motivating factor for me. It comes and it goes. I've always had what I needed, not a penny more or less.

"How much do people pay you?" I ask. "To name their kids, I mean. What does something like that run?"

She chuckles. "Why? Are you in the market?"

"Hell no." The idea of being a dad hasn't so much as crossed the stratosphere of my mind. Not to mention I wouldn't know the first thing about being a good one. The only example I had left much to be desired.

"Depends on the scope of the job. Most people want three options, and it's about a couple hundred dollars—more if there's extensive research involved like combing their family tree," she says. "Back in Chicago, clients would drop fifteen hundred bucks without batting an eye."

"That's such a weird profession."

"And what is it you do for a living?"

She flips it back on me, but to be fair, I deserved it.

"A little bit of everything," I say. "So someone actually paid you real money . . . hundreds of dollars . . . to come up with an everyday name like Benjamin James?"

"They wanted something classic and timeless," she says. "A name like that will never go out of style, and it fits with their last name. Some people get stressed out over choosing a name for their child. They feel better hiring it out. It's like hiring someone to decorate your nursery so you can worry about other things or just sit back and enjoy the pregnancy. A name is obviously more personal, but you get the point. To some people a name is just a name. To others, a name is everything. To each their own."

I shake my head and dip the roller again.

"At the pace you're going, we're going to have this whole house done in about three months," she says, watching me work.

"The sooner the better."

"You didn't answer my question, by the way," she adds.

I look back at her. "Which one?"

"What do you do for a living? You said a little bit of everything. What all does that entail?"

"I've lived in the UK for the past ten years," I say. "I've done a lot of construction, a lot of under-the-table jobs."

"Why under the table?"

"Because I never wanted to stay in one place for too long. Too much to do and see. I was constantly on the go. It's easier that way."

"So . . . are you on the run from something?" she asks.

I chuckle until I realize she's serious. "Not at all."

"You and Donovan had some kind of falling-out; then you moved to the UK and worked under-the-table jobs for ten years." She points when she talks, like she's doing some kind of mental math and piecing together an impossible equation.

"I wasn't *running* from anything. I just wanted to get away."

"Same difference." She pops a hand on her hip and dips her pointed chin. "What were you trying to get away from?"

My father.

My brother.

This house.

This town.

This life.

The accident that changed everything . . .

"Does it matter?" I answer her question with another question.

"If we're going to be living together for the next three to six months, then yes. It matters. I need to know if I'm living with a serial killer," she says in a way that suggests she's only half-joking.

"I may be a lot of things." I dip the roller brush again. "But a killer isn't one of them."

I feel the weight of her stare on my back, and the heaviness of her thoughts lingers in the silent air between us.

Turning back, I add, "I'm also not a liar."

Her pouty lips press into a firm line. "Sounds like something a liar would say."

I roll my eyes. Fair enough. It's like an untrustworthy person saying, *Trust me . . .*

"If you're around me long enough, you'll see," I say before returning to my task.

"I was an only child," she says after a pause. "So I don't really have any experience in the sibling rivalry department. I had some cousins. They were all older than me. That's about as close as I ever had to having a brother or sister. I know I couldn't possibly understand the dynamics of whatever happened between you and Donovan, but please know that my questions are coming from a good place. I'm not trying to pry. I just want to understand why he erased you from existence, that's all."

My jaw clenches, and I swallow the hard knot in my throat. Ten years apart from the bastard, and I'm still stuck cleaning up his messes.

"Maybe you didn't know him as well as you thought you did," I say, monotone.

Anneliese sniffs. "You can say that again."

"How long were you with him?" The last time I asked that question, she shot me down. One more try couldn't hurt.

"It was a whirlwind, love-at-first-sight kind of thing," she says with a breathy sigh. "He proposed after six months. We moved here and started the reno. Two months later . . . he was gone."

Her voice tapers into nothing.

"When was the last time the two of you spoke?" she asks.

"Ten years ago."

"Maybe he was mad at you for leaving? Maybe that's why he wrote you off?"

"Like I told you before, the only one who can tell you why . . . is dead. Picking apart and psychoanalyzing our dysfunctional relationship isn't going to get you any closer to the truth."

At least not the kind of truth she's looking for.

"I really thought he was a good man," she says in such a way I can't tell if she's talking to me or talking out loud to herself.

"You and every other woman who fell for his shit."

Silence fills the air between us. Maybe that was a little harsh, but it's not in me to sugarcoat, especially not where it benefits Donovan.

I snap off my gloves. It's time for a break anyway.

"At some point you have to move on," I say. "Accept that there are things he never told you. Accept that maybe he wasn't the person you thought he was."

"Don't you think I'm trying?" Her voice cuts like glass, but she maintains her composure. "I just want to make sense of whatever I can. A little closure would be nice."

"Closure is a myth. This is going to follow you the rest of your life. Even if you accept it. Even when you think you've finally moved on, it's still going to be there . . . like background noise. Some days it'll be a little louder than others. But it never goes away. Not completely."

She sniffs a melancholy laugh. "Well, that's encouraging."

"Just keeping it real."

"Do you speak from experience?" she asks, head tilted as she studies me.

"You could say that."

"And does your *experience* have anything to do with you wanting to burn the house down?" Her brows lift.

I take a second to gather my thoughts. I wasn't expecting her to shotgun that follow-up question.

"If you're fishing for information, you're using the wrong bait," I say.

Her nose scrunches. "It's just a question."

"To you, maybe," I say.

She folds her arms. "I'm not the bad guy here, Lachlan."

"And neither am I."

"I invited you into my home."

I huff. "You *accepted* me into *my* home after I invited myself. Let's not rewrite the story, Blue Eyes."

"If you want this to work, I need to know a little more about you and why you left home and never looked back," she says. "And I need to know why you want to burn your childhood home to the ground."

"You don't need to know those things; you want to know them," I say. "Big difference."

Aside from Bryce, Lynnette, and one unfortunate woman in a bar in Notting Hill a handful of years ago, no one else has heard the full story. I intend to keep it that way. It's not the kind of thing worth rehashing.

I rake my hand along my jaw before massaging the back of my neck. "I should get back to work. First coat's starting to dry."

Turning my back to her, I grab my gloves and a can opener and work the lid off a fresh container of stain. By the time I glance back, she has already disappeared beyond the plastic curtain.

After getting back to work, I finish the room by noon. I make my way to the kitchen for a glass of water before stepping out to the back porch for some fresh air. Along the way, I'm met with a silent house and no sign of Anneliese.

But it could be worse.

Things could *always* be worse.

ELEVEN

ANNELIESE

raconteur (*n.*) a talented storyteller

I arrive at the bookstore around noon, flick the lights on, and flip the sign on the door to **OPEN**. Earlier this week when Florence asked me to run the store, I told her I couldn't come in until the afternoon on Saturday. I had the Zoom with the Johnsons, plus I needed to get caught up on work around the house—this was, of course, before I knew Lachlan was going to show up at my door with an offer I couldn't refuse if I wanted to.

As quickly as he works, the renovations are going to be completed in no time and at a fraction of the cost (assuming he knows how to do half the things he claimed he did in the UK). This is also assuming we're able to make this strange little arrangement work.

He was only at the house an hour or so when he shut me down for asking questions about his past. Maybe I'd overstepped my boundaries, but given the fact that I'm living with a stranger with a complicated history, I figured I had the right to ask.

It doesn't mean he owes me an answer.

I left before I made things worse—before I rattled off the laundry list of follow-up questions dancing on the tip of my tongue. I made it to the bookshop with a few extra minutes on hand, so I spent a little time googling Lachlan . . . only to come up with nothing. He's a human question mark, and it's only a matter of time before I open my mouth again and pry a little more.

The bells on the door jangle, and I straighten my shoulders and stop replaying the conversation from this morning the instant I spot a familiar face.

"Berlin," I say with a wince, suddenly remembering my promise to her earlier in the week. Things have been so hectic I completely spaced out on brainstorming those flower-shop names. "Hi . . . I'm so sorry, but I don't have the names for you yet."

I think back to the day Lachlan was here and his comment about Berlin being Donovan's former flame. If people around here talk as much as Flo claims they do, she has to know who I am.

"Oh my gosh. No worries at all." She brushes her hand through the air. "I actually just closed my shop for the day, and I was in the area, so I wanted to stop in and thank you for those books you helped me pick out. I've read two of the four so far. Taking notes. I think it's really going to help get my shop off the ground."

"I'm so glad to hear that."

Berlin browses a clearance table, flipping aimlessly through a few coffee-table books that catch her eye.

"Are you looking for anything in particular today or just browsing?" I ask. I can't help but wonder if she came in to scope me out again—if that's what she was doing the last time.

She glances up through her long dark lashes. "Not really."

I straighten up the register area in an attempt to stay busy. I must have Windexed this thing a dozen times yesterday, but once more couldn't hurt. An upbeat Mariah Carey classic plays from the speakers above.

"Berlin, can I ask you something?" I break the silence after a few endless minutes.

"Of course." She looks up, waiting, and tucks a strand of dark hair behind one ear.

"You used to date Donovan Byrne, right?"

Her mouth arches into a confused half smile. "Yeah, actually. I did. How did you know that?"

I exhale, relieved that she probably *wasn't* stalking me the other day.

"His brother is back in town," I say. "He actually saw us chatting and said something to me."

Her brows meet, and her mouth is agape. "Lachlan's back? Really?"

Relief washes over me once more as she confirms that Lachlan is, indeed, Donovan's brother—not that I could deny their uncanny resemblance.

"I haven't seen him since"—she stares off to the side—"high school? What's he been up to?"

"Living abroad," I say, offering as much as I can. "Doing a little bit of everything."

She chuckles, shaking her head. "Always thought he was going to turn out to be some famous writer or something. He was always that artsy, quiet kid sitting in the back of the classroom, doing his own thing."

Two writers in the family . . .

Donovan once told me that his mother had loved books, that their study was once her personal library. It makes sense that she passed down her love of storytelling to both of her sons.

"I don't know if you knew, but I was engaged to Donovan when he passed," I say.

Her jubilant expression evaporates, and she walks toward me, her hand covering her heart.

"I'd heard he was engaged, but that's all I knew. I'm so sorry for your loss . . ." Frowning, she adds, "And I'm extremely embarrassed to

85

admit that I don't even know your name. You weren't wearing a name tag when I came in that day . . ."

"It's Anneliese," I say.

"Anneliese," she says. "I'm so sorry. That must have been awful for you, losing your fiancé."

Berlin places her hand over mine, her eyes softening.

"Don and I lost touch over the past few years, but I was devastated when I got the news." She studies me, her voice laced in sympathy. "Life can be so cruel sometimes."

I don't remember seeing her at his funeral. Then again, that day is a foggy blur. I spent the entire service watching from the private grieving suite with my parents, too inconsolable to get myself together enough to thank people for coming. I wanted to be strong for him, but the more I tried to hold it in, the more it forced its way out.

"Thank you." I slide my hand out from hers. "I feel strange asking this, but do you happen to know anything about a falling-out between Donovan and Lachlan?"

Berlin's mouth twists at the side as she thinks. "Um, I mean, they were brothers. They had their differences. They were never really close. It was always their dynamic, and I guess I never really questioned it because that was their normal. Every family's different, you know?"

The casualness in her tone puts me at ease—a little.

But my gut tells me there's more to the story.

"Hey, do you want to give me your number, and I can text you when I have those shop names?" I slide a pad of paper and a pen across the counter.

"Yes, actually. That would be amazing." She slings her bag over her shoulder and comes closer. A second later, she hands me a slip of paper scrawled with the name Berlin Waterford and her digits.

"Perfect. I'll text you so you have mine too." I grab my phone and fire off a happy-face emoji. Her phone chimes. "There."

"Say . . . ," she says, her hands fidgeting on the glass counter. "I just moved back here last year, and I've been so busy setting up my shop that I've been a bit antisocial. That and all of my old friends got married and had babies and moved away." She laughs, nervous almost, and her cheeks turn a rosy shade of pink. "I don't know why this feels so weird. It's like asking someone out on a date or something. But do you maybe want to get coffee sometime?"

I can attest to the fact that making friends is difficult, the older we get, so I see her nervousness and meet it with an overzealous "I'd love to."

Most of the friends I used to run around with in Chicago scattered like leaves in the wind as soon as they started getting married and having babies. I've stayed in touch with many of them, sending the occasional text or having a Facebook chat here or there. But it's never the same. The closeness eventually fades.

I could really use another friend myself these days . . .

Berlin's phone rings, and she glances down at the caller ID. "That's my mom. I should take this. Anyway, I'll text you about meeting up, okay?"

"Perfect."

She leaves, turning back and waving from the sidewalk before disappearing out of view.

She seems . . . nice.

A little lonely, perhaps, but it takes one to know one.

I could see us being friends. And who knows? Maybe she'll have some stories to share or a little insight into Donovan's younger days.

He and I never dug deep into each other's dating histories. That was one of the things I appreciated about him from those early days. He never pried. He was so secure in our relationship and his place in my life that he didn't need to. He'd mentioned once that he was a serial monogamist. He preferred to be in actual relationships rather than chasing the next one-night stand. He mentioned once that he'd dated the same girl all through high school and college, and he had nothing but nice things to say about his nameless former flame. While some women might have felt a twinge of jealousy at that revelation, knowing they would never be his first big love, it only made me fall that much harder because it implied that he was both loyal and capable of commitment.

I finish the rest of the afternoon, close the shop, and head home to Lachlan, my stomach in knots given the fact that we didn't leave things off on a great note earlier.

If I have any chance at saving this house, I need to smooth things over.

I grab a take-out pizza and a bottle of red wine from the gas station on the way home.

And before I head inside, I promise myself I won't pry again—at least not tonight.

If we get to know each other a little better, maybe the truth will reveal itself?

TWELVE

LACHLAN

toska (*n.*) an immense ache for nothing and
everything all at once

"What's this?" Anneliese stands in the back doorway of the house shortly after seven Saturday night, a bottle of wine under one arm and a pizza box in hand.

"You left without saying anything earlier, and you didn't leave me a list, so I thought I'd strip the paint off the back deck." I rise, wiping my damp brow against the back of my hand. "Started with a test corner over there." I nod to the left. "I think it's salvageable. Just needs stripped, sanded, and sealed."

"This looks . . . wow," she says, walking around and inspecting my work. "I was going to replace the entire thing, but this is great news. This'll save ten grand, easily."

Ten grand is some expensive firewood . . .

"Are you hungry?" She lifts the pizza box.

"I could eat."

I follow her inside, where she sets us up at a little folding card table before uncorking the bottle of merlot and pouring it into two plastic cups.

"All of my kitchen stuff is in storage," she says. "We didn't want to move in completely until the place was done. Hope you don't mind drinking out of this."

She places the cup in front of me, then grabs paper plates and napkins.

"Hey, I just wanted to say I'm sorry for earlier," she says, taking the chair across from me.

I grab a slice. "We're good."

No need to rehash anything—that'll only open the door for more questions.

"We are?" Her blue eyes glint.

I nod, following with a generous swig of wine.

"It's been hard, these last few months," she says. "Losing my best friend so suddenly . . . wrapping my head around the fact that the life we planned is no longer an option . . . finding out he lied to me about the bank account . . . not being able to ask him why . . ."

"I bet." I take another bite and glance out the window beside us. I wouldn't know the first thing about consoling a broken heart. I've never been on *that* side of the equation.

She leans back in her seat, running her palms along the tops of her thighs. "You know, sometimes I try to convince myself that there was some kind of mix-up at the bank. That maybe he put my name on the paperwork, but there was some clerical error, and someone else messed up."

"Wishful thinking."

"It's just . . . he was so perfect," she continues. "And I can't stress enough how perfect he was. I'd never met anyone like him. He put me on a pedestal, as cliché as that sounds."

I take another drink, my gaze meeting hers over the rim of the plastic cup.

Anneliese tucks her chin lower. "Now that I say that all out loud . . . I realize how obvious it all seems. But it was so real. At least to me, it was."

I press my lips flat. There's nothing I can say to change what Donovan did.

"You said he did this to other women?" she asks.

"I heard about a few over the years," I say. "Third-, fourthhand. Mostly from distant cousins or mutual acquaintances. Gossip doesn't take long to spread around here."

Every time I'd get a random email or text from a long-lost somebody, they always felt the need to update me on the latest with Donovan, which almost always included some kind of relationship drama that had blown up in his face or one of his pretty little liaisons looking for him after he'd borrowed some cash and then fallen off the face of the earth for a bit.

"What did he do to them?" Her eyes search mine.

"Same kind of thing he did to you," I say. "Took their money and got the hell out of Dodge."

Her shoulders deflate, and her lower lip trembles, but only for a moment.

"He gave me a ring," Anneliese says, tracing the empty space on her left ring finger. "He asked me to spend my life with him. We picked out a wedding venue and sent our save-the-dates. What was his end goal? Why go through all of that?"

"It's not worth it," I say, "to speculate like that."

"Just trying to connect the dots . . . see if I missed any warning signs . . ."

"Why? So it doesn't happen again?" I shake my head. "People like Donovan are good at what they do because they've mastered the art of manipulation. There's no such thing as staying one step ahead of them—you can only get away from them."

"Is that what you did?" she asks without hesitation.

That's what I get for engaging in this conversation.

"I'm sorry. I don't mean to use you as a sounding board for this mess," she says. "I haven't really made a lot of friends since I've been here, and that's my fault. I mean, I have Flo, but I don't want her to feel like every time we hang out it's a therapy session."

"Who's Flo?"

"She owns the bookshop . . ."

"Ah. I see." I take another drink. She hasn't touched her pizza or her wine—nor has she taken her eyes off me since she sat down.

"Berlin came into the shop this afternoon." She changes the subject. "She told me you were a writer. What do you write?"

"Haven't been one of those in a long time."

"What did you used to write?" She rests her elbow on the table and her chin on the top of her hand.

"You going to eat?" I point to her untouched dinner.

Being the center of someone's attention has never been my thing.

Anneliese sits up, reaching for her wine. "Yeah. I just thought it was neat that you and your brother were both writers."

I lift a brow.

Donovan as a writer is news to me. Growing up, he hated reading, and he loathed English class. He once paid me cash to write his papers for an entire semester. It might have been our one and only partnership, but I was happy to fatten my wallet with his dime.

"What did Don write exactly?" I ask because now I'm curious.

"Prose poetry mostly . . . he wrote a novel," she says. "He never let me read it, though. He always said he was going to, but I guess he wanted to polish it up first. He wrote it by hand."

My jaw sets when I remember *The Neon Prince*.

"My brother hated writing." My jaw is tense.

The idea of Donovan as a writer is comical.

The idea of Donovan taking credit for my work is infuriating.

"He had this dictionary of beautiful words," Anneliese continues. "All his favorites are circled in blue ink. I actually still have it by my bed, and I used to flip through it after he died, when I was missing him."

"Red book with a black spine?" I ask.

"Yeah. How'd you know?"

"That book belonged to our mother," I say. "And the circled words were *her* favorites—not his."

Anneliese is silent, leaning back in her chair, eyes drifting downward.

"Add it to the list of things he lied about," she says with a fading voice.

I take a generous swig of the semisweet liquid, finishing off the remnants.

"Our mother was an avid reader," I say, topping off my cup. "The study was her library. She was a true lover of words. She'd read anything and everything . . . poetry, classics, bargain-bin paperbacks . . . but her favorite thing in the world was coming across a word she'd never seen before. She'd always write it down on the nearest scrap of paper so she could look it up later. Sometimes she'd write it on a Post-it and place it in our lunch boxes . . . in the evenings, we had to use the word in a sentence at least once before we could have dessert. Donovan hated that game, so eventually, it was just her and me."

"There's a glass jar in the attic filled with paper scraps of words," she says.

My chest tightens, and my hand grips the plastic cup until it slightly dents. After she passed, my father tore through the house grabbing anything and everything that reminded him of her and shoved it all in boxes. I never knew what he did with them after that. As a kid, I was afraid to ask. He had a temper. And he was grieving on top of it all. The messed-up thing is that he seemed angry at her for dying—angry at her for leaving him, as if she'd done it on purpose.

"That would have been hers," I say.

I'm shocked that he kept it.

I'd be curious to see what else is up there.

Anneliese brings her plastic cup to her lips, pausing before she takes a drink. "Did she have a favorite word?"

"She did." I press my lips firm, scanning years of forgotten memories. "*Selcouth*."

"And what does *selcouth* mean?"

"Unfamiliar, rare, strange, and yet wonderful. At the same time," I answer. "Like people."

Anneliese releases a sweet sigh. "That's beautiful."

"She always used to say that most people treat strangers like they're background extras in a movie," I say. "She thought it was important that we remember that every person we come across has their own deeply complex backstory. Their own hopes and dreams and triumphs and problems."

She rests her elbow on the table, abandoning the rest of her meal. "I've never thought of it that way."

"Most people don't. They're too consumed with their own lives and their own problems. It's amazing what you can learn when you sit down and talk to a stranger. And it's easy to forget how good it feels to look someone in the eye and have an actual conversation with them that doesn't involve a screen. Or gossip."

"Connecting," she says. "That's what it's all about."

"I was renting a room on the east side of Chiswick several years ago. The woman living there was a spindly little thing with a hump on her back and a scowl on her face and this long silvery hair that she would comb back into a tight bun on the top of her head. For the first couple weeks, she didn't say more than a single word to me. I mostly came and went and stayed out of her way. Paid my weekly rent on time, picked up after myself. But that third week, I went out with some friends, got a little smashed, came home. She'd locked me out, and I ended up falling asleep against the door. I woke up several hours later to the snick of the dead bolt and the smell of bacon and eggs frying in a pan. Anyway. She let me back in, sat me down at her kitchen table," I continue, "and told me that when she was a little girl, her mother would lock her father out of the house when he came home from the bar. He got blackout drunk, belligerent, and would break things and say all sorts of horrible things. She was scared of me that night because I reminded her of her father—and here I thought she was just being spiteful."

"We're all just . . . misunderstood."

"Exactly," I say. "There was another woman I used to see at the chemist's. She was always hanging out on the corner, smoking her e-cig and chatting up anyone who'd give her the time of day. Anyway, she'd always give me a glare every time she saw me, and I could never figure out why. It didn't bother me, of course, but I was curious and about to leave for Edinburgh, so I finally confronted her."

"And what'd she do?"

"She asked me why I never called her."

Anneliese almost chokes on her drink.

"All that time, she thought I was some guy she hooked up with the year before," I say.

"Were you that guy?" she asks, one brow lifted.

"Definitely not." I distinctly recall her garish purple hair and that livid face filled with spiky piercings—not that there's anything wrong with that. It's just that I prefer to spend my nights with women who are a little . . . softer around the edges. "She didn't believe me, though. And she actually followed me home, spewing all kinds of profanities at me, causing a scene."

Anneliese cups her hand over her mouth. "I can see why that guy never called her back . . ."

"Unfortunately for her, I was already leaving town the next day. Never saw her again. Legend has it, somewhere in Chiswick, there's a purple-haired woman standing outside the chemist's looking for the *right bloody arsehole* who ghosted her."

She chuckles. "You're a great storyteller, you know that?"

I shrug. "I've had a lot of practice."

"What do you mean?"

"When I was younger, anytime I was stuck somewhere with nothing to do . . . a doctor's office or airport or whatever, I'd choose a random stranger and make up a backstory for them. It was a good way to stretch my imagination."

"That sounds fun . . ."

I tip my chin down, glancing into my plastic cup. "I've never told anyone that before."

"Why not?"

"Some people might find it strange."

"As strange as naming other people's children for them?" she teases.

My mouth cracks into a smile. "Yeah. Strange like that."

Anneliese studies me. "What would my backstory be? If you didn't know me? If you randomly saw me in the bookstore that day and had no idea who I was . . ."

I toss back the rest of my wine, buying time. It's been a while since I've done one of these.

"All right. I'll give it a shot," I say.

She settles in, clasping her hands on her lap and waiting like an eager child in line to see a mall Santa.

"Your name is Wren—like the bird—and you grew up in the Seattle, Washington, area, but the rain always made you sleepy, and you wanted to live somewhere with white Christmases, so you filled out an elaborate one-hundred-question quiz online that told you Arcadia Grove, Vermont, is your ideal location. You packed everything you owned into the back of your Subaru Forester and road-tripped across the country solo until you arrived. You've been here five years. You work at the bookstore not because you're a reader but because you love the smell of paper and it helps you pay the bills and support your hobby."

"Which is?"

"Building dollhouses," I say, motioning with my hands. "And I'm not talking your average homes for dolls. You build the kind with elaborate details. Toasters with buttons and ovens that open and rugs with rug pads under them. Wallpapered walls. Cedar-shingle roofs. Lights and doorbells that function. They're little works of art, truly."

She laughs.

"Every year you donate one to the children's hospital in Burlington," I add. "Someday they're going to name a wing after you. Many years from now, of course. After you've donated so many dollhouses they have no other choice but to honor you."

"And is that my life? Just a spinster building dollhouses until I die?"

"I can give you a family. You want a family?" I ask.

She nods. "I do."

"Okay." I crack my knuckles and stretch my arms over my shoulders. "You married a guy named Connor. The man looks like he walked straight out of a J.Crew catalog. Preppy as hell. Loves craft beer. Can grill a mean steak. Plays in the local men's rugby league on Saturdays. You met him when he walked into your bookstore looking for a present for his teenage niece. You told him he was in the wrong place, that no teenager in her right mind would want a used book for a gift. You promptly pointed him toward the trendy boutique down the street. He thanked you for your help and went on his way, but as the days passed, he couldn't stop thinking about you. He loved your honesty, and if I'm being frank, he also loved your ass."

Anneliese throws her head back, clapping and laughing. "Nice."

"Long story short, he comes back a week later, tells you he can't get you out of his head, and asks you on a date," I say. "Only, plot twist— you're already dating someone else."

She frowns, clearly committed to her fake life story.

"He tells you if it doesn't work out with that guy, to give him a call, and he leaves you his number," I continue. "You're having dinner later that night with your boyfriend, who happens to be getting on your nerves for a myriad of reasons. He's chewing too loudly. He won't stop checking his phone. He talks with his mouth full. He doesn't ask a damn thing about your day. He forgot your work schedule *again*. And all you can think about is the guy from the bookshop."

"Naturally."

"As soon as your boyfriend drops you off at home, he leans in for a kiss like he always does," I say. "That's when you break it to him. You're in love with someone else."

"But I don't even know the other guy yet . . ."

"You don't need to. You believe in love at first sight. So you leave your boyfriend completely dumbfounded, go into your apartment, and call the number. He doesn't answer, though. You get his voice mail—which you weren't expecting. The second it beeps, you choke on your words, which causes you to panic and hang up. For a moment, you're certain you've ruined it. That was your chance, your big moment, the beginning of your beautiful happily ever after. You think he's going to listen to your sputtering words and half-finished message and wonder what he ever saw in you."

"I never would've choked on my words."

I lift a finger. "Last I checked this was *my* story. Feel free to write a fan fiction spin-off on your own time . . . anyway, where was I? Oh, right. You thought you'd ruined your chance with Connor the J.Crew model. You wash your makeup off, change into your pajamas, and place your phone on the charger in the kitchen so you're not tempted to check for missed calls in the middle of the night."

"Wise move."

"When you wake up the next morning, he still hasn't called. You're one hundred percent sure it's over and done before it even began. You go about your weekend as you normally do, trying your hardest not to think about him fifty times a day. A few days later, you're working in the shop again, and in walks Mr. Wonderful, only there's something different about him this time. He doesn't smile when he sees you. But he's clearly here for you because he makes a beeline to the register without so much as glancing at a book display."

She leans in, invested more than ever.

"He tells you he's sorry he missed your call last weekend, but he was with his niece at the children's hospital in Burlington. She'd been battling stage-four brain cancer and, unfortunately, took an unexpected turn for the worse. He held her hand as she passed, and he spent the rest of the weekend comforting his family as they grieved their devastating loss."

Anneliese's blue eyes brim with tears, and she swipes them away as they slide down her cheeks.

"That's the moment you fell in love with him," I say. "*Truly* fell in love with him."

She dabs more tears on the backs of her hands.

"You're an asshole," she says with a slight chuckle and a twinkle in her damp blue eyes. "A damn good storyteller but an asshole."

Rising, she throws the remains of her pizza in the trash and dumps her wine in the sink.

"If you'll excuse me," she says, her back to me, "I'm going to go upstairs and have a good cry while I grieve for Connor's poor niece—and a beautiful marriage that will never happen because the other half of it is a fictional character."

Years ago, I took a community writing class put on by a local published author. He threw a lot of information at us at once—faster than any of us could jot down—but the advice that stood out the most was that if your writing can move someone to tears, make them laugh, or send them into a fit of rage over a character's decision, you're doing something right.

Stories should make people feel something, *anything*.

"When you're finished grieving, if you could kindly take the time to leave me a five-star review on Amazon, that'd be great," I tease.

"Thanks for the bedtime story . . . ," she calls out.

"Anytime." I've always found it easier to tell stories about other people's lives—fictional or otherwise. The second the tables turn, I lock up tighter than Fort Knox.

I watch her walk away, listen to her delicate footsteps as she saunters down the hall, and wait for the creak of the stairs as she climbs them.

It's the strangest thing . . . she's been gone all of twenty seconds, and I kind of miss her already.

There's a warmth about her, an easiness most people don't have.

Donovan dying is the best thing to ever happen to her—even if she doesn't know it yet.

I clean up our dinner situation and head upstairs to grab a shower, stopping outside her door to ensure she isn't crying. Not that I'd know what to do if she were.

It's silent on the other side.

I imagine her leaning against the headboard, paging through my mother's book of beautiful words, stopping to read the circled ones, which would be a better use of time than mourning a fictional husband.

Overhead, at the end of the hall, is the attic door. I think about the jar of words Anneliese mentioned earlier. That very well may be the last remaining artifact from my mother's time on earth—other than her ashes, which my father kept God knows where (if he kept them at all).

I debate heading up there but decide against it.

Some things are better left untouched.

THIRTEEN

ANNELIESE

apodyopsis (*n.*) the act of mentally undressing someone

I roll over Sunday morning and peek at my blurry alarm clock on the other side of the room, which tells me it's half past eleven. I can't remember the last time I slept in, but I also can't remember the last time I woke up feeling this rested.

I went to bed embarrassingly early last night, but I didn't fall asleep until almost midnight. I kept thinking about Lachlan's stories. While I still hardly know the man, he fascinates me already. And the crazy thing is he's not even trying. He isn't trying to prove himself or impress me. There are no humblebrags or gentlemanly gestures. Not that he's here to woo me or that I want to be wooed, but there's something refreshing about having a conversation that doesn't require chess-like moves.

Sitting up, I spot the red book with the black spine on the pillow beside me. I paged through it a little bit last night when I couldn't sleep, pausing to study a few of the circled words . . . words that Lachlan claims were circled by his mother. I page to the *s* section, pausing when I get to the word *selcouth*, which is double circled.

It's all the confirmation I need.

Sighing, I shove my heavy covers aside, climb out of bed, and slide my feet into a pair of house slippers before heading to the bathroom to wash up. Stealing a quick glance down the hall, I notice that Lachlan's bedroom door is open and his bed is made.

The house is still.

Too quiet almost.

Maybe last night was too much for him? Maybe he changed his mind? Or maybe he ran out for coffee? A million scenarios race through my mind—good and otherwise.

Trotting downstairs, I peek out the window at the bottom to see if his truck is still parked in the driveway.

It is.

I make my way through the main level, ending up on the front porch—which is when I finally find him pulling weeds from the landscaping.

Shirtless . . .

His body glistens with sweat thanks to the summer humidity, and his muscles ripple through his taut skin with every pull and bend. Entranced, I watch him work from behind the porch railing. He's quick and efficient, and he doesn't miss a single broadleaf weed.

"Morning," I say, snapping out of it.

But he doesn't respond.

Clearing my throat, I say it again, louder: "Good morning."

Still, he says nothing.

It's only when he changes his position that I notice the white pods in his ears. He pops one out when he finally sees me.

"What are you listening to?" I ask.

"A mix," he answers in vague Lachlan fashion. "You sleep well?"

I nod. "I was thinking about maybe grabbing some coffee, and I need to water Flo's houseplants. You want to come with?"

Maybe it's a weird little excursion to invite him on, but after a rocky start, I feel like we're finally connecting. Running a couple of errands together could almost be . . . fun?

"It'll maybe take an hour at the most," I add, sensing his hesitation and suddenly doubting the idea altogether.

My gaze accidentally drops to the sharp V of his Adonis belt as I wait for his response, but I redirect it to his glinting copper eyes. Donovan was in great shape, but he was leaner with more of a runner's build. Lachlan looks like he could single-handedly take on a gang of Marvel villains if he had to.

"When was the last time you mowed?" He ignores my invite.

I ignore the sting.

"There's a neighbor kid who mows it every week for twenty bucks," I say. "But I think his family's on vacation right now."

"Do you own a mower?"

"There's one in the shed. I don't know if it works or not. He usually brings his own."

He squints toward the side yard, quiet as if he's lost in thought.

"So that's a no . . . to the coffee?" I ask, pointing. "Just want to be sure."

He wipes his forearm against his sweaty brow, shoving his matted auburn hair to the side. "You don't want to be in a car with me right now. I've been out here since six a.m."

My jaw falls. "Doing what?"

"Yard work." He glances around as if it should be obvious. And now that I'm looking closer, I realize it is. "What else?"

"I didn't realize it was that bad . . ." I knew I had some weeds, but I didn't think it was out of control by any means.

"I'll run to the store later and get some weed and feed, which should help this thicken up a bit," he says. "I'll grab some mulch to put around the trees too."

I can't help but wonder if he's always this motivated or if he's working hard to pass the weekend trial with flying colors. Other than our brief hiccup yesterday, I'd say things are going well so far. Once I made it past his thick layer of armor, he's actually interesting to talk to. Admittedly easy on the eyes. Smart but not boastful. Direct but not arrogant. He's layered. Cultured. Fearless.

I slam the brakes on my thoughts when I catch myself cataloging his traits like he's a contestant on a dating game show.

"Thanks, though," he says before popping his bud back into his ear and returning to the landscaping.

I'm on my way to Flo's place an hour later when my mother calls.

"Just checking on you," she says over my car speakers when I answer. "You've been quiet lately. Doing okay, sweetheart?"

I picture her pacing our little galley kitchen back in Geneva, Illinois. I can almost smell the Dawn dish-soap scent on her hands mixed with her White Shoulders perfume.

"Yeah, I've just been busy," I say. "Florence had a family emergency, so I'm covering at her bookstore."

I leave out any mention of Lachlan because I don't want to worry them. They weren't thrilled when I rushed into the engagement with Donovan and moved halfway across the country to start a new life with him. They thought we should have dated longer, and they certainly didn't love the fact that I was leaving Chicago and was no longer a car ride away. Regardless, they were there for me the instant I got the news about Donovan. They even went so far as to cover his funeral expenses because there was no life insurance and no one else to step in and cover it. My plan was to pay them back—but that was before I found out about the bank account. They've yet to ask me for a single dime, but I intend to pay them back one of these days . . . plus interest.

My parents have hearts of pure, solid gold.

The last thing I want to do is give them yet another reason to worry about me.

"How's the house coming along?" Mom asks.

"I've actually made a lot of progress this week." Er, Lachlan has. "Getting the deck stripped so it can be sanded and sealed. The dining room floor is done. Working on the yard now."

"Well, isn't that wonderful?" Her tone is nothing shy of relieved as she exhales into the phone. "I know it's been quite the undertaking and it hasn't been easy doing it on your own. Your father and I were actually thinking about coming out for a long weekend and helping . . . speed things along."

All they want in this world is for me to get out from underneath this house and move back home—and that was the original plan after everything happened with Donovan. At some point this year, I was going to hire an attorney and take the necessary steps to settle his estate . . . but that was before I knew he had a brother.

It's likely an open-and-shut case now that Lachlan's here.

"You don't have to do that," I say. I grip the steering wheel, coming to a stop at an intersection.

"Don't be ridiculous," my mother laughs. "We're due for another trip to see you anyway. And your father can install some of those light fixtures."

"I don't think we should install them until all of the floors have been resanded; otherwise they're going to be collecting a lot of dust, and it's just going to be—"

"Anneliese Elizabeth," she says with a huff, in her trademark Chicagoan accent. "I love you, but let's not drag this on any longer than necessary. We're coming out next week. I'll text you our flight itineraries once your father books them. Ope . . . your aunt Linda's beeping in . . . I have to let you go. Can't wait to see you, honey. Love you bunches."

She ends the call, and the car behind me honks.

I shake out of my daze and press my foot into the accelerator. I missed the opportunity to tell her about Lachlan. She's not going to be happy about the fact that I let a complete stranger move in with me—one who is on a mission to burn down the house if I can't convince him not to. My parents aren't going to understand—but to be fair, I don't understand it either.

Losing the love of your life, your dignity, and your life savings all at the same time tends to paint things in a new light, one that begs the question: Can anything possibly get worse?

I don't think it can.

When you've been to hell and back, everything else feels like Disneyland.

FOURTEEN

LACHLAN

mágoa (*n.*) a heartbreaking feeling that leaves long-lasting traces, visible in gestures and facial expressions

"Hey." Anneliese knocks on my door Sunday night, clutching a spiral notebook against her chest. "You'll never guess what I found."

She takes a seat on the bed beside me and flips to the first page of *The Neon Prince.*

"I was going through a box of Donovan's things and found this," she says. "I think it's the book he wrote . . ."

The sharp burn of tension tightens my jaw.

"I read a few pages, and it's actually pretty good," she adds. "He was very inventive with his choice of words." Closing the cover, she hands it to me. "Anyway, I thought maybe you'd want to have it since you were a writer too? I know you weren't on speaking terms, but I feel like—"

"Donovan didn't write this," I interrupt. "I did."

Her ocean eyes fade to a dull shade of blue, settling on the empty wall space ahead of us.

"It's like it never ends," she says, monotone. "One lie after another after another. I was hoping maybe the whole novel thing was true because he talked about it so much—being a novelist and wanting to be published one day."

"He also told you he was an only child," I say. "And that those circled words in that book were his favorites, not our mother's. How are you not picking up on a pattern here, Anneliese? He was pretending to be someone he wasn't."

She buries her head in her hands, and her hair falls over her shoulders, hiding her delicate profile.

"I can tell you how this book ends if you still need proof," I say. "I can tell you the entire thing, chapter by chapter. I can even tell you there are light-blue stains on the last several pages because I accidentally spilled a bottle of Jones Soda on it."

She forces a hard breath through her fingertips.

"Curious. Did you ever actually see any of Don's writing . . . or did he just tell you he was a writer?" I ask.

She sits up, brushing her hair from her face, still staring blankly ahead.

"He never wanted to show me any of it. I just thought he was being self-conscious. Some people get that way about their art. Then we were busy planning the move and then renovating, and I never pushed it." She speaks with her hands before letting them fall into her lap, limp.

"That photo album he showed you—do you know where that is?" I ask.

Rising from the bed, she heads down the hall and returns a few minutes later with a leather-bound album I've never seen before.

"Mind if I have a look?" I flip through the first several images. "Half of these are me. We were two years apart, but we looked so much alike sometimes people mistook us for twins. I grew a little faster than he did—caught up to him in height by the time I was eight and he was ten. God, he hated, *hated*, that his little brother wasn't little anymore. I was faster than him . . . stronger than him . . . smarter than him . . ."

The only true advantage he had over me was his lack of anything resembling a conscience.

"It's interesting that he went to all the work of choosing images where we weren't standing together or posing as a family." I slide one out from behind its protective sheet—a grainy image of my mother and me standing in front of a Christmas tree covered in heavy ornaments and multicolored lights. "See."

On the back, in faded pencil, are the words: *Lachlan and Mommy, Christmas 1999.*

She inspects the inscription closer.

"I never would've thought to flip any of these over," she says. Anneliese slides the photo back into its protective sleeve with careful ease. "I get why he would lie about everything else . . . because he wanted my money, but why would he lie about you?"

"You can spend the rest of your life speculating and never come close to the truth," I say. "Honestly, I don't care what his reason was."

"Not even a little?" She tilts her head toward me, swiping at the soggy tears that slide down her cheeks as fast as they come. "He was your *brother*. That has to sting."

"Brothers don't do the kind of shit he did."

"I believed everything that came out of that man's mouth without question." She sighs, shaking her head at herself. "How could I be so naive? I mean, there were some days when I thought he seemed too good to be true, but there were zero red flags other than . . ."

Her voice tapers, and she sucks in a startled breath.

"Oh my God." Clenching her hand across her chest, she rises from the bed and paces the space in front of my dresser.

"What?"

All the color has drained from her face. Her eyes are wide, and her mouth is agape, as if she wants to speak but the words aren't coming.

"What is it?" I ask again.

"Do you think . . . do you think he proposed to me so quickly because he wanted to use my money to renovate this house?" she asks. "Do you think he was going to string me along until he could sell the house and make off with the profits?"

That's exactly the kind of thing his opportunistic ass would've done. He was always looking for easy money, never hesitating to take advantage of some poor trusting soul. I saw him do it to his own friends back in high school. The asshole was always so charming no one questioned him—until it was too late. And then he'd just gaslight the hell out of them until they let it go.

"You want my honest opinion?" I ask.

She nods, one hand clenched at her stomach.

"Knowing my brother," I say, "that's absolutely what he was doing."

"I'm going to be sick," she says before darting out the door. It swings behind her, slamming against the wall. Her trampling footsteps are followed a second later by the slam of the bathroom door.

Hunched over, I pinch the bridge of my nose as my head pounds.

Donovan royally and epically screwed her over.

If I burn this house down, I'm no better than him.

I'm the last person who should be comforting anyone, but right now I'm all she's got. I get up and knock on her bathroom door.

"You okay in there?" I call out.

The toilet flushes, and the faucet twists on with a creak.

"Yeah," she says, her voice haggard. She emerges a minute later with bloodshot eyes, breath smelling like toothpaste. "I hate him."

Join the club . . .

Tearing past me, she heads downstairs.

"Where are you going?" I follow.

"On a walk. I need some air." Perched on the bottom step, she laces up a pair of tennis shoes like a woman on a mission.

"A little late for a walk, don't you think? You want some company?"

"Yeah, sure, if you want." It's not exactly a bona fide invitation, and she hardly waits for me to get my shoes on before she's out the door, but I tag along anyway. She shouldn't be alone in her state of mind.

The full moon glows above, reflecting off the gray-white sidewalk ahead. Bullfrogs croak and crickets chirp. The humidity from earlier today has faded into something more tepid and agreeable. Funny how it can be simultaneously a beautiful night and a shitty one.

I trot ahead, catching up with Donovan's runaway former fiancée. And for the hour that follows, I tread beside her in silence: an inobtrusive show of support.

Maybe one of these days I'll tell her what the bastard did to me.

But tonight isn't about me.

It's about her.

FIFTEEN

ANNELIESE

quatervois (*n.*) a crossroads; a critical decision or
turning point in one's life

Lachlan stayed all weekend.

He stayed last night too.

I guess he's here to stay—at least until the house is finished.

I'm on my way to meet Berlin for coffee Monday night. I'm maybe
three miles into my trip, and I've already changed the radio station at
least a dozen times. I yank on my seat belt, unable to get comfortable.
For the past couple of days, I've been listless and unsettled, obsessing
over the web of lies Donovan wove. At first, I wanted to give him the
benefit of the doubt, but the lies keep stacking, piling one on top of
the other. At night, I've tossed and turned, replayed every conversation,
every memory, at least a hundred times, picking them apart until there
was nothing left to analyze.

I was always raised to trust people until they give you a reason not to.

But there were never any signs or red flags.

He showered me with love from the start, treated me kindly, and
said all the right things.

He had me eating out of the palm of his hand.

While there's a tiny part of me stuck in denial, refusing to believe the entire thing was a sham, I realize now that the Donovan I knew and loved was nothing more than a facade. The real Donovan is a stranger: a beautiful, wicked stranger who will never have to suffer for his sins.

I pull into the coffee shop parking lot, close my eyes, and take a deep breath. I can't go into this like a fidgety hot mess. I check my hair in the rearview, finger combing a strand behind my ear, and I slick on a coat of pale-pink ChapStick.

Heading in, I spot Berlin in a corner booth. Smiling from ear to ear, she flags me down with a wide wave, one so big I couldn't possibly miss it. I wave back and get in line to order a decaf cappuccino. Lord knows I don't need another reason to be up all night.

"It's so great to see you!" She gives me a hug when I make it to the table a few minutes later. "I'm so glad this worked out."

"Me too." It's not like I have an overflowing social calendar at the moment . . . "Oh, before I forget, I have something for you."

Digging into my bag, I pull out a slip of notebook paper with four flower-shop names written on it.

"So the first one is Waterford Floral," I say. "Obviously Waterford is your last name, but it goes well with the word *floral* because they share the *f* and *r* sounds and Waterford is three syllables, while *floral* is two. It also has a classy, upmarket feel. After that, we have Stem and Petal. We have the shared *t* sounds, and it fits with the modern, simple style you originally were going for while giving a nod to the original name of the shop. Next we have the Rose and Posy, which gives me English pub vibes . . . think the Rose and Crown, the Dog and Duck, the Eagle and Child, but this is obviously the flower-shop version. It's cute and playful and fresh. Lastly, we have J'adore les Fleurs, which is French for *I love flowers*—and it's also fun to say and easy to pronounce. I feel like the type of people who shop in that area will eat that up. They want to feel transported and well traveled since many of them are vacationers, and a French-themed flower shop would be just the ticket."

A barista delivers my cappuccino in a red ceramic cup. The foam art consists of two hearts, one inside the other. The irony isn't lost on me.

"Wow, Anneliese, these are amazing." Berlin studies the sheet. "I don't know what to say other than thank you. Not sure how I'm going to choose because I love them all."

"You're most welcome." I sip my coffee and settle in.

She folds the paper and places it carefully into the front pocket of her cognac-leather bag.

"So how's your week going?" She wraps her hands around her mug, letting the tag from her tea bag fall over her glossy scarlet fingernails. I can't remember the last time I got my nails done. Back in Chicago, I had a group of friends who would meet up at our favorite nail salon on the first of the month for full manicures and pedicures. I miss having a group of girlfriends.

"I'm still filling in at the bookshop," I say. "And working with Lachlan on finishing the reno."

"The reno?"

"I'm fixing up their childhood home," I say. "It was a project Donovan and I started before he passed."

I leave it at that. No need to go into detail or dampen the mood.

"Oh? I had no idea," she says. "I know his father had trouble maintaining it in his final years. My mom said something about the city wanting to condemn it. But you're saying it's savable?"

I nod. "The electrical has been replaced, and the foundation has been repaired. We tore out the kitchen cabinets, and the new ones will go in soon. Everything else is mostly sanding and staining and repainting . . ."

"Nice." She takes a sip of tea before fussing with the tea bag. "I haven't been in that house in ages."

"You'll have to stop by sometime and see the progress."

She perks. "I'd love that, actually. Lots of fond memories there . . ."

Her attention floats to the center of the table for a second, as if she's lost in thought.

"So you said you moved away and came back . . . where'd you go?" I ask.

Berlin levels her shoulders. "Oh, um . . . so after college, I took a job in Madison, Wisconsin, transferred to Indianapolis, bounced over to Cleveland . . . by twenty-eight, I was already burning out from the corporate grind, so I decided to come back home and open a flower shop. I was just craving simplicity, you know? Life was moving so fast, and I felt like this was the best way to slow it down."

"What did you do before?"

"I worked in the information-management-and-technology department of a large hospital network. I wrote a lot of code, traveled to other locations to teach our employees how to use the software whenever we had an update," she says. "Extremely boring desk job with demanding hours and an even more demanding boss."

"That's quite the leap . . . software engineer to florist. What made you want to open a flower shop?"

"My grandmother had one when I was a little girl." Her lips spread into a nostalgic grin. "She taught me everything she knew. It was always in the back of my mind, but I never really took it seriously until the last couple of years." Sitting up, she adds, "Believe it or not, the name Stem was actually Donovan's idea. Back when we were in college at Michigan State, I told him if we ever got married and moved back home that I was opening a floral shop, and he said I should call it Stem. I guess I just got it in my head that it was a great name. He could be very influential sometimes."

Among other things . . .

"Oh yeah?" I take another drink, swallowing the warm, velvety liquid. "I have to admit, we were only together half a year before we moved here. And he passed two months after that. Sometimes I think about all the things I'll never have a chance to learn about him. What was he like in his younger days?"

Her eyes light and she leans in, as if the topic of Donovan excites her. "Oh, girl. I can tell you all about him if you want?"

Yes . . . I very much want to learn all about him . . .

"Donovan was my first love," she starts, unable to remove the wistful smile from her lips. "We met when I was a sophomore in high school and he was a senior. His brother, Lachlan, was actually in my class, but Donovan was more my type, you know? He had this . . . aura. This sure-footed confidence. And every time he walked into the room, he commanded attention without even trying." Berlin pauses, glancing out at the parking lot. "He had this car . . . a black vintage Firebird. He loved it so much sometimes I got jealous of it. She was always like the other woman, you know?" She chuckles. "Anyway, his dad bought it for him for his sixteenth birthday, and it meant the world to him. They were always working on it together, adding things, modifying it, fixing it up. His dad was a little rough around the edges. Quiet. Not very affectionate. But I always thought the car was his way of telling Don he loved him. That and he loved the attention it brought him. Everywhere he went in that thing, he turned heads."

I think of the Aston Martin Donovan claimed to be restoring when we first met. He told me it was in storage back home, but as soon as we started working on the house, he said he was putting the project on hold so he could focus on one thing at a time. He never did show me the car. Now I'm inclined to believe it never existed.

"He always spoke fondly of his father," I say. "I've only ever seen him in photographs."

"I'm told he wasn't always so . . . gruff," she says carefully. "Don said after their mom died, their dad was never the same."

"He never told me how his mom passed," I say, hoping she fills in the blanks. He only told me she'd died unexpectedly when he was eleven. Like with everything else, I always thought we had more time, and I saved the conversation for another day.

Berlin glances to the side, gathering in a long breath as she squints. "Yeah. He never liked to talk about it. There were a lot of rumors; I know that. All he ever said was there was a terrible accident in the house, but he'd never elaborate, and I never pushed it because it always seemed to upset him, talking about her."

My stomach drops, and my thoughts immediately move to Lachlan.

Is that why he wants to burn the house down?

"Let's see, what else can I tell you . . ." She twists her lips to the side, moving on. "He was very particular about how he dressed. He took a lot of pride in his appearance. When most guys his age would roll out of bed in yesterday's jeans and a wrinkled T-shirt, he would wear starched button-downs and slacks. Never had a hair out of place. Always smelled like a million bucks. Sometimes he liked to pick out the clothes I wore when we went out. Or he'd tell me to wear my hair a certain way. He said we were a package deal, and he liked it when our looks coordinated."

I think back to the night he proposed in Chicago. We had dinner reservations at our favorite restaurant, and I slipped into an emerald-green bandage dress with red Louboutin pumps, but when I came out of the bathroom, he'd laid a little black dress on the bed alongside a pair of black heels. At the time, I was thrown off balance, until he pulled me into his arms, gave me a soft kiss, and sweetly told me it was his favorite look of mine.

I changed, thinking nothing of it.

Besides, I was so enraptured by Donovan that I lived to put a smile on his face any chance I got.

"He was extremely romantic," Berlin continues. "A modern-day Casanova. He was always buying me flowers—white roses mostly. At school, he'd leave me sweet little notes in my locker. He was always planning elaborate dates, and he liked to choose what we did, so all

I had to do was show up and leave the rest to him. On my sixteenth birthday, he rented a limousine and took me on an elaborate scavenger hunt around town. Every stop had a present waiting for me."

"Definitely sounds like him," I say. Donovan was a romantic for sure. I lost track of how many times I'd briefly mention a play or opera or band or movie or a new restaurant I wanted to try and he'd surprise me with tickets or reservations. He picked up on every nuance, and he always made me feel heard. It always seemed like he was one step ahead of me at every turn, but always in a good way.

Berlin gathers a hard breath, her expression growing somber. "My freshman year of college—his junior year—is when he started to change . . ."

"In what ways?"

"He was hot and cold. Some days he was the old Donovan, loving on me and being his sweet self. Other days he would be quiet and distant, and if I tried to ask him what was wrong, he would tell me I was making drama out of nothing. After a bit, he became hypercritical of my appearance—for instance, we were at breakfast one day, and out of the blue he told me gray eye shadow made me look tired. And another time he told me my head looked weird when I wore a ponytail." She tucks her chin. "I know it sounds silly, and it's such a small thing to fixate on, but I still can't bring myself to wear a ponytail without thinking about that comment."

"Ugh," I say. "I'm so sorry."

I've never wanted to hit a corpse more than I do in this moment.

"I'll never forget when we had dinner with a few friends from his dorm floor. We were laughing and having a great time—or so I thought. When it was over, he drove me back to my apartment and told me I embarrassed him." Her eyes turn glassy. "I was so confused because I thought we had fun, and he refused to elaborate. He just said he was tired and wanted to go sleep in his own bed. It wasn't long after that he started flirting with other girls in front of me. We'd be somewhere, and he would run into someone from his econ class, and he'd chat her up with a big smile on his face while I stood back, invisible."

I haven't touched my cappuccino in minutes, but I can't peel my attention off her story for one second.

"We broke up a few times," she says. "He'd always cast me out and reel me right back in. After a while I figured out that he only wanted me when he couldn't have me." A shiver runs through her, as if a decade's worth of raw emotions is clawing its way out. "It was hard, you know? Because you always love your first love in some capacity, even if they were an asshole. No matter how toxic they were, there's a part of them that'll always have their meat hooks in your heart."

"I'm so sorry, Berlin." I place my hand over hers. "Young love is complicated."

Not to make excuses for Donovan.

"What was the final straw?" I ask.

She slumps. "I was exhausted from his antics and just wanted off the damn roller coaster. He tried like hell to get me back—using all of his charm and all of his tricks and saying all of the things that always worked before. It drove him mad that I wouldn't cave that time, but I did what I had to do. Eventually he moved on, and so did I."

Berlin covers her face.

"Oh my God. I'm so embarrassed," she says. "You asked what he was like, and I gave you an entire saga worth of history. Completely did not intend for that to become a vent session, by the way."

"No worries," I say. "I find it fascinating, actually."

"Anyway, people change, and I'm sure he was a lovely person when you were with him." She takes a sip of her tea and perks up, the melancholy instantly gone.

"The way you described him in the beginning," I say, "reminds me of this guy one of my friends dated years ago. He love bombed her hard for the first year or so; then one day it was like he flipped a switch, and he started doing the things you said Donovan did to you . . . being controlling and hot and cold, gaslighting her, flirting with other women. It turns out he had narcissistic personality disorder."

She peers to the side before nodding. "I've never considered that before."

I held my friend's hand through that breakup and sat by her as we googled the hell out of NPD and gleaned everything we possibly could to understand the bizarre span of their toxic relationship. It turns out narcissists have a pattern. They're almost always charming and attractive, they tend to go for people with sweet, trusting personalities who are easily moldable, they bomb them with love and affection greater than any they've ever experienced, and when they feel they're about to lose control, their alter ego comes out. Cheating, verbal abuse, and emotional manipulation are their weapons of choice. The ironic part is they're incapable of loving someone because they don't love themselves. Their romantic partners are only there to fill their needs, nothing more or less.

If what Berlin is saying is true, Donovan must have been love bombing me too.

While I'm certainly not qualified to diagnose him, I can't help but wonder how much time we had left before his true personality came out to play. How much longer until he'd have played my heart like a fiddle too? How much longer until the mental and emotional gymnastics kicked in? Never mind the damage he was doing to my bank account right under my nose . . .

My stomach twists, disconcerted again.

"Anytime you want to talk about him, I'm here," Berlin says. "Our good days outnumbered the bad. I've got plenty of . . . more appetizing memories to share."

Her voice takes a wistful turn, but I don't want to push her. She's already shared more than enough to paint a vivid picture of the man Donovan truly was.

We finish our coffee with small talk, and an hour later, I head home to Lachlan. I find him passed out on the living room sofa, one arm above his head and the other across his stomach. The TV is muted and flickering, painting his handsome face in a myriad of colors.

Berlin's words fill my mind—about their mother dying in this house in a tragic accident. If that's truly the reason he wants to burn this place down, it must be hard for him to spend his days here, restoring it to its former glory. He spoke so lovingly of his mother the other day, about her love of books and words.

This can't be easy for him.

Careful not to wake him, I grab a throw blanket off the back of the couch and cover him up. He spent the entirety of the day prepping the kitchen so the cabinets could be installed. Tomorrow he's heading to the cabinetmaker to pick them up and bring them here to get acclimated. Wednesday will be the big install day.

Everything's happening so quickly. At this rate, we'll have this place ready to sell by the end of next month—assuming he's willing to sell it and not still hell bent on donating it to the fire department.

I tiptoe upstairs, wash up for bed, and read a text from my mom.

Just wanted to let you know, we're coming on Friday, she writes. Will send you the itinerary tomorrow.

I still need to break the news to them that I have a roommate. At this point, it might be better to do it in person. They're not going to spaz out in front of someone they've just met. They'll paint smiles on their faces and keep their thoughts to themselves like the good midwesterners they are, and hopefully by the time the initial shock wears off, they'll have warmed up to the idea of me living with a complete stranger who happens to be the brother of a man they never 100 percent approved of.

Looking back, I know I should have listened to them when they shared their doubts about Donovan, but I was too blind to see what they were seeing. I thought they were being overprotective and that it was clouding their judgment.

Lesson learned—and it's one I never intend on repeating.

If something's too good to be true, it almost always is.

SIXTEEN

LACHLAN

appetence (*n.*) an eager desire, an instinctive inclination;
an attraction

"So . . . teeny, tiny issue," Anneliese says Tuesday morning as she leans in the doorway of the kitchen. She's dressed in tight jeans and a lacy white blouse, her hair pulled back by an oversize black headband. A thin gold pendant hangs from her neck, stopping between the dip of her collarbone and the top of her cleavage. I train my gaze back to where it belongs—on her big blue eyes. "My parents are coming this Friday and staying for a few days."

I set my screwdriver aside. "And what's the issue?"

"They usually stay here . . . normally I'd give them my bed and take yours. Is there any way we can fix up one of the other rooms?" She winces, crossing her fingers.

"By Friday?" I scratch my temple. "I mean, we could clean it up. I wouldn't sand or stain it because you don't want to be breathing those fumes every night. Do you even have an extra bed to put in there?"

"No," she says. "I was going to get an air mattress. I just need your help moving things around so we can actually fit one up there somewhere."

"Put it in my room," I say as Anneliese twists at her necklace. Her fingertips graze the exposed bit of skin above her shirt, and for a brief moment, I find myself imagining my lips there instead. "You can have my bed, and I'll take the mattress."

She begins to speak but stops as if she's digesting a thought that never occurred to her before now. I've slept in every kind of bed imaginable over the last ten years . . . bunk beds, barracks, couches, futons, waterbeds, sleeping bags. A few days on an air mattress is no big deal.

"Um," she says, twisting her rosebud lips into a sly smile. "Yeah, that could work—as long as you don't mind bunking with me? Fair warning, I laugh in my sleep sometimes. It can be creepy if you're not prepared for it."

I wink. "Think I can handle it."

"This could be fun, actually . . . like a little sleepover," she says with a teasing smirk. "I'll bring the flashlight; you can tell the ghost stories."

"Deal."

Glad she's in better spirits than the other night.

She leaves, and I steal a glimpse of her perfect ass in those tight jeans before she takes off for the bookshop. Then I pop my earbuds in and put on a classic-rock playlist.

I dreaded every mile of ocean I flew over coming back to the States, hated every stretch of highway, every road sign that pointed me closer to home.

But I have to say, being back isn't as bad as I thought it'd be.

In fact, I might even be enjoying it.

SEVENTEEN

ANNELIESE

nyctophilia (*n.*) the condition of finding comfort in darkness

A Venmo alert pops up in my email when I get home from work Tuesday night.

> Florence Timmons has paid you $2,000 for one
> week of work.

I pull up my contacts and call her.

"Hey, girlie," she answers on the second ring.

"Two grand? Flo, that's way too much. I don't even think we've had two grand in sales since you left . . ."

She chuckles. "I'm lucky to break even most months. I'm not in it for the money; you know that. It just gives me something to do. Anyway, I appreciate you holding the fort down while I'm gone. I know it put you in a bit of a crimp with your renovations, but I wanted to make sure it was worth your while. Maybe you can buy that light fixture you had your eye on for the dining room? The one with the crystals that looked like little raindrops?"

"How's your mom doing?" I've yet to fill her in on the Lachlan situation, but I'll be sure to catch her up to speed the second she's back.

"Pretty well, all things considered. She's on the mend. We've got her home, and she's comfortable. We hired a home health aide to come to the house and help her with a few things. I offered to move her in with me, but she just laughed. Pretty sure we're both driving each other crazy. She's probably ready for me to go home, and honestly, I'm ready to go home too."

"I can't imagine you driving anyone crazy."

"If my husband was still here, he'd vouch for that," she chuckles. "Anyway, I've booked a flight home for the week after next, if you wouldn't mind keeping the lights on at the shop until then?"

"Of course I don't mind."

"Wonderful," she says. "I'll let you know if anything changes."

"Sounds good. Enjoy the rest of your time in sunny Arizona . . ."

"A little hard to enjoy when you can fry an egg on the sidewalk, but I'll do my best," she says, her tone sarcastic.

"And thank you again, *so much*, for the generous payment," I add.

"It was the least I could do. You're a true friend, Anneliese," she says. "Talk to you soon . . ."

I head inside my house, kick my shoes off by the door, and set my purse down. Passing the living room, I spot boxes upon boxes of cabinetry. When I find Lachlan in the kitchen, the entire place is cleared out, spotless, and marked for tomorrow's install.

Leaning against the doorway, I cross my arms and marvel at the auburn-haired Adonis.

"Color me impressed," I say. "I have to watch a dozen YouTube tutorials before I feel comfortable so much as changing a faucet handle."

"Hi," he says when he notices me. He straightens his back, stretches his arms overhead, and massages his left shoulder. I imagine he's sore. And tired.

"Long day?" I ask.

He nods, grabbing a beer from a nearby Styrofoam cooler. He hands it to me before going back for another.

"You look like you could use one too," he says.

I sigh. "Is it that obvious?"

"Little bit."

I crack the top of the can and take a sip. "So this lady came in today, wanting to return a book because it had dog-eared pages. I kindly reminded her that this was a *used*-book store and that slight wear and tear was normal and to be expected. And then I told her we only accepted returns if there was actual damage to the book . . . pages falling out, scribble marks, that sort of thing. Lachlan, I've never seen anyone's face get so red! She literally stomped her foot and huffed and leaned over the counter demanding to speak to the manager."

He laughs. "Take it you've never worked retail before?"

I take a generous gulp. "Never."

"So what'd you do?"

"I asked her to leave."

"And did she?" He cracks his beer.

"Eventually, but first she called me a 'piece of literal human garbage'—those were her exact words."

Lachlan almost chokes on his drink. "That's the best she could do?"

"I guess." I shrug. "Flo comes back the week after next, and I can't wait. I'm really not cut out for retail."

"You're a good friend," he says, tipping his can in my direction. "Filling in like that."

"Tell that to the woman who thinks I'm trash."

"You mean literal human garbage," he corrects me.

"Right, right."

He chuckles. "Oh, hey. I grabbed that air mattress today while I was out."

"You didn't have to do that."

"I was already at the hardware store. Saw one on a shelf. Not a big deal . . ."

Two weeks ago, I didn't know this man existed. Then he blasted into my life on the heels of a thunderstorm—figuratively and physically speaking. In four short days, he's become an unexpected bright spot in my day.

"You want to take this outside?" He nods toward the front door. "Don't know about you, but I could go for a change of scenery."

A minute later, we're situated on the front steps, sitting so close his arm brushes against mine every time he takes a drink.

"Looks like it might rain again soon," he says, gazing up at the starless sky and the faint glow of the moon obscured by thick clouds. The air is charged tonight, though it could be the impending storm system . . .

A tepid burst of wind kisses my face, and I inhale a long, deep breath.

"Some people love the way it smells after it rains," I say. "But I've always been partial to the way it smells before it rains."

"*Petrichor*," he says. "That earthy scent that happens after it rains. Some people can smell it before, though."

I inhale again, taking in as much of the pungent-sweet, prerain ozone as I can in one go.

Lightning flashes in the distance. I wait for a rumble of thunder that never comes. The cell is too far away yet. A car passes, and a couple of people on bikes with blinking lights whir by. Across the street, a neighbor flicks on their porch light and greets a pizza-delivery woman.

It's been a while since I sat still somewhere and observed the world around me—it makes me wonder about all the things I've missed because I was too wrapped up in my own things.

"Her name is Joan." Lachlan breaks the silence.

"What are you talking about?"

"The pizza-delivery gal." He motions toward the Nissan backing out of the neighbor's driveway. "She's a single mom of a thirteen-year-old boy, and she picks up a few evening shifts each week to help pay for his baseball camp. He's really good, but if he wants a chance at being scouted when he gets to high school, he needs to play on the good leagues, and those aren't cheap. The uniforms alone are a couple hundred bucks, plus the cost of traveling to all the different tournaments. This is her second year, and she's come to hate the smell of pizza because she can never quite wash it out of her hair or off her skin. It's always there. But the hours work for her schedule, and the tips are decent, and it beats waiting tables."

"Sounds like a good mom."

"Oh, she's the best." He lifts his beer to his lips, then adds, "Someday her son's going to make it to the majors. He's going to buy her a house with his first big check. And a shiny new car that doesn't smell like pepperoni-and-mushroom deep dish. She'll never have to deliver pizzas again."

"See?" I nudge him. "Now *that's* a heartwarming story."

"You didn't let me finish."

"No. You finished. The story is over, happy ending and all. No one dies in this story."

"So his dad—"

"Shhhh." I clamp my hand over his mouth, feeling the slow spread of his smile against my palm.

He pulls away, laughing. "Fine. The end."

I brush my shoulder against his, gifting him a playful nudge. For the briefest of moments, our gazes catch in the dark. His smile fades as he studies me, though I can't begin to know what he's thinking in this moment. I clear my throat and look away.

"Who'd have ever thought?" I ask.

"Thought what?"

"You showed up at my door less than two weeks ago, all but demanding the keys to this house so you could burn it down, and now you're staying here, and you're entertaining me with stories and doing all of the reno work and putting a smile on my face for the first time in a long time," I say. "If my life was a story, you'd be the plot twist."

"If you were anyone else, I'd tell you that's a horrible pickup line," he says, washing down his words with a mouthful of cheap beer. "But coming from you, I'll take it as a compliment. And for the record, I still want to burn the place down. That hasn't changed."

I think about Berlin's words for the hundredth time. Last night, I attempted to search for death certificate records and obituaries, but all I had was a name—Julie Byrne—and a virtual dead end. Her death occurred long before publishing obits online was commonplace. And her death record is sealed behind some hundred-dollar paywall.

"I hope you don't," I say. "It's a beautiful house, and it's turning into a beautiful home."

"There are a thousand other beautiful homes in this town. I don't think anyone would miss this one if it were gone."

"Do you plan to watch it burn?" I ask, eyeing him in my peripheral vision.

"That's the whole point." He takes another drink.

"Berlin told me your mother passed here," I say delicately. His shoulders tense, and he focuses on a fading streetlamp in the distance. Thunder rumbles from the western sky. A few minutes from now, we're going to be pelted, but I can't peel myself away from this conversation quite yet . . . or from him. "I'm really sorry to hear that. It must be hard for you, being here."

His lips press flat, and he readjusts his posture. "It's not exactly my idea of a good time, if you want to put it that way."

"What do you think your mom would say if she knew you wanted to do that?"

Lachlan rests his elbows on his knees, hunched forward. "I don't even know. It's been so long . . . sometimes I can't remember what her voice sounded like. I've got a handful of memories. The more years go by, the more she's like a figment of my imagination rather than anything else."

We marinate in quietude for a moment, and what I wouldn't give to crawl inside his beautiful mind and soak up all his thoughts so I could understand him better.

"Why do you want to burn this down so badly?" I ask. "What's going to change when it's gone?"

He doesn't answer, not at first. His chest rises and falls with a heavy breath, and he rests his elbows on his knees.

"It's a long story," he finally says.

"I've got all night."

"Another time, Anneliese." He takes a drink. "It's a bit of a buzzkill, and I don't know about you, but I'm feeling this one already. About to go in for another. You want one?"

I'm not a huge fan of beer, but I'm enjoying his company, and the rain hasn't made its way to us yet, so I nod.

"Please," I say, chugging the remains of my beer as he heads inside.

A minute later, he returns with two new cold ones.

A warm fullness blankets my body, one that tickles my insides like giddy nostalgia. It reminds me of the way I used to feel when I'd go to my grandmother's as a kid, running through the very house where my own mother had grown up, spending time with people who felt like home.

I haven't felt those tingles in forever.

In fact, I don't recall ever feeling them with Donovan.

With him, I felt an adrenaline rush, a frenzied high of sorts.

This is different.

"Did you date anyone? When you were overseas?" I ask.

He turns to me. "You and your hard-hitting questions tonight . . ."

"I'm just trying to picture you as someone's boyfriend, and I can't," I say with an apologetic frown. "You're too free spirited. I feel like you're the kind of guy who's impossible to pin down. Like nailing Jell-O to the wall."

The corners of his mouth dip. "Fair assessment."

"But did you date anyone?"

"A few women here or there over the years. Nothing serious."

"What were they like?"

He laughs through his nose. "Why do you need to know?"

"I don't *need* to know; I'm just curious. Paint me a picture. Tell me their stories."

He pauses, his finger rapping against the side of the aluminum can in his hand.

"They didn't have stories," he says.

"Everyone has a story."

"Not the kind that makes you feel anything. They were pretty ordinary people. Middle class. Average families. College degree. Steady job. The kind who've never been through trauma or tragedy. I'm a magnet for women like that. They always think they can fix me. Make me whole."

"They were never trying to fix you, Lachlan," I say. He turns, holding his gaze on mine so deeply I feel it in my stomach. "They were trying to change you into who *they* wanted you to be."

He places his beer at his side, leaning back and staring ahead.

"Trust me," I add. "A lot of women love a project. And I speak from experience. I dated my share of *projects* before I met your brother. He was the first man I thought was perfect as he was. He didn't need me to make him better. That's one of the many things I loved about him. I was so sure he was a keeper for that exact reason."

"Do we have to drag Donovan into this conversation?" he asks. "Even in death, the bastard won't let me be."

"Did you two ever get along?" I ask. "I know you don't want to talk about him, but I'm just curious if there was ever a time when the two of you didn't hate each other."

Lachlan picks the pop-top off his can before tossing it aside. "There was a time I thought he hung the moon."

My heart tightens, and I gather in a long, slow breath as I wait for him to finish.

"Sooner or later, we all find out what kind of person he truly is," he adds. "I just happened to find out a hell of a lot sooner than everyone else. Anyway."

I take his hint to change the subject and return to his dating history. "I find it interesting, though, that you're drawn to ordinary and average . . . when the life you live is anything but."

"You psychoanalyzing me, Blue Eyes?" He paints a smile on his face, though there's a thread of sadness in his voice.

"Just making an observation." I yawn and check the time. "Anyway, I need to go over some emails and work on some names. My next client wants something organic and out there—their words."

He cocks his chiseled jaw, sniffing through his nose. "Good luck with that."

"Thanks." Rising, I give his shoulder a squeeze. "Good talk."

His mouth rises on one side. "Yeah. Good talk."

I head inside and settle into my makeshift office, though I'm pretty sure I could sit out there for hours and shoot the breeze with him. Something about his presence is grounding and makes me forget about life for a while—maybe it's the depth in his gaze or the occasional semblance of a smile he offers or the way he seems so sure of who he is when some people live their entire lives never knowing.

Aside from a handful of passersby, it felt like we had the whole world to ourselves.

I think of what Berlin said yesterday, about being in Lachlan's class but falling for Donovan instead because he was more her type. While I still hardly know the man, if I had been here back then, it would've been Lachlan.

No question.

EIGHTEEN

LACHLAN

metanoia (*n.*) the journey of changing one's mind, heart, self, or way of life

I finish installing the first wall of cabinets Wednesday afternoon, and I stop for a lunch break and to take a minute to stand back and admire the progress. Anneliese chose a vintage-inspired dark green—a bold choice, but it works. The cabinets are decent quality, too, soft-close doors and dovetailed joints, made of solid white oak with a smooth painted finish. I should be able to wrap up the other half of the installation by the end of the day if I work straight through until night. Once the counters and appliances are in, this room should be in good working order—and that much closer to being finished.

I grab a bottled water, wipe the sweat off my brow, and take it all in.

It's nothing like the kitchen of my childhood. Anneliese completely reconfigured the layout, making it more functional and moving the sink under the window, where it looks out onto the backyard. My mother would've loved this arrangement. When she wasn't reading or chasing after us, she was in the kitchen, making every meal from scratch. She was traditional in every sense of the word.

I think of what Anneliese said last night, that I'm drawn to ordinary women when my life is anything but. Maybe on a deeper level, I'm chasing the very thing I lost—the security and safety that I knew for the first nine years of my life.

Taking a swig of water, I try to imagine what my mom would think of Anneliese. She's anything but traditional. She's quirky and naive, wears her heart on her sleeve, asks way too many questions, and has an addiction to busyness. I bet Mom—or the idea I have of her, anyway—would be amused.

I finish my lunch and check my phone, listening to a voice mail from the repair shop informing me the replacement window is in. Scrolling through my messages, I find a few from friends back in the UK asking when I'm coming back, one from Lynnette asking how things are going, and then a third from Anneliese—a picture of an open book, with her finger pointing to a word.

I zoom in to get a closer look . . . *eccedentesiast.*

ANNELIESE: I was paging through this book today out of sheer boredom and came across this word that I thought you might like, so I looked it up. It means someone who hides pain behind a smile.

I write back.

ME: What are you implying?

ANNELIESE: Not implying anything, just thought it was pretty and that maybe you could use it in one of your stories.

ANNELIESE: I found another one if you're interested.

ME: Go on . . .

ANNELIESE: psychomachy . . . a conflict between soul and body.

Head cocked sideways, I rake my hand along my jaw. Am I supposed to be reading between the lines here, or is she simply sending me big words because she knows I like them? Either way, she's at the bookstore right now, and she could be doing anything else, but she's thinking about me.

ME: I have one for you . . . kalon—beauty that is more than skin deep.

ANNELIESE: Love it. The world needs more kalon. Did I use it correctly in that sentence?

The world needs more kalon—and I need more Anneliese.

ME: You did. A+.

ANNELIESE: Appliances are being delivered Saturday, BTW.

She changes the subject. Whether that's intentional or not, I have no way to know. Nor do I know if we are flirting or straddling the precipice of something that neither of us anticipated.

All I know is that when I'm with her, I find myself not wanting to be anywhere else.

NINETEEN

ANNELIESE

paraprosexia (*n.*) constant distraction

"Hi, sweetheart. Oh, it's so good to see you." My mom clasps her hands on my cheeks and kisses my forehead.

"How was your flight?" I ask before giving my dad a hug.

She shoots him a look, raised eyebrows and all, which is never a good sign.

"Three hours of screaming babies and gassy travelers and a little bit of turbulence over Lake Michigan, but we made it in one piece," he says.

My mom steps past the landing, inspecting the house for progress—like she always does. She finds it absurd that I feel the need to finish this project (alone), but she offers encouragement anyway.

"My goodness, Anneliese, the dining room looks great," she says. "The floors turned out amazing."

"You should see the kitchen . . . cabinets went in this week, and appliances are coming tomorrow." I picked them out months ago, since the cabinetmakers needed the dimensions, but I didn't want to store them in my house, so the appliance store agreed to keep them on hold until I needed them. Countertops are being templated next week, then hopefully installed the week after.

It's all coming together so quickly . . . thanks to Lachlan.

"Okay, so there's someone I want you to meet," I say, leading them to the study, where I told Lachlan to wait.

My mother's gaped expression is one of horror, and my father's complexion turns the pale shade of unfinished Sheetrock.

I forgot that was how I introduced them to Donovan last year . . .

"What's going on? Are you dating someone?" my father asks, hushed.

Waving my hands, I say, "No, no, no. It's not like that."

"Then what's it like, Anneliese?" Mom crosses her arms.

"I recently found out that Donovan had a brother," I say before correcting myself. "*Has*. Has a brother."

"You didn't know?" she asks.

"He never told me," I say, "and before you ask, no, I don't know why. Anyway, his name is Lachlan, and he's staying here to help me fix up the house. He's actually the one who did the dining room floors . . . and the landscaping out front . . . and the kitchen cabinet install . . . he's also stripping the back deck to restore that . . ."

I motion for them to follow me into the study, where Lachlan is waiting by the window, hands shoved into the front pockets of his ripped jeans.

My parents stop in their tracks and stare, and my mother slips her arm into my father's for support. They're usually friendlier than this, but I didn't think to take into consideration the shock that comes with seeing a Donovan doppelgänger for the first time.

"Lachlan, these are my parents . . . Rob and Linda," I say. "Mom and Dad, this is Lachlan Byrne."

He extends his hand to my father first, his gaze direct and warm. "Great to meet you."

"You look just like him," Mom says, her voice tapering into a whisper. "It's uncanny."

"I used to get that a lot," he says. "People used to mistake us for twins, but I'm actually younger."

"Lachlan's been living in the UK for the last ten years," I say, hoping they'll accept that as the answer to why he didn't attend his brother's funeral. Now is not the time to get into the nitty-gritty of a situation I still don't fully understand.

"Really?" My father straightens his shoulders. "Whereabouts?"

"All over," Lachlan says, dropping the names of familiar cities and tacking on a handful of towns I've never heard of.

"I studied abroad for a year in Glasgow," my father says. "Stayed with a lovely family. The Petermans. One of the best years of my life. We talk on the phone every New Year's to this day—they get a kick out of calling me from the new year while I'm stuck in the old one for a few more hours."

I exhale, relieved. My father is an introverted high school math teacher who rarely finds common ground with anyone, let alone complete strangers. This is good.

I'm starting to wonder if Lachlan just has that effect on people. He can't be bothered to be anyone but himself, which takes the pressure off having to be a perfect conversationalist or making the best first impression.

That says a lot about the man.

Not to mention it puts him in a category light-years from Donovan.

"Rob, can you take our things up?" Mom asks. "I don't know about you all, but your father and I are starving. Airport food is not for the faint of heart, so we tend to avoid it. We were thinking about going to that little Mexican restaurant you took us to last time, Anneliese?"

"Cabo Sol?" I ask.

"Yes, that one," she says before turning to Lachlan. "We'd love for you to join us."

"I don't want to impose," he says without hesitation.

"Nonsense." Mom waves her hand in front of her face. "You're coming with us. Anneliese tells us you've been tremendously helpful with renovations. At least let us feed you."

"She's really bad at taking no for an answer, so you might as well plan on joining us," I tell him, speaking under my breath.

Ten minutes later, we're riding in the back of my parents' rented Kia sedan, en route to Cabo Sol, listening to my father tell stories from his time abroad.

I catch Lachlan's gaze for a second and give him a friendly wink, then shoot him a quick text while my dad continues to wax poetic.

ME: You're a good sport.

LACHLAN: They're not that bad.

ME: No one wants to hang out with someone else's parents on a Friday night . . . I'm sure you had other things you wanted to do.

LACHLAN: You know me—I'm all about living an extraordinary life.

ME: Fine. But I think it's only fair that I should warn you to avoid the following topics at dinner tonight (or we'll be there until close): capital gains taxes, core curriculum, and the pope.

LACHLAN: Triple noted.

We pull into the crowded parking lot of the only Mexican restaurant in town and put our name in for a table. Twenty minutes later, they seat us in a cozy booth. Lachlan slides in beside me, his arm brushing against mine and causing the tiniest thrill to run down my spine. That nostalgic warmth follows—the same one I felt the other night sitting outside with him. That feeling that has no business interjecting itself in my life right now; that feeling that can only be described as *home*.

I place my confusion aside and reach for a chip.

I've spent the past several months grieving. And alone.

My mind is playing cruel tricks on me . . .

For the hour that follows, we drink salted lime margaritas and stuff ourselves full of chips and salsa while the conversation flows . . . and all of it feels oddly *natural*.

When we get home, my mother insists we watch a ninety-minute documentary about three identical strangers. While I fully expect Lachlan to excuse himself for the evening, he stays.

He takes the chair on the other side of the room and settles in.

I cozy up on the end of the sofa, grab my phone, and send him another text.

ME: You don't have to do this.

LACHLAN: I know. I want to.

ME: Why?

LACHLAN: Because I heard this doc is good and I'm a sucker for a real life plot twist.

He darkens his phone screen, places it facedown on the coffee table, and lifts his pointer finger to his lips before pointing to the TV screen.

My cheeks turn red hot, and I'm thankful for the darkness of the room because it hides the sheepish expression on my face. I can't believe any part of me hoped he was sticking around for any other reason besides the fact that he actually wanted to watch the doc. If there's anything I've learned about Lachlan so far, it's that the man loves a compelling human-interest story.

Pulling in a cleansing breath, I get myself together and snap out of it.

I can't entertain these kinds of thoughts anymore.

Crushing on someone I hardly know is the last thing I should be doing.

Didn't I learn my lesson the first time?

TWENTY

LACHLAN

basorexia (*n.*) the overwhelming desire to kiss

"Oh." Anneliese stands in the doorway of my room Friday evening wearing a matching pajama set covered in little pink hearts, her hair pulled back from her freshly washed face.

I think it's safe to say she won't be trying to seduce me tonight . . . not that I expected her to. But she's dressed like a girl about to play truth or dare at a slumber party. If she's trying to send a message, it's been received: loud and clear.

"I said I'd take the air mattress," she says when she spots me on the floor.

"I might be an asshole, but I'm not a dick. Take the bed. I insist."

I punch my pillow a few times to fluff it up before lying back and getting situated. The plastic squeaks under the sheet, and a faint whistling sound fills my ear. Holding perfectly still, I listen for it once more, only to feel the thing deflating in real time.

In less than an hour, I'll be sleeping on the cold hardwood floors.

No good deed goes unpunished . . .

Anneliese climbs under the blankets of the twin bed, reaches up to shut off the lamp by the nightstand, then turns on her side, facing me. Despite the darkness, I can make out the shape of her body and the angles of her pretty face. With her cheek resting on top of her hand, her lips glide into a sly smile.

"What?" I ask.

"I'm ready for my bedtime story." There's a tease in her tone.

"Looks like you forgot your flashlight." I roll to my side, and the air mattress releases another steady stream of air. Sitting up, I drag my fingers along the side to find the valve to ensure it's sealed—it is. And then I pull up the sheet to feel around for any rips or tears.

"What's wrong?" She sits up.

"This thing isn't holding any air." I follow the sound, searching for small rips or tears, only it seems to be coming from the valve itself. Grabbing my phone off the ground, I turn on the flashlight feature and inspect the thing. "Looks like it's the valve. It's ripped on the underside. Can't believe I didn't notice that when I was filling it earlier."

Anneliese is quiet.

I stand up, grabbing my pillow and blanket.

"Where are you going?" she asks.

"To sleep on the couch . . ."

"The frame is warped—you'll wake up with a kink in your back. Maybe not the first night or the second, but by the third you'll be hurting," she says. "Trust me. I speak from experience."

"Then I guess I'll sleep in my truck . . ."

She scoots to one side of the twin bed, patting the other half. "It'll be a tight fit, but we can make it work."

"You want me to sleep there? With you?"

"Don't be weird about it, just . . . I'm trying to come up with a reasonable solution to this little predicament," she says, using the very same words I used the day I came to seize the property. In retrospect, I could've been a little less brash, but I came in guns blazing because I didn't know this woman and she represented someone who'd already taken so much from me.

Anneliese peels the covers back and makes room for my pillow. There isn't much room on the open side of the bed, but I climb in beside her anyway and attempt to make myself as narrow as possible—easier said than done.

"You comfortable? Need more room?" she asks, inching closer to the edge of the bed.

I'm still hanging off my side, and one wrong move in the middle of the night will have me face-planted on the floor in two seconds flat.

"I think I'm falling off the bed over here," Anneliese says a few seconds later.

"Me too."

She laughs. "Okay, so let's scoot in a little bit and meet in the middle. I promise I don't have cooties."

"That's a relief," I say. "Just so happens I had my annual cooties test last month. Came back clean."

We slide closer, until our faces are mere inches away from one another and our bodies are all but fused from our feet all the way up to our middles.

"Would you rather lay like this and stare into my eyes, or would you rather me flip around and then it's like we're spooning?" she asks. "Which would be less awkward?"

I almost opt for the latter until I imagine her waking up to my morning wood poking her backside.

"Here, sit up." I slide my arm underneath her and guide her closer. "Just come in a little, lay on your side, and rest your head on my chest."

This way we're not gazing into one another's eyes, nor is my cock pressed up against her perfect little ass.

"Can I wrap my arm around you like this?" She slides her hand over my stomach. "Otherwise it just feels weird if I rest it straight."

"I'll allow it," I say with a chuckle.

"Your heart's beating really fast . . ."

I hadn't noticed, but now that she says something, I'm suddenly aware of the steady thrum against the inside of my rib cage.

"Am I making you nervous?" she asks.

"Not at all." I'm just not used to the lack of personal space and sleeping in such close quarters.

"It's starting to settle down now." She presses her cheek firmer against me.

"Thanks for the update."

"Feel free to tell me that story whenever you're ready."

"I don't know if I have it in me tonight. I'm still processing that documentary . . ."

"Yeah, that was a wild ride. I think my mom really appreciated how into it you were," she says. "You know, my dad probably said more words to you tonight than he ever said to Donovan the entire time we were together."

There she goes again, bringing him into a space where he's not welcome.

"Interesting," I say, monotone.

"Donovan always did most of the talking," she adds.

"Most bullshitters do."

"I always thought he was just rambling on because he wanted my dad to like him. Maybe on an unspoken level he could sense that my dad was seeing through him," she says. "My parents tried to warn me not to make this move, but I had stars in my eyes, and I thought they were just being overprotective. Their only child wanting to run off with some guy she hardly knows would make any parent nervous."

"You live, you learn, then you move on. That's all you can do."

"It's going to be hard moving on," she says, breathing me in. "With someone new, I mean. Romantically. Whenever that happens . . . I'll probably be scrutinizing every word that comes out of their mouth, paranoid that I'm missing a red flag or that the bottom's going to drop out at any time."

"You're too soft. Too trusting. Most people have their own interests at heart. Just keep that in mind, and you'll be all right."

"That's very . . . uninspiring."

"I'm a realist."

"So you're saying I'm an idealist?"

I adjust my shoulders against my pillow. My arm is falling asleep beneath her, but she seems comfortable, so I won't make her move just yet.

"You see things for what they can be," I say. "I see things for what they are. You're better off letting go of any expectations, and that applies to everything, everyone, and everywhere."

"So that day you came to my door to tell me this house belonged to you, you had zero expectations?" A hint of sarcasm resides in her voice.

"I had zero expectations that this was going to go smoothly," I say. "And that was confirmed when you slammed the door in my face."

I also had zero expectations that I would catch myself daydreaming about how her lips would taste against mine or how soft her skin would feel beneath my palms. The last thing I ever expected was to be attracted to my dead brother's would've-been widow.

As much as I enjoy my own company—and have for the past decade—a part of me is starting to enjoy hers more. And that's something I haven't had with anyone else. Even the slew of "ordinary" women I dated in the UK began to grate on my nerves after a few days together. After a long weekend, I'd always need a break or a breather before going back for more—and it wasn't their fault. I just don't tend to like most people.

But there's something about Anneliese . . .

Something that makes me want to talk to her a little longer, forget about life for a while.

She's just . . . so damn nice.

Easy to like.

Intelligent.

Different.

Interesting.

Just as sexy in a pencil skirt as she is in a paint-stained T-shirt.

"You still want that story?" I ask, keeping my voice down.

She doesn't answer.

When I glance down, I find that her eyes are closed and her breathing has slowed to a steady pace. She's out cold, her arm draped across my chest. And it's probably better this way. Had we stayed up all night talking, I can't promise I wouldn't have made a move by morning. Those petal-pink lips are begging to be claimed by someone who actually gives a shit about her.

Anneliese once mentioned that she intends to go back to Chicago after we sort out the fate of this house. My plan has always been to return overseas—though I'm leaning toward Spain for this next go-around. We're on two very different trains leaving the station in opposite directions—but if things were different, I'd make her mine.

TWENTY-ONE

ANNELIESE

phosphenes (*n.*) the colors or "stars" you see when rubbing your eyes

"He's good, isn't he?" Mom asks as we watch Lachlan and Dad seal the deck Saturday afternoon. The two of them have been going at it since sunup. "At fixing things, I mean."

Better than Donovan was, that's for sure.

"He certainly knows his way around a sander," I say, watching the way his tanned and taut muscles ripple through his white V-neck T-shirt.

"They make a great team."

"Lachlan's pretty easy to get along with."

"I'll say." Her eyes sparkle for a moment. "I have a feeling your father would've been happier had you fallen for Lachlan instead of Donovan." She makes the sign of the cross before her expression grows somber. "God rest his soul."

Such a weird thing to say.

"Mom . . ." I shoot her a look.

"Look at them," she says. "I've never seen your father talk to anyone as much as he's been talking to Lachlan. You'd think they'd run out of things to talk about by now, but nope. Every time I peek out there, they're gabbing away like they've known each other their whole lives."

She's right—that's not my dad's normal modus operandi.

"Dad's probably telling him every story he can think of from his year in Glasgow." I run my hand along the smooth ceramic top of the new range that was delivered this morning. It's crazy that a few weeks ago this room was nothing more than a dorm fridge, microwave, and folding table, and now all we need are countertops and light fixtures. "He's probably just tickled to be able to tell his stories to someone who hasn't heard them a million times."

Mom sighs. "I suppose you're right."

Falling asleep in Lachlan's arms last night came easier than I thought it would. I was worried he'd feel too much like Donovan, but the more I settled in and concentrated on the comforting thrum of his heartbeat against my ear and the soft rumble of his voice in the dark, the less I thought about . . . anything else.

Despite their uncanny resemblance, Lachlan doesn't feel like Donovan's brother to me.

He's his own separate entity.

"What's the plan after this?" Mom asks, stealing me from my thoughts.

I take two glasses from one of the new cabinets and fill them with ice water from the brand-new french door refrigerator for the guys.

"We still need to sand and stain a few of the interior rooms," I say. "One of the bathrooms needs remodeled. And then we'll paint . . . inside and out . . . after that it's light fixtures. Then we'll need to order an appraisal."

"No, I mean, what's after *this*," she says, motioning wide with her arms. "Are you planning to stick around Arcadia Grove, or are you looking for a change of scenery? I know we've talked about this before, but the offer still stands: you can always come home."

In a perfect world, I'd recoup my savings and move back to Chicago. I'd have enough for a decent apartment in my old neighborhood as well as time to relaunch my business. If I walk away from this empty handed, I'll have no other choice than to move back home with my parents until I can get on my feet again.

"Everything's kind of up in the air at the moment," I say.

She frowns, studying me. "It pains me to see you struggling. And we hate what that man did, leaving you in the lurch like that. You didn't deserve it."

My parents have said a million things since the truth came out about Donovan's deception, but not once have they uttered the words *we told you so.*

I slide my arm around her shoulders and give her a squeeze. "I know, Mom. Thank you."

She follows my gaze to Lachlan.

"He's a nice young man, isn't he?" Her voice is laced with sorrow, pitiful almost.

"He is," I say. "He's been a godsend."

Funny, if someone had told me the first time Lachlan and I met that I'd be calling him a godsend weeks later, I'd have never believed them.

"It may seem like he's your white knight," she says, choosing her words carefully. "And I see the way the two of you look at each other. But sweetheart, whatever you do, don't go romanticizing any of this."

"The way we look at each other?" I choke on my laugh.

Mom leans in, swatting her hand between us. "Anneliese, your father and I weren't born yesterday. The way you two flirt, the way you text each other when you think no one's paying attention, that smile you can't take off your face when he's around . . . *sharing a bedroom . . .*"

My jaw all but hits the floor. "You're just reading into it."

"A mother knows her own daughter," she says, almost disapproving. "I know how you get around men you like, Anneliese. I've seen it before. This is no different." Leaning closer, she adds, "I just want you to be careful. I'd hate to see you hurt all over again. That one's got heartbreak written all over him."

I don't disagree with her statements at all, but she has it all wrong.

"I don't like him—not like that," I say. "He's nice, and he's helping me out around here. Period. End of sentence."

He may be ridiculously, unfairly, distractingly good looking, a skilled storyteller, and a top-notch conversationalist, but I'm not looking for a relationship, and if I were, it wouldn't be with my dead fiancé's estranged brother. Not because I'm loyal to Donovan but because I'm not interested in a buy-one-get-one-free Byrne-brother special.

One Byrne is more than enough for this lifetime.

"Are you sure that's *all* he's doing?" she asks, keeping her voice low.

"What are you talking about?"

"He's clearly keeping you company," she says. "And I see the way he looks at you, how his eyes linger a little too long and his lips crack a sly smile whenever you walk into the room. I've been around long enough to know what attraction looks like."

"Again, you're reading into everything," I say. "Promise."

She lifts a brow, skeptical.

I leave before she can say another ridiculous word.

Carrying the waters outside, I sense my mother's watchful stare, and with each step, I tell myself she's wrong. I don't *like* him.

I couldn't.

I wouldn't.

I shouldn't.

And he doesn't like me . . .

I'd know if he did.

The man's certainly not shy about asking for what he wants in this life, nor does he hesitate to go after it.

Besides, there's no possible scenario I can conjure in my mind of the two of us running off together into the sunset. The man hasn't been stateside in a decade and clearly has attachment issues, and I'm still nursing a shattered heart and bruised ego.

Two broken halves do not make a whole.

"You guys thirsty?" I deliver their drinks with a smile and make a conscious effort not to let my gaze linger anywhere on or near Lachlan's vicinity.

They thank me, stopping to rest for a bit, and my father begins to say something, only I head back in with the swiftness of a hummingbird.

I lose myself in busywork the rest of the day, sanding and staining and cleaning and prepping before rinsing and repeating. I stop for an email break and manage to make it to inbox zero. And for that handful of hours, I almost forget Lachlan's even here.

But at the end of the workday, just before dinnertime, I catch him exiting the upstairs bathroom, his hair shower damp and a towel tied tight and low at his hips. My stomach ties in a million knots at the sight of him, and I draw in a long, slow breath, holding it tight in my chest. He doesn't notice me; he simply veers into his bedroom and closes the door, leaving a foggy trail of woodsy aftershave in his wake—a scent that has lately become one of my favorites.

The stairs creak, and I snap out of it, turning to find my mother making her way up.

"Anneliese, what are you doing just standing here in the dark?" she asks, chuckling. She places her hand on the small of my back before brushing past me in the hallway. "Is everything okay? Dinner's about ready. First meal cooked in your new kitchen . . ."

"I'll be down in a bit. Just need to clean up," I say.

She disappears into my bedroom, and I head into my bathroom to grab a quick shower and change for supper. I'm almost done when I catch myself dabbing on a touch of makeup to make the bags under my eyes a little less noticeable . . . which only serves to make my pale lashes paler, so I slick on a couple of coats of mascara . . . but then my eyebrows scream for attention. I fill them in lightly before deciding a few pats of cream blush on my cheeks might put a little life into my complexion.

By the time I'm finished, I've given my mother every reason to hold close to her opinion, but at least I look halfway human.

I head downstairs, confused, with butterflies in my middle that have no business being there. Everything was so simple before—relatively speaking. Now I'm going to spend the rest of the night hyperaware of every look, glance, touch, or word that comes out of my mouth and ends up in Lachlan's direction.

Not only do I not want to give my parents the wrong idea, but I'd hate to give him the wrong impression as well.

I take a seat at the unfolded card table in the kitchen—while the room might be finished, I'm still lagging in the furniture department. Mom pulls a casserole from the oven, and my father spreads a paper napkin over his lap, studying me.

"Sounds like someone had quite the productive afternoon," he says to me. "I've always found that productivity has a snowball effect. Sometimes all it takes is a little momentum to keep it going."

I bite my tongue, deciding not to remind him that for the past six months, I've been renovating a six-thousand-square-foot home by myself while running a side business and pinching pennies to keep the lights on.

"Won't be much longer, and you'll be on your way to wherever life takes you next," he says.

Mom shoots him a look: a dead giveaway that they've been talking.

"I'm praying life takes her home for a bit," Mom says.

My dad chuckles. "If it were up to you, Linda, she'd still be living at home."

She places the casserole dish on a trivet in the middle of the table before checking her watch. "Is Lachlan joining us for dinner? I set a place for him."

"He said he was," Dad answers.

"Anyway, Anneliese." Mom brushes my shoulder in passing on her way to the fridge. "I just think you've had such a trying year, and there's no shame in coming home, putting your feet up, and decompressing for a bit."

"Appreciate the offer," I say. "I'll let you know what I decide when the time comes . . ."

Mom places a plate of dinner rolls and a tub of spreadable butter at the table before taking a seat next to me.

"Should we wait for Lachlan?" Dad asks.

"No need," he says, appearing in the doorway in a muscle-hugging button-down and dark, nonripped jeans. He takes the seat across from me, and our eyes lock. From the corner of my eye, I sense my parents' watchful gazes.

I do my best not to squirm under all this heat.

Anyone can make something out of nothing if they try hard enough.

And that's all this is—*nothing*.

It's all it'll ever be.

Period. End of sentence.

TWENTY-TWO

LACHLAN

dormiveglia (*n.*) the space that stretches between
sleeping and waking

"Look who it is," I say softly when my bedroom door opens Saturday night. A sliver of hallway light paints the background of Anneliese's curved silhouette as she lingers in the doorway.

Reaching for my phone on the nightstand, I check the time.

"It's one a.m.," I say.

She steps inside, turning to close the door softly behind her. "I wasn't tired, so I worked on some names."

I sit up and scoot a few inches to my side of the tiny bed, waiting for her to make her way over.

"Find it a little strange that you worked *literally* all day long and you're not tired," I say.

She peels her sweatshirt over her head, revealing a wispy white tank top that stops in the middle of her thighs and practically glows in the dark. I direct my attention from the distracting curve of her legs.

"I also find it strange that you didn't say more than ten words to me all day," I add.

"Believe it or not, Lachlan, not everything is about you." She gives me a teasing smirk as she climbs in beside me. Her body heat fills the space around us, and the faint scent of her gardenia shampoo permeates the air.

"Oh, so the whole no-eye-contact thing and radio silence whenever I was around . . . *wasn't* about me?"

"Are we bickering right now?" She sits up a little. "What is this?"

"God, no."

"Just wanted to make sure." She punches her pillow, fluffing it a bit before attempting to get comfortable.

For someone who avoided me most of the day, she's doing a top-notch job at pretending everything's fine . . . at least between us.

For a while, I thought maybe I'd done something to upset her, though I couldn't imagine what that could be. Was I too friendly with her dad? Too polite to her mom? Did I do *too* good of a job finishing the deck? I wasn't trying to be a kiss-ass. Lord knows that's not my style. But I wasn't about to make the next several days miserable for all involved.

I chuckle to myself.

"What's so funny?" she asks.

"I thought you were mad at me earlier."

Anneliese chews the inside of her lip, her eyes stuck on mine in the dark room that wraps itself around us.

"You're . . . not . . . mad at me, right?" I ask. Not that it would matter. She wouldn't be the first, and she won't be the last.

She draws in a deep breath, squinting. "Have we been flirting?"

"What?" I almost choke on my words before they make their way out.

She lies on her back, her hands resting on her upper stomach as she stares at the ceiling.

"Just something my mom said earlier," Anneliese says.

"She said we were flirting?"

"She's convinced that we're . . . I don't know . . . together or into each other or whatever," she says.

"Why would she think that?"

Turning, she props her head on her hand, and her gaze settles onto mine again. "She claims we smile too much when we're around each other. And she sees us texting. She says I get this look in my eyes when you're around, and she also says she's caught you checking me out . . . I told her she was imagining things."

I press my lips firm, scrutinizing the events of the past couple of days.

Is she, though?

"She's overprotective," she adds. "Especially with everything that happened with your brother. She's seeing things because she's worried. Anyway, I told her it's all in her head."

"Is it?" I sit up, move to my side, and prop myself up on my elbow until we're face to face, so close I can taste the cool peppermint of her toothpaste when she exhales.

Her big eyes widen.

"Yes. It's very much in her head." The amount of conviction in Anneliese's voice makes me think she's trying to convince herself more than she's trying to convince me. "Anyway, I don't want to make things weird. I just . . . you asked me why I was quiet all day. I was just trying to keep my distance from you to prove a point to my mom."

"To your mom?" I ask. "Or to yourself?"

"Don't flatter yourself, Lachlan." She playfully swats my chest. "Ugh. I'm sorry. Was that flirting?"

"You're all over the place tonight," I say. "Pull yourself together, Blue Eyes. Haven't seen you this rattled since the day I showed up on your doorstep."

Her lips glide into a slow, pretty smile, and she exhales.

"You're disarming," Anneliese says. "I think that's the problem. You make everyone you meet feel like they've known you their whole lives.

My dad, for instance? He's never like that. With anyone. And my mom adores you—despite wanting to ensure that you're not trying to sweep me off my feet."

"I wouldn't dare." I wink.

"There's a familiarity about you that I can't figure out. I used to think it was because of how much you looked like Donovan." She bites her lower lip. "I don't think that's it, though."

"You know what I think?"

"What?" She blinks.

"I think you're exhausted, which is making you delirious. I think it's been a long damn day. And I think this is way too heavy of a conversation to have at one o'clock in the morning." I pat her pillow. "Get some shut-eye, roomie."

She lies back, attempting to get comfortable, tugging on the covers and fidgeting. Finally, I slide my arm under her shoulders and pull her closer. Not because I'm trying to "sweep her off her feet" but because this is the only way either of us is going to get any rest tonight, and my alarm is set for 6:00 a.m.

"You never did tell me a bedtime story last night," she says with a yawn.

"Anneliese," I say with a soft groan.

"Just a quick one, until I fall asleep?"

"I'm sorry, are you a grown woman or a six-year-old little girl?"

"I just want my mind to shut off," she says, her face half-pressed against me.

"I can put on some music."

"I just really like your voice," she says, yawning again.

Gathering a big breath, I relent. She'll be out soon enough.

"Fine," I say. "Fiction or nonfiction?"

"Surprise me."

"All right," I say, buying a little bit of time. "Once upon a time, there was a young man named—"

"Once upon a time? Is this a fairy tale?" She pops up.

"Not even close," I say. "Can I continue?"

"Yes. Sorry." She settles against me, her eyelids fluttering shut.

"*Once upon a time*," I say again, with added emphasis, "there was a young woman . . . we'll call her . . . Anneliese."

"Hey . . ."

"Anneliese couldn't sleep, so she begged her extremely exhausted roommate to tell her a story even though he wanted nothing more in the world than to get some sleep because Anneliese had worked him to the bone all day."

"I'm guessing this is a nonfiction story."

"Anyway," I continue, "Anneliese was a bright young woman who lived in a ruined castle. She was hell bent on restoring it to its former glory, despite the fact that no one was ever going to live there long enough to enjoy it."

"That remains to be seen," she interjects, eyes still closed.

"Not only was this bright young woman stubborn, she was also funny. And generous. And a little sad sometimes."

"So what you're saying is Anneliese is sweet but psycho," she says.

"I'm not saying that at all. Also, has anyone ever told you it's incredibly rude to interrupt someone when they're in the middle of telling a story?"

"Sorry." She zips her fingers across her lips before resting her arm across my stomach.

I clear my throat three times, for dramatic effect. "*Anyway.* Anneliese worked in a bookstore, even though she hated books."

"I never said I hated books," she interrupts again before clapping her hand over her mouth and squinting up at me. "Sorry."

Squirming and fighting a good laugh, she slides her leg against mine, brushing my inner thighs in the process. Not only that, but her breasts are all but popping out of her tank top. Never in my life have

I spent days upon days with a beautiful woman, held her in my arms while we slept, and not made a move.

If she were anyone else, I'd have kissed her by now.

Hell, I'd have done more than kiss her . . .

My heart hammers in my chest. Knowing I can't have her—that I shouldn't have her—only makes me want her that much more.

My cock pulses, a warning sign, a threat that I'm about to reach the point of no return. I turn my thoughts to the least sexy ones I can find—British politics, rugby, craft beer, international layovers, and water polo.

It's no use.

The damn thing gets harder by the second.

I adjust myself, praying she doesn't notice any strategic maneuvering—and she doesn't.

"Are you going to continue the story?" she asks. "I kind of want to learn more about the crazy chick's roommate."

"The crazy chick's roommate," I say, "as you put it ever so eloquently, was two seconds from going absolutely insane, right along with her. Not only was he living in a house he promised himself he'd never set foot in again for the rest of his life—but he was fixing it up . . . all because the crazy chick wanted to."

"But she didn't force him. No one was forcing him. We should make that clear."

My gaze falls to her lips as I think about all the ways I could silence them, though one method sticks out more than the others. "Anneliese, I swear to God, if you interrupt me one more time—"

"You'll what?"

Lifting my hand to her face, I trace the pad of my thumb across her pillow-soft bottom lip.

"Either you give this busy little mouth a rest, or I rest it for you."

Her eyes glint in the dark as she sucks in a tight breath. The outline of her hardened nipples presses through the thin fabric of her top.

"I'm going to be completely honest with you, Anneliese," I say. "I'm hard as a fucking rock right now."

She writhes again, laughing under her breath, only this time her knee brushes against my cock.

"Plot twist." She breaks the silence first.

"You're damn right it's a plot twist."

"Does this mean we *have* been flirting? And you *have* been checking me out?" she asks.

"It means there's a beautiful woman in my bed, pressing her body against mine, for the second night straight, and knowing I can't have her makes me want her that much more."

"Now that's a pickup line."

"Not trying to pick you up," I say. "Just being honest."

I trace my thumb along her lips once more, and mine burn in response. I've never wanted to taste anyone this badly in my life.

She lifts her hand to my wrist, wrapping her fingers around me softly as her eyes plead with mine, though I'm not sure if she's pleading for me to stop or start something neither one of us will know how to finish.

"Promise me something," she says, her voice a bare whisper. "Whatever happens next, good or bad, something or nothing, just swear you'll never lie to me about anything, ever."

Easiest promise I've ever made.

"I promise," I say without hesitation before leaning in to taste those juicy pink lips.

Only she places her hand against my chest, leaning back. "Say it like you mean it."

"I do mean it . . ." I frown before reminding myself of what this woman has gone through, how many times she's opened her heart to men only to have them shit all over it. Some men see women like her as a dime a dozen. To me, women like her are one in a billion. Not everyone can wear their vulnerability on their sleeve and make it look sexy as hell. "Anneliese, I swear to you, I promise you, I'll never lie to you about anything, ever."

Her body softens against me, and her lips part slightly, a silent invitation.

Pulling her closer, I narrow the space between us inch by inch, until we're breathing the same air and our mouths are almost touching.

Cupping her cheek, I angle her chin upward, until we're perfectly aligned, and then I press my mouth hard against hers, slipping my tongue between her lips until we collide. She's peppermint and soft skin, sweet sighs and beautiful tragedy. I pull her onto my lap, and she tugs her tank top over her head, revealing only a pair of satin shorts so thin I can tell she's wearing nothing beneath them.

She sweeps her hair off the back of her neck, leaning back and grinding against my hardness until it aches, pushing against the thick cotton of my sweats.

I grip her hips before sliding my hands up her sides and stopping at her full breasts, taking her pert nipples between my fingertips until she releases the softest moan.

Leaning up, I silence her with a kiss before brushing my lips against her ear.

"Your parents are down the hall," I remind her.

The bed creaks with our movements. A metal groan here or there is nothing, but a series of them in rhythmic order is enough to give us away.

Slipping my hands around her wrists, I deposit her hands over my shoulders. She wraps her legs around my hips, and I carry her to the small chest of drawers on the other side of the room, placing her on top.

"What are you doing?" she asks.

I taste her mouth once more before dragging my fingertips along her inner thighs. When I get to her knees, I spread them wide. Anneliese runs her fingers through my hair, grabbing a fistful, as I lower my mouth to her sex.

The taste of arousal meets my tongue as I sample what I've done to her. Focusing on her clit, I circle it before gently sucking—a move that sends her stomach caving and her thighs locking around me. She grips the edge of the small dresser as I continue to devour her.

And as I'm lost between her legs, immersed in her addictive scent, the world around me fades.

A guy could get used to this—even if a guy shouldn't.

TWENTY-THREE

ANNELIESE

pistanthrophobia (*n.*) fear of trusting people due to past experiences with relationships gone bad

"Anneliese, hi!" Berlin stops by the shop Monday afternoon, a leather portfolio tucked under one arm.

"Hey, stranger." I lean over the glass counter. "What's new?"

She fillets the portfolio and pulls out a sheet of white paper covered in brightly hued logos.

"So," Berlin says, "I settled on Stem and Petal for the name. I thought it would be a cute nod to the original name . . . so as not to confuse customers . . . and I just adore it."

"Love it."

"And I had a local graphic artist whip me up some new branding." She flips the paper so it faces me. "Which one do you like? I'm leaning toward the second one. It captures that modern vibe that I was originally going for."

I place my hand over my heart. "First of all, I'm honored that you came all the way down here to share this with me. And secondly, I'm thrilled that you want my opinion on the logo, because no one ever asks my opinion about anything other than names . . ."

She laughs. "Don't be so modest. You have great taste and an eye for this stuff. I trust your judgment."

I pore over the logo variants for a few moments before settling on the third one from the bottom. "Number two is great, and I'm not ruling it out, but this one feels like something that would fit right in among your neighboring shops. The second one might be too metropolitan for Arcadia Grove?" I wince. "Just my two cents."

She frowns, spinning the page back to her and homing in on the third one from the bottom.

"You have a point," she says with a sigh.

"Don't let me sway you. If you love number two, then by all means . . ."

"No, you're right. No need to reinvent the wheel. Arcadia Grove does have a certain vintagey nostalgic feel that people go nuts for. The logo you like captures that." Berlin traces her finger over the logo I chose before stuffing it back into the portfolio. "All right. Easy enough. We'll go with that one."

Glancing at my watch, I get a thrill through my middle when I see it's almost time to close up for the day . . . which means going home to Lachlan.

The other night was unexpected to say the absolute least, but it wasn't as weird as it should've been. His touch didn't feel foreign; it felt natural. And despite Lachlan being a dead ringer for Donovan, I didn't once experience anything remotely akin to emotional déjà vu.

When I woke up this morning, it took me all of five seconds to realize I'd overslept. I had no more than twenty minutes to get showered and to the shop on time, so I ran out of there without so much as a goodbye. Two hours later, Lachlan texted me a picture showcasing the demo he and my father had done so far on the main-floor bathroom.

I don't expect things to be weird between us—we're both grown adults.

But I can't deny that every time I've thought about him today, I've felt a little niggle deep in my center that hasn't quite left since last night. It's stuck there. Swirling. Tickling. Demanding attention like a petulant child.

"Hey, you want to grab dinner tonight?" Berlin asks. "There's this new Italian place on the north side. I hear their zucchini parmesan is life changing."

"Aw, I'd love that, but it's my parents' last night in town." I log out of the iPad, turn out the "open" light, and lock the front door. "Maybe tomorrow?"

"Can't. I have my hot-yoga class," she says. "You want to come?"

"I'm probably the least flexible person you will ever meet. I'd be a huffing, puffing distraction."

"Oh, come on. I'm sure you're not that bad." She laughs.

"No, I promise—I am that bad, and then some," I say. "Are you free Wednesday night? Maybe we can do something then?"

Her brows rise. "For sure."

I walk her to the door, unlatching the lock to let her out. "I'll text you."

She gives me a smile and a finger wave before trotting to her car. I lock up once again, draw the shades, and hit the lights before exiting out the back.

My stomach somersaults the whole drive home, anticipating the moment I walk in the door and see Lachlan again. The text he sent earlier regarding the bathroom demo made me think it was his way of acting like everything was cool between us, that nothing was going to change or be awkward. Which is great. That's what I want. I'm not trying to date him, but I'm also not trying to pretend like the other evening wasn't one of the most enjoyable, exhilarating nights I've had in a long time.

Turning the corner to my street, I pass a handful of houses before realizing his truck is noticeably absent from the driveway, but my parents' rental is still there.

Heading in a minute later, I'm hit with the scent of my mother's famous goulash and the sound of her and my father singing some old Frank Sinatra tune from the kitchen.

"Hey," I say when I catch them dancing.

Kitchen dances have always been their thing. It's kind of their trademark.

"Hi, sweetheart," Mom says as my dad spins her. "You hungry?"

"Starved," I say before adding a casual "Where's Lachlan?"

"Hey, you should check out the bathroom," Dad says.

No one's answering me.

"Lachlan and I gutted the entire thing today," he continues. "Tomorrow he's going to install the new toilet and pedestal sink. Once fixtures are roughed in, all it'll need is tile and paint. It's going to look sharp by the end of the week."

"Awesome," I say, though I have to ask again. "Where is he, anyway? I saw his truck was gone?"

My parents stop dancing for a moment, exchanging a glance that makes my stomach plummet.

"I believe he said he was going to get dinner with an old friend," Mom says, her words moving at a snail's pace. "I can't remember her name . . ."

Her.

Her name.

"I don't think he gave a name," Dad adds. "Just said she was a very special friend of his."

I can feel the color draining from my face, and the room begins to tilt. I take a seat at the table to steady myself and catch my breath. I know we're not anything, and I know I have no right to be jealous, but the other night he was devouring every inch of me and whispering about how sexy I was, and now he's spending the evening with another woman? It's not like he owes me anything—we aren't together, and the plan was always for him to bounce eventually. But there's no denying this burns . . . worse than I expected it to. And it serves as a reminder that the side of Lachlan I've come to know is merely one of his many facets.

The rest are question marks and blank spaces he refuses to fill in.

I think back to the text he sent earlier with the bathroom picture. Maybe instead of acting like things were back to normal between us, he was simply trying to act like nothing had happened?

Either way, I use this as an opportunity to remind myself not to get attached because I never want to feel the sick swirl in my middle and the hot burn of adrenaline in my veins and the storm of confusion in my head.

Mom fixes my plate, placing it in front of me.

"Mom, you didn't have to do that," I say.

"You look like you've had a long day, hon." Her mouth presses flat, and her eyes hold sympathy.

Dad grabs his food and sits across from me, spreading his paper napkin over his lap and peering over the top of his glasses toward me.

"Your dinner's getting cold," he says.

Picking up my fork, I push the pasta mixture around my plate before taking a bite. I don't taste a thing, though. And my mouth is so dry I have to wash it down with a mouthful of water. The oven timer beeps, and Mom slips on a couple of oven mitts before retrieving a loaf of garlic bread.

"These appliances are so efficient, Anneliese," she says as she slices the bread. "I've never heard of this brand before."

"It's Italian," I say, monotone.

"Rob, you're going to have to get me some of these Italian appliances."

"They look expensive . . . ," he says.

"I got mine at the scratch-and-dent place," I say. "Otherwise they'd have cost twice what I paid for them."

"Well, they look amazing." Mom inspects the microwave before moving to the fridge. "I don't see anything wrong with them."

My father goes on to explain that sometimes the dents are in the back or on the sides, but the more he talks, the farther away he sounds. Everything around me fades into background noise. All I can think about is Lachlan meeting up with another woman; I conjure up an image in my head of some mysterious brunette with legs to her neck and a sensual aura lapping up Lachlan's worldly charms and addictive stories and laser-focused attention that makes you feel like you're the only one in the room.

"Anneliese, you're extra quiet tonight," Mom says, sitting beside me.

"I'm just . . . tired." I manage a smile and force the rest of my goulash down before retiring to the living room with my laptop to catch up on some emails.

But while my eyes scan the words on the screen, nothing computes.

My thoughts are stuck on every worst-case scenario.

I can't shut them off.

I can't stop thinking about his charming smile and the familiar yet mysterious gaze he has when he's looking at me like I'm the only person he sees. I liked that feeling. I liked being *seen*. Acknowledged. Wanted.

I never should have let him kiss me; I never should have gotten myself caught up in how good it felt to be unapologetically *desired* for the first time in forever.

While I could talk myself out of liking him until I'm blue in the face, the most frustrating part of it all is that my worries have no basis in reality . . .

They're only rooted in the fact that he *is* a Byrne.

And if history is the best indicator of the future, nothing good can come from getting wrapped up with one.

TWENTY-FOUR

LACHLAN

laconic (*adj.*) expressing much in few words

"So?" Lynnette crosses her pencil-thin legs before lighting a Virginia Slim. "How's it going with the whole house situation? You went radio silent on me for a while. Thought maybe you'd changed your mind about burning the place down and skipped town."

I deserve that.

Settling into her sagging sofa, I drag my palm across my five-o'clock shadow. I've been here since four o'clock this afternoon; I changed the oil in her mower, ate two heaping servings of tuna casserole, fixed the leaking faucet in her bathroom, and replaced the busted lock on her back door. I'm surprised it took her this long to bring up the house.

"Actually took your advice," I say. "I'm living there."

Her brows lift. "No shit? With the girl? What's her name . . . Annielynn?"

"Anneliese," I correct her. "And yes. I'm living there. Staying in my old room, actually."

Lynnette winces. "That's rough."

"It's different," I say. Just being in that hellhole conjures up a lifetime of memories best forgotten, but I do a decent enough job at tamping those down when they crop up. It's a skill I've almost mastered over the years. "Better than the Pine Grove Motel."

She exhales a plume of smoke. "That's the spirit, kid. You helping her fix it up, then?"

I nod, my jaw set. "That was part of the agreement."

"So you'll sell it when it's all done, then? And not donate it to the fire department?"

"Jury's still out on that one."

Lynnette rolls her eyes. "What's the latest with the whole estate-lawyer thing?"

"Swank filed. Just waiting . . ." I clear my throat. "Once I'm officially named administrator of Don's estate, I can check into his financials. I'm hoping there's something left in that bank account that he opened with her money. Maybe that'll be enough for her to walk away from the house."

"Is it about money for her? Or is she grieving your brother?"

I sniff. "Pretty sure the mourning period is over."

She takes a drag, squinting my way. "Oh yeah? And how would you know that?"

"We've been together every day for the past couple of weeks almost. Pretty sure I've got her figured out."

She crosses her legs the other direction, leaning against the opposite arm of her recliner. "Lachlan . . . please tell me you're not taking advantage of this poor woman."

"Taking advantage?" I chuff. "I'm letting her live in my house, rent-free, while I do all of the manual labor, also for free. Pretty sure she's getting the good end of the deal here."

"You know that's not what I'm talking about." Her voice is low, scolding almost. "The girl lost her fiancé in a horrible car accident, and then you show up, looking like a better version of the man she fell in love with . . ."

I pull in a hard breath.

Nothing gets past Lynnette.

Ever.

I learned that the hard way in sixth grade when Bryce and I propped a bunch of pillows under his bunk bed covers and sneaked out in the middle of the night to go skateboarding at the park. She was out cold when we left, snoring up a storm in her room. It took forever to tiptoe to the back door without making a sound, but we managed. By the time we came home an hour later, every light in the house was on, and Lynnette was pacing her living room, chain-smoking, so furious she was shaking.

The thing that stood out the most about that moment, though, was that the verbal lashing she gave to me was worse than the one she gave to her own son.

Looking back, I think she was doubling down, trying to say the things she thought my own mother would want her to say: that someone gave a shit about me.

"Everything's fine," I say.

She stubs her cigarette out before cracking open the sweaty can of Diet Pepsi on her side table. "You're a shitty liar, Lachlan. Always have been."

"What are you talking about?"

She shoots me some side-eye. "You kissed her, didn't you?"

How she can infer that from this fragmented conversation is beyond me, but the woman has an impressive knack for picking up every last nuance.

"You grin like a goddamned Cheshire cat every time you talk about her," Lynnette says.

I hadn't realized . . .

"How much longer until the house is done?" she asks.

"A month, at most," I say. "I've been working ten-, twelve-hour days since I got there."

"And this court, probate, estate thing is going to take a few more months, yes?"

I nod.

"So what are you going to do when the house is done and it's just the two of you, biding time until you can get the house stuff situated?" she asks.

"Haven't thought that far ahead. If it's going to be a long, drawn-out process, I'll probably go back overseas and come back when I have to."

"I'm going to be frank with you, kid." Lynnette straightens her shoulders and cracks her neck. "You're acting like an asshole."

"I don't follow."

Last I checked, my father was the asshole for leaving the house solely to Donovan, and then Donovan was an asshole for conning Anneliese into emptying her life savings into that dump. As far as I'm concerned, it's not my problem.

"Number one," she says, counting on her fingers. "You disappear for ten years without so much as a proper goodbye. Number two, you show up after your brother dies because you want the house that his would-be widow occupies, and not only that, you only want it so you can burn it down. Never mind all the work she's put into fixing it up. What number am I on now . . . three . . . you show up with your tattoos and your muscles and your Mr. Fix-It persona, and you white knight yourself into her life—and likely her bedroom—and you plan on jetting off again if the court process takes too long? You're just going to leave her like your brother did, high and dry."

"First of all, it's not like that with her. We're not dating. We kissed. Once," I admit, leaving out the details of what followed after that impressively unforgettable kiss. "Secondly, I'm not a white knight. I'm not here to clean up my brother's hot mess of a life. Whatever money is in the account . . . it's all hers. But the house is mine. It's all I want."

"Kid." Lynnette slumps, her eyes searching mine. "Burning it down won't bring your mother back. And it won't erase what happened to her. It's also not going to undo all the things your dad and brother did to make your life a living hell. Even if the house is gone, those memories aren't going anywhere."

"Well aware."

She sniffs, like she's taken aback at my snark. "Then what's your endgame here, huh?"

"My endgame is to never have a reason to set foot in this town again," I say. "My endgame is to know that the one place that stole everything from me no longer exists."

Lynnette cocks her head. "It stopped existing the first time you got on that plane."

"Figuratively, maybe."

Sinking back into the recliner, she throws up her hands. "I can't tell you what to do."

She does a damn fine job at doing it anyway . . .

"You're your own person," she adds. "I just think it wouldn't be the worst thing if you had a little heart for once. Hurt people hurt people. Healed people help people."

"What are you, a therapist now?"

"No. I heard that on Oprah the other week. It's a good one, though, isn't it?" She chuckles. "Anyway. You're getting all shifty over there, and you keep looking at your watch. I feel like you're about ready to bolt, so before you go, I wanted to tell you that Bryce is coming home later this week. His job in New Hampshire is wrapping up earlier than expected. Thought maybe we could swing by the house when he's back, take a look at all the work you've been doing."

"Stop over anytime."

I check the time again and rise from the saggy sofa before dipping my hands into my pockets and making sure I have my things.

"Thanks for dinner," I say.

"Thanks for fixing all the shit my son was supposed to fix months ago." She rises from the recliner, shuffles across the living room, and wraps her lanky arms around my shoulders.

"I'll be sure to rub that in Bryce's face when I see him."

"I hope you do, kid."

Lynnette walks me to the door, her hand rubbing small circles against my shoulder blade the way she used to when I was younger and I'd had a rough day.

"Remember," she calls out when I make my way down the front steps a few seconds later. "Try not to be an asshole. Your father was an asshole. Your brother was an asshole. Break the damn cycle, for crying out loud."

Once again, Lynnette has a point.

I've spent the past ten years doing everything in my power to not be like them . . . only to become exactly like them.

I give her a wave on my way to my truck and head home to Anneliese and her parents. It's their last night in town, and since I owed Lynnette a visit anyway, I figured I might as well let them have some time alone and kill two birds with one stone.

The house is dark when I arrive, and I recall Rob saying that their flight leaves pretty early tomorrow morning. I kick my shoes off at the front door and head up the staircase, skipping the creaky steps, and then I make my way to my room.

I twist the knob softly, on the off chance Anneliese is asleep, and then I step into a black void. Tugging out of my clothes, I manage to find a clean pair of sweats in my top dresser drawer and slide them on before crawling in bed beside her. She stirs, her eyelids flittering open.

"Go back to sleep," I tell her. God knows she needs the rest.

A soft sigh escapes her lips as she rolls to her side to face me.

"If you want a bedtime story tonight, I'm afraid I'm all out," I say.

She brushes a wayward strand of hair from her forehead. "Did you have fun tonight?"

I snicker at her random question. "Of course I did. Why do you ask?"

She half shrugs one shoulder, her eyes half-open. "My parents said you went to see an old friend."

"I did. Though I wouldn't call her a *friend* . . . she's a little more than that."

Anneliese swallows. "What'd you guys do?"

"We hung out . . . I fixed a few things around her house . . . she made me dinner . . . we did some catching up . . . she gave me shit like she always used to . . . ," I say. "Nothing too crazy."

She locks her sleepy gaze on me, quiet for a moment. "I bet she was happy to see you."

"Always is."

"Did you keep in touch with many people after you left?" she asks.

"Not really," I say. "I kept in touch with her, but not as much as she probably wanted me to . . . not as much as I should have. It really hurt her when I left, but I was eighteen then. I wasn't thinking about anyone other than myself."

"So you broke her heart?"

"You could say that, yeah." I add, "She's tough as nails, though. I don't think my leaving set her back. Didn't stop her from living her life either."

"She sounds like a strong person."

"Strong as hell," I say. "Which is funny because she's maybe five foot one on a good day, smokes like a chimney, swears like a sailor, and buys all of her shoes from the children's department."

"You must've had interesting taste in girls when you were younger."

I cock my head. "What's that supposed to mean?"

"She doesn't sound like the ordinary women you dated in the UK," she says.

"Wait . . . you thought I was visiting an ex?"

She glances to the side. "Yeah . . . you . . . you made it sound like . . . you said she was more than a friend . . . she made you dinner . . . I just assumed . . ."

"Wow." I study her. "Anneliese, were you *jealous*?"

"No," she says without hesitation. "I just don't want to be played. You were kissing me the other night, and then tonight you were spending time with another woman. I know we're not dating, but at least have the decency to—"

"Anneliese." I cut her off before she makes an even bigger fool of herself. "The old friend I visited tonight? My childhood best friend's mother. She was a second mom to me growing up—the only mom I had for a long time. That's why I said she was more than an old friend."

Her eyes widen as she realizes the error of her ways.

"Her name is Lynnette," I add, reaching to tuck a messy wave behind her ear before cupping her cheek. In the dark, I trace the details of her perfect face before brushing my lips against hers and stealing a tender kiss.

I know I shouldn't.

And I know damn well I'm playing with fire.

But for reasons I can't quite understand, I'm drawn to this woman. I crave her when she's gone.

I think about her contagious laugh and the way she smiles with her whole face when she thinks I've said something funny. I think about her honesty and her generosity—especially to strangers. I think about how she puts everyone else's needs above her own. How she stayed in a house that reminds her of unspeakable betrayal because she wants to turn it into something beautiful. And maybe to some, those traits would be weaknesses. But to me, she's one of the strongest women I've ever known, and I still hardly know her.

"You don't have to do this," she says when I kiss her harder.

I run my hand down the side of her body, gripping her hip and pulling her closer against me.

"You're right," I say. "I don't have to—I *want* to."

She sighs, her peppermint breath mixing with mine. "I'm sorry I assumed you were hooking up with an ex-girlfriend. I know we're not dating, and I have no right to be jealous, and I hate how I sounded when I was asking all of those questions . . ."

I silence her with another kiss. She doesn't need to qualify her apology. I'm not holding this against her, especially after what my brother did to her.

Anneliese pulls back, placing her hand on my chest. "I don't think this is a good idea."

"You tired?"

"No," she says. "I just don't think *this* is a good idea. You and me. If I kiss someone and then go into a blind rage at the mere mention of them hanging out with another woman, I have no business inviting that kind of dysfunction into my life. I'm just not in a good place . . . and the night we shared was fun; don't get me wrong. But I've learned from past experience that casual hookups aren't my thing. I get attached way too easily, and I'm always the one who gets hurt."

I slide my hand off her and give her some space—which isn't much given the size of this bed.

Running my hand through my hair, I exhale. "Yeah, no. I understand."

This morning while she was working at the bookshop, her father told me that she's the kind who falls in love easily and gives everyone she meets the benefit of the doubt.

"She can't help it," he said. "She's soft like that. Too soft for her own good. Makes for a lot of heartbreak, though."

As much as her father seems to like me, I couldn't help but feel like that was a warning.

"I like you, Lachlan," she says. "As a person, I mean. And I want to keep it that way."

Anneliese rolls over, her backside flush against me, and a few moments later, her breath steadies. But while she's out cold, I'm wide awake a world away, lost in my thoughts, replaying Anneliese's words alongside Lynnette's advice about breaking the cycle.

I watch her sleep, inhaling her soft scent, knowing I can never be what she needs—or who she wants. Knowing she's right—if we mess around, she's the one who'll get hurt in the end because I'm the asshole who always leaves before shit gets real, before I get attached enough to get my heart trampled on.

I've swallowed more hard pills in my life than I can count, but this may be one of the hardest.

I'm not capable of loving someone, not in the traditional sense of the word, but if I were, I'd want to love someone like her.

TWENTY-FIVE

ANNELIESE

akrasia (*n.*) lack of self-control

I toss and turn in my bed Tuesday night, rolling to my side to reach for my phone. At half past eleven, I'll be lucky if I get six hours of solid sleep before my alarm goes off.

My parents left early this morning, and I shared an awkward coffee moment with Lachlan in the kitchen before jetting off to the bookshop. Flo returns next week, which means he and I will be spending much more quality time together over the coming weeks . . . or months.

As much as I wanted him to kiss me last night, I had to hit the brakes.

I know myself.

And I know when I'm getting in over my head.

Monday evening, when I should've been playing cards with my parents or bonding over some heartwarming Hallmark movie my mom put on, I was there but I wasn't present. My mind was ruminating on Lachlan, convincing myself he'd played me for a fool. And by the time he came home, smelling like cheap perfume and cigarettes and talking about how he'd spent the evening with someone who meant more to him than a friend and someone whom he'd hurt badly when he'd left . . . it took all the strength I had not to burst into a jealousy-fueled inferno.

Of course, it was all a misunderstanding.

Getting the rug pulled out from under me this year has cast shadows of doubt over any little thing that brings me joy lately.

But as I came down from that emotional cliff, I cringed and realized that the side of me who reared her ugly head that night was the still-broken side of me.

I wish I could throw caution to the wind and shamelessly hunt for carnal pleasure at every turn. I wish I could be as fun and sexy as Lachlan makes me feel when he reaches for me in the dark or when he flashes that gleaming copper gaze of his.

But at the end of the day, I'm still in a state of repair—much like this house—and I'm bad at love—much like that Halsey song. Not that I love Lachlan. But I have a tendency to put the cart before the horse when it comes to men. I get my hopes up. I trust too easily. I only see the good until the bad is staring me in the face, smacking me over the head with a hard dose of reality.

I don't want to be *her* anymore.

I fling off my comforter, head downstairs to make a cup of chamomile, and grab my laptop from the study before curling up on the sofa under some dim lamplight. If I can't sleep, I might as well be productive.

I fire off a handful of quick emails before checking my schedule for next week. I'm due to present names to a Californian influencer couple who is requesting female monikers that are earthy and organic. I pull up their Instagram page, where every curated picture is filtered in dreamy creams and soft tans and pale-blue skies. Their matching bleached hair and surfer-chic vibe are further complemented by their brilliant smiles and heavenly beachside backdrops.

I wonder if they're as happy as they look.

I wonder if *anyone's* as happy as they look . . .

I spend a few more minutes on their social media page, zooming in and out on an image of the two of them doing child's pose on matching yoga mats. And then I open a blank Word doc, brainstorming the first names that come to mind: Honey, Saffron, Goldie, Luna, Maple, Soleil, Sunny, Briar, Dove, Indigo.

Next, I pair each name with their last name, Hendrix, narrowing down the contesters to Honey, Goldie, Sunny, Dove, and Indigo.

I place asterisks next to my top three: Honey, Dove, and Indigo.

The creak of a stair interrupts me from my flow, and I glance across the hallway, past the foyer, and toward the bottom of the steps, where Lachlan fills the darkness.

"Can't sleep either?" I ask.

He steps closer, until the lamplight highlights his V-neck T-shirt and low-slung sweats, and he brushes his messy hair from his forehead.

"Yeah. It's weird having all that bed to myself again," he teases before taking a seat in the armchair beside me. "I don't know what to do without someone kneeing me in the kidney every five minutes."

I roll my eyes, grateful that after last night's talk, we can keep our playful banter. It's actually the highlight of my day sometimes. Everything aside, there's no denying the man knows how to put a smile on my face.

Whatever happens after this, and once we go our separate ways, I'm going to miss that.

"What do you think of the name Indigo Hendrix?" I ask.

"You're asking the wrong person."

"A simple yea or nay will suffice."

"Nay," he says. Though I couldn't disagree more. I think it sounds like exactly the kind of thing Santa Cruz residents Talon and Shalom Hendrix would adore.

"What about Dove Hendrix?" I ask. "Or Honey Hendrix?"

"Are these names for a real human or a dog?"

"Who would name a dog Dove?"

"Who would name their kid Dove?" He answers my question with one of his own. "I met a girl named Sunday once. Asked her if that was her real name, and she said it was. Her parents chose it because to them, Sunday was the day of peace and serenity, and that's what she represented. Anyway, I always thought it was a badass name. She even looked like a Sunday, if that makes sense. Guess she grew into her name."

"Sunday Hendrix," I say out loud, "*Sunday Hendrix* . . . that actually works."

It doesn't have my mismatched syllables, but it begins and ends with the same sound, and it fits their whole carefree-surfer-vibe persona. Indigo could easily slide in there as the middle name; then all three names would share the *d* sound.

"Congratulations, Lachlan. I think you may have just named someone's baby." I type the name into my document and put three asterisks next to it. Closing my laptop, I place it on the coffee table and adjust my posture toward him. "So what really has you up tonight?"

His lips twist at one side as he stares at the lifeless fireplace on the other side of the room.

"I talked to my attorney today," he says.

"Yeah?"

"Things are moving quicker than he expected with opening the estate," he says. "He's thinking sometime in the next couple weeks."

"I thought he said it could take months?"

"He did," he says. "Are you still planning on filing that claim?"

"Depends. Are you still planning to burn the place down?"

He rakes his hand along his jaw before pinching the bridge of his nose. "Once everything goes through, I should be able to access that bank account. I plan on giving you everything in it, down to the last penny."

"And what if it's empty?" My throat turns dry, and my gut twists. I haven't let myself get my hopes up because I have no indication one way or another. I'd rather expect nothing and get a little something than expect a little something and get nothing.

"I have some money saved away." He rubs the back of his neck. "Not as much as what you probably lost, but enough to get you moved back to Chicago or wherever you're trying to go next."

"I don't want your money. I want my money. I don't know why that's so hard to understand," I say. "And why should *you* have to pay for something your *brother* did? I can't let you do that."

"Donovan was an asshole," he says. "I'm not trying to atone for his sins, but I don't want to be just another asshole doing an asshole thing to you. If I'm taking the house, the least I can do is give you some cash to get on your feet."

"Is that what *you* decided was fair?"

"Nothing about any of this is going to be fair, Anneliese. Any way we slice it, neither of us are going to walk away winners."

"Really? Because it sounds like you're getting what you wanted and I'm getting a consolation prize so you can sleep a little easier at night."

His mouth presses flat, and his jaw clenches. "It's not like that."

"Yeah? Because that's exactly what it sounds like." I shove myself up from the couch, pacing the living room as my mind spins. "You know, it's not fair that Donovan gets to rest in peace without ever answering for what he did, and now you come along with your offer and try to slap a shiny red bow on it so it seems a little less shitty than it really is."

I was screwed over by one Byrne. I'm not about to be screwed by another.

"I hate him," I continue, dragging my fingers through my hair before making a fist in the air. I'm sure I look like a lunatic, but I feel like one too. Three months of pent-up rage can do that to a person. "I used to lie in bed at night and fantasize about all the ways I'd get him back if he were still here. I'll spare you the details because, honestly, some of them were pretty juvenile and I'm not in the mood to embarrass myself. But at the end of the day, the truth is . . . there is no getting back at a dead person. It just doesn't work that way."

Lachlan is statue still in his chair, though I can tell he's listening to every word I'm spewing.

"And even if I did somehow get revenge on a dead person, what's going to change?" I carry on. "Nothing. Absolutely nothing. So what's my next best bet? Salvaging anything I can from this project and moving on. You don't understand, Lachlan—it's not just about the money. It's about proving to myself that I'm no longer the lovesick moron who fell in love with a con man. I can't be her anymore. I refuse. And if I leave here with nothing but your pity money . . . I . . . I don't even know . . ."

My thoughts fade, leaving me exhausted from their unapologetic weight.

I collapse back onto the sofa.

"What would you say to him if he were still here?" he asks.

"A million things, all at once."

"Do you have any of his clothes?" he asks. "Did you save anything?"

I scrunch my nose. "There are a few things in my closet . . . what are you getting at?"

"Stay here." Without another word he heads upstairs, disappearing up the dark stairs.

I'm left alone with nothing but footsteps, closing doors, running water, and the tick of the clock in the kitchen echoing through the hollow house.

Ten minutes later, he's back.

Only it isn't him.

I mean, it is—in the literal sense.

But the man standing before me looks every bit the part of Donovan, from the neatly parted hair, shiny with Brylcreem, to the crisp white button-down, navy sport coat, pressed khaki pants, and Italian-leather loafers. Every tattoo is covered. And the faint scent of Donovan's cologne permeates the air.

I try to speak, but nothing comes out.

"I know it's not the same," Lachlan says, tugging on the cuffs of Donovan's sport coat before clearing his throat and straightening his shoulders. "But it might be the only chance you get."

He's either insane, a genius, or a frighteningly dangerous combination of the two.

"Anneliese," he says, lifting a finger and curling it, beckoning for me to come closer. I remain frozen on the sofa, still processing this moment. Stepping toward me, he takes my hand and helps me up. Chuckling, he adds, "Please don't tell me I'm wearing my dead brother's clothes for nothing."

Dragging in the heady cologne wafting from his shirt, I'm flooded with nausea. I take a string of deep breaths until the room stops spinning and my stomach doesn't feel like it's about to turn inside out.

"Well? Is there anything you'd like to say while you have me?" Lachlan lifts his wrist, pretending to check an invisible watch. "This ridiculous excuse for an outfit expires in ten minutes."

"Donovan never would've called it an outfit," I say.

"You're stalling."

He's right.

"Fine." I gather a lungful of Donovan's favorite Creed cologne—a bottle of which I kept for some unknown reason—and gather my thoughts. "You are pathetic. You disgust me. You're a habitual liar. You're a vile human being, and I deserved better than you. I gave you everything: my trust, my love, my time, my attention, my energy, my life savings . . . and you took it all without a second thought. You were a malignant bastard in an expensive suit, and now you're six feet underground, rotting like the maggot you were."

Lachlan doesn't flinch, doesn't react. If he's in character, he's doing a damn fine job. I don't think Donovan would have shown an ounce of emotion. He'd have calmly talked me out of my own beliefs, taking me on point for point and dismantling all my logic and reasoning. He'd have insisted I was overreacting—like the time I happened to be having one of the worst days I'd had in forever, and he told me I should just try to be happy and that most people wouldn't get as upset as I did over such little things.

The man gaslighted me seven ways from Sunday, but he did it so kindly, so gently, I never realized it at the time.

"I wish I never met you," I say. "I wish I could go back to the day we met, walk out of that hotel bar, and never have given you a second thought. But I was bored. And you were charming. And you knew exactly what you were doing. It's my fault for falling for it, but everything else is on you."

Without warning, Lachlan—Donovan—the man standing before me gently reaches for my face, catching a tear that slides down my left cheek.

I hadn't realized I was crying.

I brush my other cheek as my vision blurs and my eyes brim hot.

"I'm sorry for hurting you, Anneliese." He speaks the words his brother never had the courage to say, the words his brother will never have a chance to say, the words I never thought I'd get to hear.

Even if they're not from Donovan's lips, they land just the same.

I swipe my tears as fast as they fall, stifling the ugly sobs threatening to escape.

Shrugging out of the navy jacket, Donovan tosses it on the floor before unbuttoning the starched white shirt and doing the same. He pulls me into his arms, holding me warm against his inked chest.

"He's gone now." Lachlan speaks into my hair, kissing the top of my head and wrapping me tight.

Without another word, he slips his hand over mine and leads me upstairs. Only he doesn't stop at my door—he continues on to his.

"Didn't think you'd want to sleep alone tonight," he says, pushing his door open.

I fall asleep with my cheek against his chest, to the steady thrum of his heartbeat, my mind a little less heavy than it was before.

A girl could get used to this, even if she shouldn't.

TWENTY-SIX

LACHLAN

ramé (*adj.*) both chaotic and joyful at the same time

I'm grouting the tile floors on the main-floor bathroom Wednesday evening when there's a knock at the front door. Rising up, I wipe my hands on a nearby wet rag before heading to the kitchen sink to wash them.

The visitor knocks again, three times, harder.

"Just a minute," I call out.

Trotting to the door a few seconds later, I spot two shadowy figures on the other side of the privacy glass: one slight, one burly and an entire head taller. They could only belong to two people.

I haven't seen Bryce in a decade. We've texted off and on throughout the years. Talked on the phone here and there. With each conversation, it was as if no time had passed.

"Open the door, you sorry bastard," he says from the other side, though I can hear the smile in his voice. Insults have always been Bryce and Lynnette's go-to love language, which I've always appreciated, as I'm not one to profess my love for anyone.

"A call would've been nice," I tease him back when I get the door.

Bryce meets me with an instant high five, which turns into a one-handed hug where he squeezes all the air from my lungs. He ruffles my hair when he's done.

"Look at you. Inked up. Muscles." He nods, smiling. "Figured maybe you'd lost your hair and tacked on fifty pounds and that's why you were hiding out for so long, but I thought wrong."

Lynnette elbows her son. "Anyway, we're here for the grand tour."

"Yeah." I step aside. "Come on in. Excuse the mess. I was in the middle of tiling the main-floor bathroom when you knocked."

Bryce scratches his chin, peering around. "God, this place used to terrify me. Now it looks like some bright and cheery Airbnb."

"*Bryce*," Lynnette says before turning to me. "I love the lighter paint colors. It really opens the place up. And all the old window coverings are down."

"Can't take credit for any of that, but yeah," I say. "Let me show you around."

I take them upstairs, walking them through the bedrooms and bathrooms, pointing out a handful of things still needing installed . . . light fixtures, a new faucet in the guest bathroom, fresh paint in two of the bedrooms. On the main level, I take them through the living room, dining room, study, and kitchen.

"Anneliese's father and I finished the deck last weekend. Just stocked the fridge with beer . . . you want to sit outside a bit?" I offer.

A minute later, we're perched on the back steps, cracking beers and cracking jokes like old times. I'm in the middle of retelling Lynnette the classic Bryce tale of the time he stole her car to go drag racing on Eleventh Street. He was fifteen, and the ink was still drying on his learner's permit, but he's always been overly confident in all his endeavors. He got halfway there when a cop pulled him over, one who happened to be crushing on Lynnette at the time. He threatened to call Bryce's mom, but in the end, he let him off. The only caveat was he had to shift it into neutral and push it the entire five blocks home.

"Hardest half mile of my life," Bryce says just before the back door opens.

"Hey." Anneliese appears in the doorway.

"You must be the famous Anneliese," Lynnette says before I have a chance to introduce them.

"Famous or infamous?" Anneliese asks, walking toward us. She leans down and gives my shoulder a squeeze. "I know Lachlan can be quite the storyteller."

"You can say that again." Bryce takes a sip of beer, sneaking in glimpses of her when he thinks I'm not looking. I don't blame him, though—she's gorgeous. Today, in her red gingham sundress and her hair twisted and piled on top of her head and delicate gold studs accenting her ears, she's a sight for sore eyes. Not to mention the sun-kissed glow on her face and the tops of her shoulders.

"You must be Lynnette and Bryce?" Anneliese says. "Lachlan painted quite the picture of you two the other night."

Lynnette laughs, her voice raspy. "I can only imagine. The kid sure has a way with words, doesn't he?"

"House looks good," Bryce says. "Much better than I remember it."

Anneliese leans back against the railing, completely at ease, her hands cupped around the rail. "Did Lachlan give you the grand tour?"

"He did," Lynnette says. "Except for your room."

Anneliese shoots me a look.

"You could've shown them," she says with a shrug before turning back to Lynnette. "You want to see? I'll take you up."

If I know Anneliese, she's only trying to be polite. If I know Lynnette, she's only gunning for a chance to be alone with her. They disappear inside, and I gather a breath and let it go, staring into the backyard where we used to run around as kids. The tree we climbed still soars high above the rest, twenty years bigger than the last time we scaled it.

"Must be weird for you," Bryce says. "Living here again."

190

"I try not to fixate on it." I pull at the pop-top of my can until it stands straight up. "It was either this or the Pine Grove Motel."

"You doing okay?" Bryce asks. "You happy and all that? In life, I mean. Obviously you're not happy to be back here. At least I don't think."

I take a mouthful of beer and contemplate my definition of happiness. I wouldn't call myself a happy person, but I have pockets of contentedness. I'm happy *enough*.

"Yeah," I say.

"Just *yeah*?" He huffs, like he doesn't believe me.

"What about you?"

"I mean . . . I'm twenty-eight . . . living in my mom's basement . . . working sixty-hour weeks in construction . . . single as fuck . . . I think that pretty much speaks for itself." Bryce laughs, but it's only there to disguise his bruised pride.

"Sounds like you're living the dream," I say. "No bills, no one telling you what to do, no one breathing down your back to be the person they want you to be."

He takes a drink from his can. "I don't know. Sometimes it's like . . . is this how it's going to be forever? Am I going to be fifty-five years old someday, never married, my best years behind me, no kids or grandkids to spoil on Christmas, no one to call and tell me happy birthday once my mom's gone? No one to fight with over what movie to rent or what restaurant to go to?"

"I'm sure there's someone out there looking for a guy to fight with over movies and restaurants. Maybe put that on your Tinder profile?"

He swats his hand, chuckling. "I stopped using those stupid dating apps years ago."

"You're not going to find the future Mrs. Hornsby hanging out in your mom's basement."

"No shit, Sherlock." He finishes his beer. "I've had a few girlfriends over the years. Nothing serious. A couple of regular hookups. I actually, uh . . . it feels weird saying this, but, um, I was hooking up with your brother's ex for a while last year."

"Which one? Berlin?"

He nods, dragging his thumb across his lower lip. "She'd just moved back to town, and I ran into her at one of the bars on a Friday night. We got drunk, started reminiscing; she ended up coming home with me. We hooked up a few times after that and talked a bit. It didn't work out, but I just thought it'd be wrong not to mention that to you."

"Couldn't give a shit less about any of my brother's exes," I say, before realizing that isn't true.

I give a shit about Anneliese.

I check the time on my phone, swirl back what's left of my beer, and give Bryce a nudge.

"Going to head in and grab another. You want one?" I ask.

"Yeah, if you're headed that way."

Once I'm inside, the sound of Lynnette's voice trails from another room.

"You know, underneath it all is a guy with a heart of gold," she says. "You just can't see it with all that damn ink in his skin. It's like his armor."

I find them standing in the hallway, outside the study.

"Were your ears burning?" Lynnette asks.

"Something like that." I rest my hands low on my hips as my gaze passes between them.

Anneliese offers a smile, though her stare is deeper than usual, as if she's looking at me in a different light. I can only imagine what else Lynnette filled her head with while they were venturing around the house on their own.

"Well, thank you for the tour, Anneliese." Lynnette brushes her hand along Anneliese's arm. "I'll let you check your emails. If, God willing, Bryce ever gives me a grandkid, I'll be sure to pass your naming services along. He swears if he ever has a son, he's naming him Stiles . . .

after the character in that *Teen Wolf* movie. He used to watch it with his dad back in the day, and so I think it's sentimental to him. But this day and age, the only Styles people think of is that boy band kid . . . what's his name?"

"Harry?" Anneliese asks.

"Yes, Harry Styles." Lynnette wrinkles her nose. "Anyway, hon, I'll let you get some work done. Lach, you got any more of these?"

She lifts her empty beer can.

"Yep. Was just about to grab another round," I say, leading her to the kitchen as Anneliese heads into her office and closes the door behind her.

"She's nice," Lynnette says when we return to the back deck, cold beers in hand. I give one to Bryce and take a seat on the top step. "Not sure what the hell she saw in your brother, but other than that, she seems to have her head screwed on straight. She's smart, well spoken, friendly, driven . . . Bryce, why can't you find a girl like that?"

"Girls like that don't want a man who's working on out-of-state job sites most weeks of the month," Bryce says.

"Girls like that just want a nice, honest, trustworthy guy," she says.

"But maybe one that doesn't live in his mom's basement," I say before adding, "No offense to either of you."

Lynnette punches my shoulder. "You act like he lives there rent-free."

"He doesn't?" I ask.

She frowns. "Hell no. He pays rent and half the utilities. I'm not stupid, and I'm sure as hell not raising a mooch."

"Still not helping me land any nice girls," Bryce says. "It's probably time I start looking for a place of my own anyway. Just been putting it off."

"Yeah, for ten years," Lynnette quips. Leaning toward him, she pinches his chubby cheek. "As much as I don't want to kick my baby bird from the nest, it might be the only shot I have at getting a grandkid."

Turning back to me, she says, "What about you, Lachlan? You ever think about settling down one of these days?"

Bryce chuffs. "That'll be the day."

"It's not something I've thought about, no." I crack my beer.

She throws her hands in the air in frustration. "You two are at that age when you think you have all the time in the world, but I swear you're going to blink and you'll be forty. And everyone in your dating pool will either be married or thrice divorced and in the midst of a midlife crisis."

"A person can be happy on their own," I say.

"Of course they can. Why do you think I never married after Bryce's dad left? Marriage is work. I always said I'd try it and if it didn't work out the first time, I wasn't going to do it again," she says. "One and done."

"A woman of her word," Bryce chimes in.

Lynnette changes the subject, asking her son about some weird sound her car is making. Meanwhile the setting sun darkens the sky minute by minute. I glance back at the house, watching the light in the study go out. A few minutes later, the light above flicks on—Anneliese's room.

"We should probably get out of your hair," Lynnette says after following my gaze. She pushes herself up and taps Bryce on the shoulder.

He rises next. "I'll be around at least two weeks before they ship me off again. Don't be a stranger."

"I won't," I say.

"Maybe we can grab drinks this weekend?" he asks.

"Yeah. Shoot me a text, and we'll figure it out."

I walk the two of them around the house and out to the street, where Bryce's old Monte Carlo is parked beneath the big oak tree. After sending them off, I head back in and find Anneliese in the kitchen, microwaving a frozen dinner. The summer dress is gone, and in its place is a loose-fitting tank top and polka-dot pajama shorts.

Still hot as hell.

"Hey," I say.

"Hey." She leans against the counter as the microwave hums. Once again, she studies me the way she did earlier in the hall outside her office.

"Sorry. I had no idea they were stopping by, or I'd have given you a heads-up."

"Not a big deal at all . . ."

The timer beeps, and she turns to retrieve the little black tray of God-only-knows-what. After dumping the steaming contents into a ceramic bowl, she leaves it on the counter to cool.

"So . . . Lynnette told me something," she says, pressing her lips together.

"I'm sure she told you a lot of things."

"She said your mom passed in this house." Anneliese takes her time, choosing her words. "At the bottom of the stairs."

My jaw clenches. I'm sure Lynnette meant well, but it wasn't her story to tell.

"She didn't say much more than that," Anneliese offers. "We were talking about you, and she said that it was a miracle you were staying under this roof at all, having to walk past the spot where your mom died, living with that reminder multiple times a day."

"She shouldn't have said anything."

"In her defense, she thought you'd already told me. She shut it down when she realized I had no idea, and she told me to ask you about it." Anneliese shifts. "I told her you tend to clam up anytime I ask you about your childhood or your mom or your past, and that's when she told me you had a heart of gold . . ."

Ah, so *that's* the conversation I walked into earlier.

"Please don't be upset with her," Anneliese says. She takes a step closer, reaching for my hand. "Is that why you hate this place so much? Because of what happened to your mom here?"

The image of her body lying crooked at the bottom of the landing is forever seared into my memory.

"Part of the reason, yes," I finally answer, since Lynnette already let half of the cat out of the bag anyway.

"That would've been nice to know," she says. "Not that I blame you for not talking about it, I just—would it have changed your mind about renovating?

"I don't know. But it would've made it a lot easier to understand where you're coming from," she says.

Exhaling, I throw my head back. "I'm sorry, Anneliese, but I don't have the energy to argue with you about the house tonight."

"Lachlan," she says, closing the space between us and squeezing my hand tight. "I don't want to fight with you. I want to be here for you."

Her eyes search mine as she lifts her hand to gently cup my face.

"It must have been awful for you," she says, her voice a broken whisper.

"Donovan pushed her." I say the words I haven't said since a lifetime ago. "I saw him. He was angry with her over not letting him go to some pool party, and he shoved her hard. She lost her balance, screamed, tumbled down . . . by the time she hit the landing, she wasn't moving. The fall broke her neck."

She clasps a hand over her mouth. "I'm so sorry, Lachlan."

Little tremors run through my body, as if the story is making its way out of the depths of my memory and into my reality.

"I called 911, but it was too late," I say. "There was nothing they could do. She was already gone. I'll never forget the look on my father's face when he got home from work just in time to watch the paramedics zip her into a black bag. I'd never seen the man shed a tear in my life, and he just . . . collapsed onto the floor, wailing the kind of sound that no kid should ever hear coming from their parent."

Anneliese burrows her nose into my neck, breathing me in, listening, holding me. She doesn't pry. She doesn't ask questions. She's simply here for me.

"Donovan told our dad that I was the one who pushed her." My voice chokes with ancient resentment. "And of course, he believed him because everyone always believed Donovan. After that, my father refused to look me in the eye. He'd pass me in the hallways at home and look right through me. I was dead to him."

She holds me tighter.

"My father spent the rest of his miserable life making sure I knew I meant less to him than the mud on the bottom of his work boots. And Donovan took every cheap shot he could, staking his claim as the golden child," I say. "Leaving this town, getting the hell away from those two, was the best thing I ever did."

She holds me. "You didn't deserve any of that. You were just a kid. An innocent kid."

My chest constricts, and my throat closes in, but I focus on her warmth against me and her sweet, familiar scent, and it pulls me out of it.

"I've never talked to anyone about this besides Lynnette and Bryce," I say. "No one else would listen. No one else cared."

Tilting her head back, she peers up at me through her long, dark lashes and sighs.

"You've been running away from your legacy all this time," she says. "Only to be forced back into it. But you're not them, Lachlan. You are so much more than what happened to you."

I'm tired of talking, sick of the sound of my own voice.

All I want is to lose myself with this beautiful woman—a woman who looks at me and truly sees me, a woman who makes me forget about life for a while.

I crush her mouth with a greedy kiss, pulling her hard against me. Her pillow-soft lips separate, and she meets my tongue with hers.

"I know you said this was a bad idea," I breathe. "But you're wrong. Being with you is the only thing that makes sense to me. You're all I think about every minute of every hour of every day. Every day, I watch the clock, waiting for you to get home like some pathetic puppy dog. And the second that front door opens, it's like my day is finally beginning because you're home. Neither one of us went into this arrangement knowing something like this could happen, but it's happening. I want you, Anneliese. And you want me too."

She presses her forehead against my shoulder, unnervingly quiet.

"Just promise me something," she says when she finally looks up.

"Anything."

"Whatever happens from here, promise I'm not going to be some story you tell to a pretty girl in a London bar."

"Falling for my dead brother's former fiancée isn't exactly the kind of story you tell to impress people you're trying to sleep with," I say, "and even if it were, you're not just some story, Anneliese. You're a whole damn novel."

Her full mouth arches at one side. "Did you just say you're falling for me?"

"I did."

"Plot twist," she says.

"Nah." I scoop her into my arms and carry her upstairs. "I saw this coming from a mile away."

TWENTY-SEVEN

ANNELIESE

twitterpated (*adj.*) lovestruck

"Hey, hey!" Berlin waves from several yards ahead, stepping away from a sidewalk sale table covered in clearance shoes.

It's the third time we've met up in the past week. First it was mani-pedis, then we tried that new Italian place, and now we're shopping Arcadia Grove's Annual Summer Sidewalk Sale. Though I'm doing more window-shopping than actual shopping. Still, it's nice to spend time with her, aimlessly walking the city sidewalks, latte in hand, feeling like a normal twentysomething hanging out with a good friend.

"Oh, did I tell you I met Lachlan's friend Bryce the other day?" I ask as she plucks a pair of violet suede heels from an open shoebox and slides one onto her left foot.

She glances up. "Bryce Hornsby?"

"You went to school with him, didn't you? He would've been in your class? With Lachlan?"

Berlin steps her foot into the other heel, suddenly towering at least four inches above me.

"Yeah, actually . . . he and I briefly had a thing last year," she says. "It was more of a hookup kind of thing. It was never serious. At least that was how it started. He kept pushing to take things to the next level, and I wasn't really feeling that same way about him. In the end, he didn't take the rejection that well. It got a little intense. I had to break it off for good."

"Bryce?" I ask. "He seemed so chill when I met him."

"Ha." She steps out of the vibrant shoes and places them back in the box. "Don't they all?"

"Did he ever do anything crazy?"

"If you mean calling my phone fifty times a day and driving by my apartment to see who I was hanging out with is crazy, then yes."

I wince. "I'm sorry. That's really unacceptable."

She flicks her wrist and bunches her lips at one side, continuing on to the next table of shoes.

"It's water under the bridge," she says. "He leaves me alone now. It's all good." Going back to the last shoe table, she grabs the purple heels. "On second thought, I think I'm going to get these. They're kind of badass, aren't they? Completely impractical, but at fifty percent off . . ."

"Get the shoes," I say.

"Did you want to try any on before we move on to the next shop?" she asks.

"Nothing's really catching my eye today," I say. And it's true. I'm not in the market for new shoes anyway. I have a small collection of dressy shoes from my Chicago days and an assortment of sneakers and Keds to get me through renovations and long days at the bookshop—which are fortunately coming to an end as of tomorrow, when Flo officially returns.

We browse a few more shops before calling it a day, and I return home to a six-foot-two auburn-haired Adonis cooking shirtless in the kitchen, nothing but a pair of tight jeans and my floral apron tied around his muscled waist.

"This is an interesting look for you," I say, wrapping my arms around him from behind.

"You like?" He tends to whatever the heck he's sautéing on the stove. I don't know what it is, but it smells divine.

A week ago, he dressed up as his dead brother so I could get some closure. Six days ago, he professed that he was falling for me before carrying me upstairs and claiming my body once and for all. The following morning, he gifted me with a triple orgasm before I'd so much as set one foot off the bed. Four days ago, he took me out on our first official date, at some overlook pass on the edge of town, where we watched the sunset and waited until the sky was full of stars before camping in the back of his truck.

Lachlan sets the heat to low before turning to face me. "I want to take you with me when I leave."

I feel the smile practically melting from my face. I've been so caught up in the excitement of everything this past week, so focused on having zero expectations like he once said, that I haven't thought about what comes next.

Or maybe I didn't *want* to think about what comes next . . .

"Think about all the interesting people you'll meet, all the freedom you'll have; every day will be yours and mine," he says. "To do whatever the hell we want."

"That sounds like a great vacation . . ." My mouth turns dry. I can already envision the conversation that's about to follow—one where we realize despite our rampant attraction to one another, our lifestyles are tragically incompatible. "I'm more of a roots kind of girl. I don't think I could drift from city to city with a backpack for the rest of my life. I'm adventurous, but not that adventurous."

"Once you spread those wings, Anneliese, you'll wonder why you didn't do it sooner." He cups my face in his hand before tipping my chin up until our eyes lock.

"Sell this house, and I'll fly anywhere you want," I tease. "We can take a trip. A trial-basis kind of thing."

I haven't told him yet, but I've been thinking more and more about what he went through with his mother and the kind of closure he so clearly needs. It's a devastating loss that has haunted him for nearly two decades, compounded by the emotional and psychological abuse of his father and brother. If I were him, I'd want to light these memories on fire too.

Months back, when I was attempting to research the history of this house, I found a microfiche article about the doctor who built the place. He and his wife had seven children, but only one of them survived past infancy. When the baby was two years old, the father passed of tuberculosis.

Maybe this place is cursed.

Maybe the people who live here are doomed to experience loss and tragedy.

Maybe we'd be doing the world a favor if we just let it . . . burn.

TWENTY-EIGHT

LACHLAN

cryptadia (*n.*) things kept hidden

I pull up to the savings and loan Monday afternoon, a packet of paper-work on the truck bench beside me. Earlier this morning, I received a call from Swank, saying the estate had been established and I'd been officially named as the administrator, which means we can begin the process of transferring the house—and any bank accounts—into my name.

Heading inside with my papers in hand, I approach a cheerful red-haired bank teller and explain my situation. She picks up the phone, punching in an extension, and a moment later, she directs me to a personal banker in a private office.

After I've explained my situation yet again and filled out a small mountain of paperwork, the personal banker prints off a series of statements, each one longer than the one before. I scan the itemized lines; nothing but cash withdrawal after cash withdrawal separated by a handful of payments to various contractors and material vendors.

At the bottom of the final page is the most recent balance . . .

$27.23.

"Is there anything else I can help you with today, Mr. Byrne?" he asks.

"Are you sure this is the only account in his name?"

"Yes," he says. "At this bank. There are a few more around town that you could try if you suspect he had others?"

"Thank you." Collecting the statements and my packet of paperwork, I show myself out—only to bump into none other than Bryce in the lobby.

"Hey, stranger," he says. "What's up?"

I'm in no mood for casual conversation, but I'm not about to blow him off, so I force a smile and shoot the breeze with him for a few minutes.

"Where's Anneliese?" he asks.

"She's out and about with Berlin," I say. Those two are glued at the hip lately, but I'm happy for her. Anytime they hang out, she comes home practically walking on air. It's almost like Berlin is some missing piece in her life, but I don't try to understand it. I've picked up on enough female friendship drama over the years to know that women's friendships are intricate, complex, and nuanced. And for that reason, I tend to mind my own business when it comes to them.

"Berlin Waterford?" Bryce asks, his expression falling.

"That'd be the one."

"That's messed up," he says.

I sniff. "Weird thing to say, don't you think?"

He cocks his head. "No, what's weird is that the two of them are friends . . ."

"Why? Because they have an ex in common? They've obviously moved past that."

Bryce's hands move to his hips, and he lowers his chin. "You know Berlin was screwing your brother when he died, right?"

"Um, *no* . . ."

"Yeah . . . remember when I said I was messing with her last year and I thought we were hitting it off, then all of a sudden she went cold on me? Turns out Donovan was back in town, and the two of them were hooking up. The night he died, he was leaving her place. I know this because I drove by and saw his car parked outside her apartment. Don't judge me. Anyway, you can read the police report if you want. He was on I-93, just north of the Wells River exit. That's where Berlin was living at the time, in those new apartments on the east side of town."

"Are you sure?"

"One hundred percent," he says. "When she was breaking it off with me, she told me she was talking to Don again, that he was her first love and she was always going to love him. I guess he was promising her they'd get back together soon; he just had to sort a few things out." Bryce lifts his palms in the air. "I had no idea Don was even engaged until I showed up at his funeral with Mom and there was this sobbing blonde in the front row with a diamond ring. Heard someone say that was his fiancée. It was news to us, that's for damn sure."

I think about Anneliese, how she adores Berlin. The two of them text all the time, get dinner at least twice a week, and last I heard, they were talking about doing a girls' weekend in Manhattan.

If what Bryce says is true—what Berlin is doing is beyond wrong. Nefarious, even. I don't want to assume I know her motivations, but if she's intentionally misleading Anneliese, I imagine she won't be fessing up of her own accord.

"You really didn't know?" he asks.

I shake my head.

"Figured the way people talk around here, it would've gotten back to you by now," he says. "Anyway, you going to tell her?"

"It'd be wrong not to." I run my hand through my hair, grabbing a fistful. There's a chance that if I tell her the truth and she goes to Berlin—Berlin might accuse me of being the liar.

It wouldn't be the first time.

"Agreed." He grabs a check from his pocket. "Hey, I need to cash this check, but you still want to grab beers? We missed each other last weekend . . ."

"Yeah, for sure. Saturday?" I ask, though my mind is still processing the bombshell he just dropped.

I drive home in a daze, more or less on autopilot. And when I arrive, Anneliese's Prius is parked in the driveway.

I don't know how I'm going to bring this up.

Not only that, but I'll also have to let her know that Donovan's account was cleaned out . . . save for that twenty-seven bucks.

No one ever said life was fair, but this is bullshit.

I didn't do any of these things to her, yet I'm the one tasked with breaking her heart all over again.

Staring ahead at the house that has brought me so much misery, I take my time heading in, trying to choose the right words, debating over which bad news to deliver first. But she greets me at the door with a mile-wide smile on her pretty face and her laptop pressed against her chest.

"I just found one-way tickets from Burlington to Manchester for six hundred apiece," she says, giddy and rising on the balls of her feet before she leans in to kiss me hello. "And Flo just paid me for the last two weeks of work." She kisses me again, leaving the taste of chocolate on my tongue. "Alternately, we could fly to Morocco for fifty dollars more, but there's an eight-hour layover."

"What's with this?" I ask. "Finally decide to spread your wings?"

"Berlin and I were talking about trips, and she was telling me about all the places she's been to, and I realized I'm almost thirty years old, and I haven't even been to Canada or Mexico or Hawaii. I've never left this country. And yeah, maybe your method of getting around is a little terrifying because I'm a planner and I prefer to travel with itineraries and hotel reservations, but I think we could do this. A trial, like I said. Maybe two weeks?"

There's nothing more I want in this world than to travel it with her by my side.

Anneliese places her laptop down before slipping her arms over my shoulders. Her fingers twist the hair at the nape of my neck as she sweetly smiles up at me.

This moment is perfection. Pure bliss. I want to capture it in a bottle. I want to drink it down until I'm stupid drunk. I want to keep that grin on her lips and that sparkle in her eyes for as long as possible because, truth be told, it's all I'm living for these days.

"You're in an exceptionally good mood today," I say, hooking my hands around her waist. "You have fun with Berlin today?"

"Always," she says.

"You really like her, don't you?"

"I've never clicked with anyone like this before," Anneliese says. "At least, not since college. We just . . . have a lot in common. We're similar ages, similar stages in our lives, small-business owners, trying to find our places in this world and have a little fun while we're at it."

The words linger, burning on the tip of my tongue.

But I can't bring myself to tell her.

Not yet.

I'll break it to her, but not here. Not now.

I need to bask in her oblivious sunlight for a little while longer.

"What's wrong?" she asks. "You seem kind of . . . I don't know . . . deflated?"

"Do I?" I deflect her question with a question of my own.

"Is everything okay?" she asks, her expression growing somber as she studies me. "Did you have a good day today?"

"It was productive," I say, skirting the question as best I can.

I think about the bank statements folded in my back pocket and how I hold the power of ripping apart her newfound friendship *and* her chance at recovering her life savings all at once.

It hits me now that the choice is clear—I'll sell the house. I'll reimburse her for her investment and her time. And when the dust clears, I'll sweep her off to Europe and show her what it's really like to live a truly untethered life.

My head throbs, tension threading across my forehead.

"Think I'm going to take some aspirin and lie down," I say.

"You don't feel well?"

"Just need to sleep off this headache." I head to the kitchen.

"You sure nothing's wrong?" she asks, following me. I find a bottle of Bayer in the medicine cabinet, and by the time I turn around, she's handing me a bottle of water.

"Don't worry about me, all right?" I kiss the top of her head before tossing back my aspirin and heading to the sofa to put my feet up and figure out when to break the news to her. At least when I do, I can cushion the bad with some good.

I'm settling into the couch when she climbs next to me, curling under my arm and resting her cheek against my chest.

"I missed you today," she says. "Mind if I lie with you for a while?"

"Not at all." I hold her tight, and she exhales, eyes closed, a dreamy, contented smile on her face.

I just want to keep it there a little longer.

TWENTY-NINE

ANNELIESE

kalopsia (*n.*) the delusion of things being more beautiful than they really are

I'm on my way to run a few errands the next day when Lachlan asks me to drop off a socket wrench set he borrowed from Bryce. Parking outside a white single-story house with a green front door, I double-check the address Lachlan gave me before grabbing the tools and heading up the front walk. My phone vibrates in my pocket, and I manage to slide it out and catch a text from Berlin.

BERLIN: Lunch? Got a table at Cabo Sol . . .

She follows up with a picture—a cheesy selfie of her sitting solo at a checkered-tablecloth table, making an egregious kissy face.

I type back a thumbs-up emoji and slide my phone away before ringing the doorbell.

"Hey there, pretty lady," Lynnette answers a minute later, surrounded by a fog of stale smoke and sprightly perfume.

"Lachlan asked me to drop these off for Bryce." I hand them over.

"How nice of you to do his bidding," she says with a wink. "How's the house coming? You want to come in for a bit and chat?"

"Aw, I'd love to, but I actually promised Berlin I'd meet her for lunch," I say, shrinking. "She's already at the restaurant . . ."

"Berlin?" The expression on Lynnette's face turns sour. "So you forgave her?"

"What do you mean?" I ask.

"Bryce said he ran into Lachlan yesterday at the bank . . ."

I had no idea he went to the bank yesterday. He must have *forgotten* to mention that when I asked how his day was . . .

A cold sweat blankets my forehead, and the back of my neck grows hot from the midday sun beating down from above.

"Did something happen with Lachlan and Berlin?" I ask.

She spreads a petite hand across her chest, her mouth forming a small circle. "Oh my goodness, honey, no. Not Lachlan. Donovan."

"What about Donovan?" I ask. "I know they dated a long time ago . . ."

She rests her palm across her forehead, staring down at an overgrown bush to the right of the front stoop.

"I've said too much," she finally says. "You should ask Lachlan about it."

My knees weaken.

Is this why he was acting so strange yesterday? Because he knew something and didn't want to tell me? When he gave me the impression that everything was fine . . . was it not?

"Please, Lynnette, tell me," I say, my hands turning to fists at my stomach, but only to keep it from turning inside out. "What's happened with Berlin?"

The corners of her mouth dip down, and she leans against the doorjamb, arms folded, looking every bit the part of a person about to deliver life-altering news.

"Berlin was sleeping with Donovan the night he died," Lynnette says, her delivery soft and apologetic.

I wrinkle my nose, refusing to believe. "There's no way. She told me they hadn't spoken in years."

"Then she's lying to you, sweetheart. She and my son were dating last fall. Berlin broke things off with Bryce because she was getting back with Donovan." She rolls her eyes. "Apparently he was telling her he was getting a few things in order and then they could finally be together again."

"It doesn't make sense . . ."

"What? That Donovan was messing around?"

"No," I say. "It doesn't make sense that Berlin lied to me."

"I believe my son," she says. "But maybe you should talk to her yourself, get some answers?"

Tears blur my vision, and I thank Lynnette for sharing that with me before jogging to my car. I can't get out of there quickly enough. But I also can't go meet up with Berlin, not like this. I swipe my tears away long enough to compose a text to her, canceling lunch. She asks if everything's okay, and for the first time since I've known her, I leave her on read.

After hightailing it home, I'm both disappointed and relieved to find Lachlan's truck there. Heading inside, I search the quiet house, ending up in his room last. Only he isn't there. On my way out, a stack of papers on his dresser catches my eye.

More specifically—the logo catches my eye.

Arcadia Grove Savings and Loan.

Biting my lip, I try to talk myself out of looking. I tell myself perhaps he was there to open his own personal account yesterday? If that's the case, of course he wouldn't be obligated to share that with me.

But a cocktail of impatience and desperate curiosity gets the better of me, and I scan the top sheet until my frantic gaze finds the words: ACCOUNT STATEMENT FOR DONOVAN N. BYRNE. I pore over the credits and debits, most of which are cash withdrawals mixed with a handful of renovation purchases. I flip through the first few pages before settling on the final page, which declares an account balance of twenty-seven dollars and twenty-three cents.

It's gone.

All of it.

Lachlan knew this yesterday and didn't tell me.

He also knew the Berlin-Donovan connection and withheld that as well.

When I asked him if everything was okay, he lied.

"Hey, what are you doing home so early? I thought you were running errands?" Lachlan's presence fills the doorway, and his gaze darts to the papers in my hand.

"When were you going to tell me about this?" I ask.

"Today, actually."

"That's convenient."

"It's the truth," he says.

"Interesting choice of words coming from someone who lied to me yesterday."

"What are you talking about?"

"I knew something was wrong when you came home, but you brushed it off and acted like everything was fine," I say. "It wasn't fine. At all. And you knew it."

"It's not as cut and dried as you're making it sound."

"Really? Because I think it's pretty cut and dried that you knew Berlin and Donovan were messing around behind my back and you let me carry on this friendship with her like a damn fool . . ." My voice breaks, and my throat tightens so hard that speaking is painful.

"I found out yesterday," he says. "At the bank. I was just as shocked about all of it as you, and when I came home, you were in such a good mood, and I was still processing how I was going to tell you."

"You don't get to play God with other people's emotions, Lachlan."

The red-hot sting of betrayal pours over me, head to toe, igniting my skin and my thoughts all the same. The room grows ten degrees warmer, and suddenly his imposing stance in the doorway makes the space feel that much smaller.

I need air.

I need space.

"Anneliese." He follows after me, his footsteps heavy on the creaking stairs by the time I reach the front door. I step into a pair of tennis shoes and yank the front door so hard it smacks the wall behind it. "Anneliese, wait."

Stopping in my tracks, I turn to face him. "I'm going for a walk so I can cool off. Please don't chase after me. I just . . . I need to be alone right now."

He doesn't move a muscle. He simply stands there quietly, observing me, his expression so blank I can't tell if he feels remorse for breaking the only promise that mattered to me or if he's watching the inevitable play out.

And to think I was planning on telling him I didn't even want the house anymore, that it was rightfully and lawfully his and I understood his reasons for wanting it to go up in smoke.

Deep down, I think we both knew . . . whatever this is, whatever it was, was destined to go down in flames.

THIRTY

LACHLAN

hamartia (*n.*) a flaw that causes the downfall of a hero

I watch Anneliese grow smaller in the distance before completely disappearing around the corner when she reaches the end of the street. She asked for space, so space she'll get. By the time she gets back, she'll have come to her senses. She's just in shock right now. As soon as she calms down and listens to me, she'll understand my reasoning, and we can pick up where we left off.

I head to the kitchen to grab my truck keys off the counter, along with my wallet, and then I pluck out the business card I found on the gas station bulletin board this morning and dial the number.

"Arcadia Grove Realty, this is Debra. How may I direct your call?" a friendly voice answers.

"I'd like to speak with Callie Hodges," I say.

"Just a moment, please."

Hold music fills my ear for all of ten seconds before an even friendlier voice takes the call.

"This is Callie. How may I help you?" she asks.

"Yes, I'm looking to sell my house in the next couple of months, and I was wondering if you could run a quick market analysis for me?" I ask. "Just trying to get a ballpark estimate for now. It's an old house that's mostly renovated, and I haven't the slightest idea what it's worth."

"Sure," she says. "And you're in luck because I just happen to have the next couple of hours free. Why don't you come down to my office, and we can pull some quick comps and go from there?"

"Will be there shortly," I say before hanging up.

My plan was to deliver the bad news to Anneliese later today, when she was back from running her errands, and then I was going to soften those blows by telling her my intentions to sell the house so she could recoup her money.

I should know better than anyone that even the best-laid plans often miss their mark.

I'm flooded with discontent on the drive to the realty office, playing out Anneliese's emotional outburst and hating that she's out strolling the neighborhood, cursing my name, but everything will come together soon enough.

It has to.

I can't leave this town without her.

THIRTY-ONE

ANNELIESE

ignify (*v.*) to form into fire, to burn

"Anneliese, hey," Berlin says from behind the register of her flower shop. Concern colors her dark gaze, and rightfully so. With my sweat-dampened face and bloodshot eyes and breathlessness, I'm sure I'm looking every bit a cause for concern. "Is everything okay?"

She doesn't answer, peering out the shop door instead.

"Where's your car? Did you walk here?" she asks. "That's, like, five miles. And we're in the middle of a heat wave . . . do you need some water?"

"I need to know why you lied to me," I say, pacing and breathing, breathing and pacing. "You were sleeping with Donovan. He was leaving your house the night he died. But that's not what I'm upset about right now, crazily enough. It's the fact that you made a genuine effort to befriend me, to insert yourself into my life, knowing damn well you didn't belong there. And you lied, Berlin. You told me you hadn't spoken to Donovan in years . . ."

Her eyes turn glassy, and her attention flicks to the tiled floor.

Is she crying because she hurt the one friend she had, or is she upset that she got caught in this twisted little web she wove?

"Why did you pretend to be my friend?" I ask. "What was your goal? What were you expecting to get from this?"

"Anneliese, first of all, I was never pretending to be your friend." Her voice is jagged, but I don't buy the crocodile tears sliding down her rosy cheeks. "I was your friend. And I considered you mine. I still do."

"I confided in you," I say. "I trusted you. I shared very personal things with you. And the whole time you knew. You knew what you did, and you played me."

"I'm so sorry. I know it's wrong. And I don't expect you to understand it," she says. "I came into the shop that day, and I recognized you from the funeral. And then you were so kind. And I felt so awful. And then you offered to help me name my flower shop, and I thought, What kind of person would do such a generous thing for a complete stranger? Out of the goodness of their heart? I genuinely liked you from the first time we spoke, Anneliese. I swear to you, I wasn't expecting to get a friendship out of this. Believe me when I say the last thing I wanted was to hurt you."

There's no way to know if I should believe her or not. All I know is that it seems like everyone in this town has a tendency of lying and taking advantage of people without thinking better of it.

"Why'd you sleep with him?" I ask. "After everything you claimed he put you through . . . the narcissistic abuse . . . the horrible things he said and did . . . or were those all lies too?"

Berlin shakes her head. "No. All of it was true."

"Then why did you go back to him?"

"First of all, I had no idea he was engaged. I ran into him at the store one day, and we reconnected. It felt . . . different this time. He was older, wiser, calmer, kinder. I thought maybe he'd matured. Changed his ways. Anyway, we started hanging out again," she says. "Next thing I knew, he was promising me the future I always thought we were going to have. He said he was fixing up his childhood home—which was his reason for never inviting me over—and as soon as it was done, he was going to propose. I had no idea you existed until the funeral, Anneliese. He never talked about you. I guess I know why."

"He stole my life savings . . . so he could fix up the house . . . that he was using to bait you with the happily ever after."

"God, he was the worst. Truly. But he had his moments. I try to focus on the good over the bad. It's easier that way. Ruminating on all the negative doesn't change what's already been done." Berlin's gaze grows distant. "But honestly, when I look back at everything, I feel like the biggest fool for not seeing through it all. I'm embarrassed. I should've known better than to trust him after everything we'd been through before. And if I could take it back—my involvement with him this past year—I'd do it in a heartbeat. Again, I'm *so* sorry."

As much as I wish she'd come clean sooner, I try to put myself in her shoes—there never would've been the perfect time to drop a bombshell like that. If she truly saw me as a friend and cared about my feelings, her avoidance of sharing this information is understandable. She wasn't deceiving me to gain an advantage over me—she simply didn't want to hurt me.

"Thank you," I say. "For coming clean. For sharing all of that with me. For owning it."

She places her hand over mine. "I hope you'll be able to forgive me one of these days."

I offer a pained yet appreciative smile. I've never been a grudge holder, and the fact that she opened up about everything instead of gaslighting me puts her miles above Donovan in my book.

"If it makes you feel any better, odds are as soon as he ditched you and went back to me, he'd drop me as soon as the next exciting catch came along. Knowing him, he only wanted me because he couldn't have me. I'm the one who broke it off with him last time. Maybe he wanted to be the one to break my heart this time," she says. "Either way, I guess it doesn't matter anymore. He's dead. And he died driving from my place back home to you—which is poetic justice in a sick sort of way."

"Never thought of it that way, but that's actually a pretty perfect send-off for that asshole," I say.

"Ugh. I hate him for what he did to you," Berlin says, wrapping her arms around me. "And I hate myself for having any part in it."

"You couldn't have known." I hug her back. "I should probably get back home. I said some pretty harsh things to Lachlan earlier . . . and then I ran off. Without my phone, of course. He's probably worried about me."

"You want a ride?" she asks.

"Your shop doesn't close for two more hours."

"Good thing my boss likes me." She winks. "Come on. I'll get my keys. You're not walking five miles home."

Berlin closes up the shop for the day, and we load up in her little red Jetta, heading back to the house so I can apologize for going off on him earlier. Being blindsided by Donovan's actions has made me hypersensitive to anything remotely akin to betrayal, and that's something I'm going to have to work on.

"You okay?" she asks on the drive.

"Yeah," I say. "Just mentally practicing my apology."

She turns onto a side street, not far from my place. We're a block and a half away when the wail of ambulance sirens in the distance is followed a moment later by the honking of a fire truck.

"Huh," she says, pointing to the billows of thick black smoke rising above the tree-lined streets. "Is that a residential fire? It's all houses over here . . ."

A police car flies up behind us in full lights and sirens. Berlin pulls over to let him pass.

My heart lurches up the back of my throat, beat by beat, second by second.

It almost stops beating altogether when we round the corner to my street . . . and I realize the house on fire . . . is mine.

"Oh my God, Anneliese," Berlin gasps, slowing down to a crawl. I jump out before she gets to a full stop, dashing toward the house, past yellow tape and uniformed officers.

"Ma'am, you can't go beyond these lines," a younger officer shouts.

"This is my house," I yell back. "I need to know if anyone was inside?"

He steps toward me, motioning for me to move behind the barricades.

"Please! My roommate!" I beg, pointing frantically. "There could be a man in there!"

The west side of the roof caves in, sending a thousand sparks up into the clear blue sky. The window in the front of the house explodes.

Berlin parks her car down a ways before chasing after me.

A chaos of flashing lights and shouting emergency workers blurs together to complete the scene.

"Come on." She grabs me by the arm and leads me across the street, away from the chaos of flashing lights and shouting emergency workers and fire trucks so big they block the view of my driveway so I can't even see if Lachlan's truck is here . . .

"My phone was inside," I say.

"Honey, phones can be replaced . . ." She slips her arm around my shoulder.

"No, I mean, I can't call Lachlan."

"You can use my phone."

"No . . . I don't have his number memorized," I say as another section of roof caves in.

"I . . . I can reach out to Bryce." Her tone is hesitant, but I know she'll put her issues with him aside for this—for me. "I'll have him check on Lachlan and let me know."

She pulls out her phone and moves farther down the sidewalk to make a call.

I take a seat on the curb next to her car and watch the place burn down.

I only pray he didn't burn down with it.

THIRTY-TWO

LACHLAN

agathokakological (*adj.*) composed of both good and evil

Two hundred grand.

That's what Callie thinks the house will pull, maybe even two twenty-five if we price aggressively from the start and manage to snag a bidding war. Luck and timing are half the battle, she said, but she seemed excited about getting the listing.

"Thanks, Lachlan," she says, walking me to the door. "I'll see you tomorrow at ten a.m."

I leave with a printout of the quick market analysis she did—I wanted to make sure I had something to show Anneliese when I got back, something to put a smile back on her face and give her a little bit of hope that she didn't have before. Tomorrow morning, Callie's going to come by to personally tour the home and check out the renovations that have been completed so far and to get a better idea of where exactly we should price it.

Folding the paper, I slide it into my back pocket and climb into my truck to head home. I can only hope she'll be waiting for me when

I get there. She took off without her phone, but if she's home now, I might be able to reach her.

I take my phone out to call her—only to get an incoming call at the same time—from Bryce. I hit the red button and attempt to call Anneliese, but her phone goes straight to voice mail.

Bryce calls again.

Once more, I ignore it.

I'll call him back in a sec.

I try Anneliese a second time, getting her voice mail once again.

"Hey," I say after the tone. "I know we didn't leave off on the best note earlier, but I have good news. Great news, actually. Call me when you get this."

I hang up, only to get a third call from Bryce.

I start my truck, back out of my spot, and answer, putting him on speaker.

"What's up?" I ask.

"Your house is on fire." He speaks so quickly that the words jumble together into one big, long word.

"What'd you say?" I ask, certain I misheard him.

"*Your house is on fire, Lachlan,*" he says, clearer this time.

The stoplight ahead flicks to yellow, but I slam my foot into the gas and make it through.

"Where's Anneliese?" My knuckles turn white against the steering wheel, and I hold my breath as I wait for him to answer.

"She's with Berlin," he says.

"I'm on my way." I end the call and blast through another yellow light. The closer I get, the stronger the scent of burning wood. Up ahead, the crystal-blue sky is filled with ominous black-gray clouds of smoke.

By the time I get there, there are so many cars and emergency vehicles lined up and down the street that I have to park almost a block away. Sprinting toward the scene, I scan the crowd of neighbors, onlookers, and hometown heroes for Anneliese.

The heat from the fire stretches far, and I stop to glance at the house, but only for a moment. Flames shoot from every busted window, licking up the siding and spreading across the roofline. A large portion of the house has completely collapsed. For the longest time, this was all I ever wanted, and now that it's happening, all I want is to find her and make sure she's safe.

"Lachlan!" a voice I don't recognize shouts from behind. I turn to follow it, spotting Berlin flagging me down. "She's over here."

I find Anneliese crouched on a curb, her elbows on her knees, staring ahead with tear-streaked cheeks. The instant she spots me, she scrambles up and throws her arms around me, squeezing so tight I can't breathe.

"I was so worried you were inside," she says, her words muffled against my neck. "I'm sorry. I'm so sorry for going off on you earlier."

Berlin watches us from a careful distance. I take it the two of them patched things up, but now's not the time to discuss that whole situation.

She peels herself off me, turning her attention back to the inferno across the street.

"I can't believe it's gone," she says.

"Me either." I wrap my arms around her waist, holding her from behind as we watch the place go down.

"I don't understand how this happened," she says.

"Two hundred grand up in smoke, just like that."

She turns back. "Two hundred grand?"

Reaching into my back pocket, I show her Callie's market analysis.

"What's this?" she asks.

"When you were on your walk, I went to see how much we could get for this house if we sold it. After seeing the number on that bank statement, I decided to sell the house so you could get your investment back. It was the right thing to do."

Anneliese presses the paper against her chest, turning back to face me. "You were going to do that? For me?"

I brush a strand of tear-dampened hair from her cheek. We exchange a look that says so much without saying a damn thing.

The fire roars, lighting the early-evening sky.

But all I see is her.

An older man shuffles past on the sidewalk with his wife, giving her a nudge before pointing to the fire and saying, "This one's going to be a slow burn. These big houses always take a while. All that wood, it's all kindling now."

"They seem to have it pretty well under control, Herb," his wife says.

"It's the hot spots they really have to look for," he says. "That's a lot of property to search."

The couple continues on, and Berlin keeps back, chatting on the phone with someone.

"You want to sit down and watch it burn?" Anneliese asks.

"Might as well, right?"

She slides her hand inside mine, leads me to the curb where she was perched a few minutes ago, and we take a seat. I stretch my arm around her shoulders, and she leans in, resting her head on my chest.

The fire is both wondrous and terrifying: a fitting demise for a house that was equally beautiful and ugly, filled with good memories and evil.

Now it no longer exists.

Everything is just . . . gone.

We stay until most of the crew clears out, we've said our goodbyes to Berlin, I've assured Lynnette half a dozen times that we're safe and sound, and we've had a chance to speak to both a police lieutenant and a fire chief. It isn't until the last fire truck leaves that we discover

Anneliese's Prius—which was parked in the driveway—did not survive the fire.

"Hope you had full coverage," I say, taking her by the hand and leading her to my truck.

Anneliese gasps, stopping short at the end of the driveway.

"What is it?" I ask, turning back.

"I had renters' insurance," she says. "Everything inside the house was covered . . . all of the furniture, the lights we hadn't installed yet, the appliances I bought . . ."

"So you might not walk away from this empty handed after all."

"It won't be close to what I lost, but it'll be enough for whatever comes next . . ."

I take her hand again, pull her in, and kiss the top of her smoke-scented head. "What do you say we grab some clean clothes at the big-box store and look for a place to crash for the night?"

"As long as it's not the Pine Grove Motel . . ."

"Tomorrow we'll get you a new phone," I say when we get to the truck. "And we'll start calling the insurance companies."

Anneliese climbs in next to me, slides to the middle of the bench seat, and rests her head on my shoulder as we head to the outskirts of town, to a twenty-four-hour Walmart.

Today we lost everything but this old beater of a pickup truck.

And each other.

For now, it's all we need.

THIRTY-THREE

ANNELIESE

feelstoria (*n.*) a story that is heavily influenced by the author's emotional state at the time of its writing

"Tell me a story." I roll to my side and slip my arm across Lachlan's bare chest, our legs tangled in hotel sheets and the blackout curtains pulled so tight it still feels like nighttime. We've been camped out at the Hampton Inn north of Arcadia Grove for the past week. It's no Ritz-Carlton, but it's a world above the Pine Grove Motel.

I'm pretty sure I'd take a tent or a tree house at this point, though—anywhere with Lachlan. He's been a godsend through all of this, offering his support and encouragement, hyping me up for living a life with the "bare necessities," unencumbered by *things*.

Also, Berlin, Flo, and Lynnette have rallied the Arcadia Grove troops, telling everyone they know about the house fire and setting up donation funds both online and all around town. Last I checked, we've been given more than we could possibly need, and we intend to make sure the excess goes back into the community and is put to good use.

Funny how life can break you apart, only to put you back together again—better than you were before.

"What kind of story?" he asks.

I begin to answer, only to be interrupted by his vibrating phone on the nightstand. He leans over, checking the caller ID.

"It's a local number," he says. "Might be the arson investigator. They said they'd be calling within the week."

Sitting up, he takes the call on speaker.

"Mr. Byrne," a man on the other end says. "This is Jim Connor, arson investigator for Arcadia Grove FD. We spoke earlier last week."

"Yes, Mr. Connor," he says. "I've got Anneliese Nielsen here with me."

"Ms. Nielsen, hi," Jim says. "We've concluded our investigation, so I'll cut to the chase here. We've determined the cause of the fire was a faulty wire connected to the gas range in the kitchen."

Lachlan and I exchange looks. For the past week, we speculated and guessed, wondering what it could possibly have been. I worried I'd left a curling iron plugged in, or perhaps one of the varnish cans had been left in direct sunlight and combusted. We went through every scenario we could think of—but the brand-new range was not one of them.

"I'll email you a copy of the report," Jim says. "Your insurance company will ask for it when you submit your claim."

"Thank you," I chime in.

"You have my number if anything comes up or you have any questions," Jim says before ending the call.

"Wow." Lachlan places his phone aside, turning back to me. "The range . . ."

"I thought I was saving a few grand by going with a scratch-and-dent model," I say. "Somehow it ended up costing me everything and giving me everything at the same time."

Lachlan takes me in his arms, tucking the messy covers around us as the ice-cold AC hums from the opposite side of the room. We've been holed up for a week now, only leaving the hotel to get fresh air, food, and a few replacement electronics—a phone and laptop for me, charging cords and earbuds for him.

"We should probably get out of here, don't you think?" I ask.

"Where do you want to go? Don't let me forget to top off my gas tank while we're out."

"London? Morocco? Florence?" I shrug.

"Oh, you mean get . . . out . . . of . . . *here*." He pulls me into his lap, and I gather the covers around me for extra warmth. "Tell me where you want to go, and I'll book us on the next plane there. I'll take you anywhere you want to go."

"This could get expensive for you . . ."

"*Parlez-vous français?*" he asks.

"*Oui . . . un peu,*" I say. "I took four years of French in high school. I could get around if I had to."

"Paris it is," he says, leaning in to steal a kiss. "The City of Light . . . the City of Love."

"I'm in." I kiss him harder, my hips circling against his hardness, teasing. Last night, out of sheer boredom, we decided to get drunk on cheap wine and try the most ridiculous *Kama Sutra* poses we could find online—which in retrospect was a terrible idea on my part given my intense lack of flexibility.

My muscles burn this morning as if I completed an Ironman Triathlon overnight, but it doesn't stop me from wanting him all over again.

"Who gave you permission to be this addictive?" I ask, kissing my way down his rounded shoulder.

He cups my chin, steering my lips to his, and when I come up for air, our gazes catch, lingering in something unspoken.

"I have to tell you something," he says.

My stomach drops. Those six words are rarely followed by anything good.

"It's something I've only ever said to one person before . . . and in a completely different context," he says.

I lose myself in his copper-hued irises, waiting with bated breath, growing more impatient with each torturous second.

"I love you, Anneliese," he says.

Fullness floods my chest, and I throw my arms around him so hard and fast I knock him back into our messy pile of pillows.

"You love me?" I ask, but only because I want to hear him say it again. I wasn't ready the first time. I didn't get to fully appreciate the beauty of those words on his lips.

"*I love you*," he says, his mouth curling at one side. "Just thought you should know."

"I love you too." I think it's time I spread my wings. "Take me to Paris."

EPILOGUE

LACHLAN

belamour (*n.*) one who is loved; a beloved person

Five years later . . .

"There you are. I was looking for you." My wife steps through a curtained doorway into the inner courtyard of the eighteenth-century Spanish home we've been restoring for the better part of the last year. With its sweeping views of the Montserrat mountains, charming locals, authentic cuisine, and centuries of history, we feel as if we've stumbled into a hidden paradise. "I should've known you were out here working."

She shifts her notebook to her right arm before checking her watch.

I close my laptop lid and place it aside.

"How's it coming?" she asks with a wince.

"Eight more chapters to go before she's ready for her first read," I say before soaking her in. Maybe it's the midday sun, but she's radiant today—more than usual.

"Progress is progress," she says. "Are you still stuck on the title?"

Ever since Anneliese took her naming business to social media, it's grown by leaps and bounds. With a wait list a mile long and a full-time assistant keeping her organized, she's spread paper thin these days—and yet she still found time to whip up a list of title options for my newest manuscript. Given the fact that she named my last book—which was an instant bestseller—I figure she knows what she's doing. That and she's my personal good-luck charm.

"I'm going back and forth between *The Midnight Apartment* and *The Crooked Key*," I say, spouting off two of the top contenders.

"Both are intriguing," she says, her lips bunched at one side as she takes the spot beside me on the sun-soaked bench. "I don't know that you could go wrong either way."

I run my palm along her thigh. "I just feel stuck without a solid title. The other ones were so easy."

"I don't know that you're stuck as much as you're finding every reason under the moon not to write," she teases. "You do this every time."

"Do what?"

"You get to the end of a book, and all of a sudden you're stuck on this or that, or you've got a laundry list of more important things to do." She says all of that with love in her voice and a tender gaze. "I get it, though. It's scary finishing a project, putting it into someone else's hands, waiting for the official critique before it goes to the masses, where you'll get hundreds of thousands of new critiques."

I sniff a laugh. She knows me too well. My whole life I never cared what anyone thought of me—until I became a published writer.

Five years ago, when my childhood house burned to the ground, it took *The Neon Prince* with it. A week later, Anneliese presented me with a brand-new Moleskine notebook and monogrammed fountain pen and encouraged me to write something new and fresh. The more I declined, the harder she insisted.

She loved my stories, she told me. She also called me selfish for not wanting to share them with the rest of the world. I swore to her my oral stories were miles better than the ones on paper, but she wouldn't hear it.

A bet was made.

I would pen a story, and she would tell me if it was better or worse than the ones I made up on the fly. She pledged her brutal honesty as long as I promised to submit it to an agency if it ended up being halfway decent.

In the end, a middle-grade fantasy tome called *The Wicked Ones* was born, and a year later, it was sold at auction for a generous seven-figure deal.

"I'm kind of liking *The Crooked Key*," Anneliese muses. "I think it fits your brand better."

"I think you're right."

She claps her hands. "Then it's settled. You have your title. Now you can finish your damn book and get back to work on refinishing those Saltillo tiles in the kitchen . . ."

"You just want to see me with my shirt off." I wink. "Covered in sweat and dust."

"Busted." She chuckles. "Anyway, the reason I came out here"—she flips open her notebook and clicks her pen—"is because I'm working on a name list for these new clients, I'm feeling kind of stuck, and I wanted to get your input."

I lift a brow. "All right. What are they like?"

"So they're American," she says. "But they're living here in the village."

"Okay." I scratch the side of my temple. "And we haven't met them yet?"

"You'd probably recognize them if you saw a picture," she adds. "But anyway, they're super down-to-earth people. Very lovely couple. The woman's a little more outgoing than the guy. He's very quiet until you get to know him. Maybe a little intimidating to some?"

"What's their naming style?" In the past, she's always labeled them in colorful terms like *New England chic, East Coast prep academy, California surfer baby, southern debutante,* and *millennial influencer.*

"I don't know that they have a style," she says. "That's the thing. They weren't planning on having a baby. At least not yet. So the pregnancy was kind of a surprise to them both. They haven't chatted about styles yet. That's why they need help."

"What do they look like?" I ask, if only because you can tell a lot about a person by the way they do their hair or the clothes they choose to wear.

"They're pretty laid back," she says. "Not formal or stuffy. I'd describe him as more of a hip professor type with tattoos. Very resourceful. Good with his hands. Adventurous."

I sniff. "Okay . . ."

"And she's more of a . . . hummingbird."

"Hummingbird?"

Anneliese nods. "She's very busy. Flits around a bit. Always talking, always bouncing from one task to another."

"Reminds me of someone I know . . ." I give her a nudge.

"Yeah, I see a lot of myself in her." Anneliese gives me a side glance, peering up through her dark lashes. "You could even say . . . it's like looking in a mirror."

I frown, but not because I'm upset. I'm just unfamiliar with this cryptic side of her.

"So the guy," I say. "The one with the tattoos . . . does he happen to write books?"

"Yes, actually. He's a published author," she says, eyes glinting as her lips fight a grin.

My mouth runs dry and my heart hammers in my chest as I figure out where she's going with this.

"What about his looks," I say. "Is he dashing or . . .?"

"I don't know what his looks have to do with anything, but he's quite handsome."

"About six foot two?"

She nods. "On the nose."

"Auburn hair?"

"Yes," she says. "With eyes like whiskey and a jaw that could cut steel."

"He sounds awful," I tease.

"Well, he's kind of the greatest thing that ever happened to me." Her words are pillow soft and music to my ears. Anneliese runs her hand over mine before steering it to her lower stomach. "And in seven more months, I'll be having his baby."

I pull her into my lap and tip her chin lower, until her mouth aligns with mine and our gazes are locked.

"We're having a baby?" I ask.

Her eyes water, and her lips press together for an endless moment.

"We're having a baby," she confirms. "I know we didn't plan this . . . I hope you're not . . ."

I claim her soft lips before she can utter another word. Cupping her face, I taste her tongue and pull her close against me.

My wife.

My unborn child.

My whole damn world.

Everything I want, everything I need, everything I have, is right here in my arms.

And I'm never letting go.

ACKNOWLEDGMENTS

Eternally grateful for my editor at Montlake, Lauren Plude, for her infectious passion and saintly patience and for helping me out of those corners I sometimes write myself into. And to my developmental editor, Lindsey Faber. Working with you the second time around was just as enjoyable (and painless) as the first time!

To my agent, Jill Marsal, thank you for your tireless support.

To my readers who have supported me from day one and have stayed with me through this whirlwind journey I've been on since 2015, thank you times infinity! I could not do this without any of you. Your kind words, reviews, and messages are always the bright spots in my day.

To Neda Amini of Ardent Prose and to the bloggers and bookstagrammers, librarians, and reviewers who help spread the word about my work, thank you! You are such a vital part of the book community, and your efforts do not go unnoticed.

To Kcee, my PA, thank you for all you do! You're amazing, and I appreciate you more than words can convey.

To Max and Kat, two of the best author friends a girl could have.

To Ashley—best beta in the biz. Period.

To my parents, friends, and family, and to my husband and our three kids—your support gives me life. I love you.

To my new readers, thank you for giving this book a chance. I hope you enjoyed your time in Arcadia Grove!

ABOUT THE AUTHOR

Photo © 2017 Jill Austin

Wall Street Journal and #1 Amazon bestselling author Winter Renshaw is a bona fide daydream believer. She lives somewhere in the middle of the USA and is rarely seen without her notebook and laptop. When she's not writing, she's thinking about writing. And when she's not thinking about writing, she's living the American dream with her husband, three kids, the laziest puggle this side of the Mississippi, and a busy pug pup that officially owes her three pairs of shoes, one lamp cord, and an office chair.

Renshaw also writes psychological and domestic suspense under her Minka Kent pseudonym. Her first book, *The Memory Watcher*, hit #9 in the Kindle store, and her follow-up, *The Thinnest Air*, hit

#1 in the Kindle store and spent five weeks as a *Washington Post* bestseller.

She's represented by Jill Marsal at Marsal Lyon Literary Agency.

Visit her website at http://winterrenshaw.com, or connect with her on Facebook at www.facebook.com/authorwinterrenshaw or on Instagram (@winterrenshaw).